ETHAN'S OBSESSION (SPECIAL FORCES: OPERATION ALPHA)

TACTICAL OPERATIONS SERIES
BOOK TWO

ANNA BLAKELY

Editing by: Tracy Roelle
Proofreading by: Angie Springs, Kim Ruiz, and Judy Wagner

Dear Readers,

Welcome to the Special Forces: Operation Alpha Fan-Fiction world!

If you are new to this amazing world, in a nutshell the author wrote a story using one or more of my characters in it. Sometimes that character has a major role in the story, and other times they are only mentioned briefly. This is perfectly legal and allowable because they are going through Aces Press to publish the story.

This book is entirely the work of the author who wrote it. While I might have assisted with brainstorming and other ideas about which of my characters to use, I didn't have any part in the process or writing or editing the story.

I'm proud and excited that so many authors loved my characters enough that they wanted to write them into their own story. Thank you for supporting them, and me!

READ ON!
    Xoxo
    Susan Stoker

To everyone who waited patiently (and impatiently) for Ethan's story. This book went from being the bane of my existence to a story I absolutely love and am proud to share with all of you. Thanks so much for hanging in there with me on this one. I think you'll find it was worth the wait!

XOXO~

Anna

AUTHOR'S NOTE

Thank you so much for choosing to read Ethan and Nicki's story. These two star-crossed lovers are destined to be together, but if Ethan and his teammates—along with Ghost and the rest of your favorite Delta Force team—can't get to Nicki in time, their chance of happiness will be ruined. Along with the world as we know it.

I hope you enjoy your time spent with these characters, and that this is a story you will come to love. Thanks so much for all you do to help me have the best job ever!

Hugs and Happy Reading!

PROLOGUE

10 years ago...

"The party's inside, you know."

Nicki Castille's heart flipped, but she forced herself not to react. She didn't have to turn around to know who'd just joined her. She would recognize that low, rumbly voice anywhere.

"I know." She continued staring up at the stars.

"So, what are you doing out here?"

Trying not to think about the fact that you're leaving. Again.

"Just taking a breather." Nicki shifted slightly on the patio bench. A casual move. "It was starting to get a little crowded inside."

The familiar scent of woodsy male rolled with the passing breeze as Ethan McAllister—one of her two best friends and the man she was secretly in love with—sat down next to her.

Stretching one of his strong arms behind her, Ethan rested it along the bench's tall wooden back. The air in her lungs stilled, and it was all Nicki could do not to react when his hand inadvertently brushed along the curve of her bare shoulder.

"This from the girl who's always the life of the party?" His deep voice resonated to the depths of her bones.

"It's not my party." She forced herself to look at him. "It's yours."

"It is." Ethan dipped his dimpled chin. "And yet, one of my closest friends is sitting out here all by herself instead of being inside with me. Wanna tell me what's really going on?"

Dark chocolate eyes that always saw everything—everything except the *one* thing she wished they'd see—stared expectantly into hers.

Nicki frowned. "That's so annoying."

"What?"

"You know darn well *what*." She narrowed her gaze. "You're doing that thing you always do."

"That *thing?*" One of his dark brows arched, making her want to physically growl.

How was it possible for a guy to be both teeth-clenchingly frustrating and heart-stoppingly attractive, all at the same damn time?

"Yes, Ethan. That thing. You know, where you study someone a little too closely and try to look for something that isn't really there?"

Only this time, it *was* there. More than he or anyone else knew.

"I'm just trying to figure out what has you hiding out here instead of enjoying the party."

"I'm not hiding," Nicki insisted a bit too defensively before licking her nervous lips. "I needed to get some fresh air."

Liar, liar.

After another assessing glance, Ethan drew in a deep breath and pulled his arm away. Resting both hands on his denim-covered lap, he lifted one shoulder in a casual-yet-telling shrug.

"My mistake."

Great. It was his going-away party, and now she'd upset him. Not exactly how she was hoping this evening would go.

You should tell him. Now, before he leaves town for good. Once that happens, you may never get the chance.

Nerves danced low in her belly. At eighteen—almost nineteen—she'd been on her fair share of dates. Nothing serious or fancy. Mostly a simple movie night here and there.

But thanks to strong warnings from the man currently sitting next to her—warnings she'd learned about *after* the fact—the boys she'd dated up to this point had been nothing short of complete gentlemen.

Nicki didn't want a gentleman. Okay, she did, but she also wanted...

More.

The other boys at her school were nice enough, but most were annoying and totally immature. Mainly because they were all still a bunch of...well...*boys*.

When Nicki pictured herself as one half of a couple, she always saw herself with someone who was strong and brave. A man who was unafraid to stand up for what he believed in, and who went after what he wanted without hesitation or remorse. Someone just like...

Ethan.

Tell. Him.

"Will you come back?" She cleared the crackling out of her dry throat. "To Woodlyn Falls, I mean?"

She and her father had moved here when she was nine. Her mom had just passed away after a long, heartbreaking battle with ovarian cancer, and her grieving father had needed a change. A fresh start for them both, he'd called it.

They'd packed up their things and headed south, trading

the fast-paced way of life in Cincinnati for the Norman Rockwell quaintness of Woodlyn Falls, Kentucky.

"Of *course*, I'll come back." Ethan frowned. "This place is my home, Nic. My folks are here… You and Trey are here. I came back after boot camp, didn't I?"

Trey Ward was the third member of their self-monikered Three Musketeers. Where one was, usually all three were. Or at least that's how things used to be.

It's all about to change.

"Didn't I?" Ethan repeated himself with a playful nudge of his broad shoulder.

"Yeah." Her answer was soft. "But that was just boot camp, Ethan. This is BUD/S."

BUD/S, or Basic Underwater Demolition and SEAL training, was arguably the military's hardest, most intense training a Navy man could endure. Only the best of the best made it through to the end, and that's exactly what Ethan was…

The best.

"So?"

"*So*…" She brought her forlorn gaze to his. "I watch T.V. I know what that means."

A touch of humor glinted in his soulful eyes. "And what exactly do you think that means?"

"That you'll be sent off to who knows where to do all sorts of dangerous missions. You'll be gone for weeks at a time. Maybe months. I'm guessing you'll need to get a place close to whatever base you're assigned to so when you get back from all those undisclosed locations, you'll go there. Not here."

Okay, so maybe she'd put a little too much thought into all of this, but why wouldn't she? Ethan was her person. Her confidant. And he was about to head off to a world that didn't include her.

I need him to stay in my world.

Ethan's dark eyes sparkled with a sideways smirk that drove her wild. "Who says I won't come back here?"

"Come on, Ethan." Nicki pushed herself up from the bench. Crossing her arms at her chest, she turned back around to face him. "I'm not stupid."

"Never said you were, sweetheart."

Sweetheart.

Her chest tightened. God, she loved it when he called her that. Even though it meant something entirely different to her than to him.

But hearing it now only made the aching in her heart more profound.

"Once you leave tomorrow, things will never be the same." Nicki sighed, her shoulders falling slightly. "I just..." She bit her bottom lip. "I just hate how everything's changing."

Ethan rose from his seat to join her. Shoving his hands into the pockets of his well-worn jeans, he stepped closer. "Change is one of the few constants in life, Nic. Sometimes it's good. Other times, not so much. All we can do is roll with it and hope that everything turns out the way it's supposed to."

"But what if it doesn't?" Nicki gave her lips another nervous lick. "What if we make the wrong choice, and it leads us down a path we were never supposed to travel?"

It was the same question she'd spent the last few days contemplating.

Tilting his handsome head slightly to the side, Ethan considered her question. Drawing in a deep breath through his perfectly straight nose, he exhaled slowly with a simple shrug.

"That's always a risk, sure. But I figure it's better than living the rest of my life with regrets and what-ifs. It's why I'm going to BUD/S now instead of waiting another year or two. Hell, I still may end up bowing out and ringing that damn bell. But I won't know unless I try."

Nicki knew which bell he was referring to. Men who chose not to continue on with their dream of becoming a SEAL rang a brass bell, signaling their concession and the end of their time in BUD/S.

"You won't ring it." She shook her head with confidence.

"I don't know." He rubbed the muscles at the back of his neck. "The next twenty-four weeks are gonna be hell."

"I *do* know." He would complete the intense training with flying colors. Of that, Nicki was certain. "You can do anything you put your mind to, Ethan." He always had. "There's no doubt in my mind, you'll be the best Navy SEAL there's ever been."

As they stood there, staring at one another under the light of the moon and stars, she couldn't help but take his previous words to heart.

I won't know unless I try.

He was right. About so many things.

In less than twenty-four hours, he'd be flying across the country to California. If she didn't make her move now, she may never get another chance.

The risk was massive. Just the *thought* of losing her best friend was crushing. It was also a very real possibility.

On the one hand, Ethan could pull her into his arms and tell her he loved her, too. In her head, that's how this terrifying moment always played out. Best case scenario and all that.

But the worst case—the one that always seemed to barge its way into her blissful fantasies—would be if he rejected her. If that happened, things between them would never be the same.

A possibility that left her insides quaking with trepidation.

"There's something else, isn't there?" Ethan's deep voice rolled straight through her.

Nicki nodded; the emotional ball stuck at the base of her throat preventing her from speaking.

Concern darkened his gaze as he rested one of his strong hands on her shoulder. "What is it, Nic? You know you can tell me anything."

Could she, though?

You have to. You'll hate yourself forever if you don't.

This was it. The most definitive moment of her entire life. And despite the fear swirling around inside her, Nicki knew what she had to do.

She took a step forward. With mere inches between them, she lifted her hesitant gaze to Ethan's. *It's now or never.*

"Nicki?"

Swallowing back the urge to blow off the whole crazy idea, she sucked a steeling breath and went for it. "There *is* something I wanted to say. But I think maybe...m-maybe it would be better if I just showed you."

"Okaaay..." His voice trailed off, and it was clear he had no idea what she was about to do.

Please, God. Please don't let this be a mistake.

Shuffling her sandaled feet across the remaining inches separating them, Nicki raised a trembling hand to Ethan's muscled chest. She could feel his big heart beating strongly beneath her palm.

With her hand resting steadily against the soft fabric of his dark gray t-shirt, she rose onto her tiptoes, closed her eyes, and pressed her lips to his.

Ethan's entire body became stiff beneath the unexpected touch. His mouth brushed against hers as he started to ask, "Nicki, what are you—"

"I want to be more than just your friend, Ethan." She opened her eyes and met his gaze. "I have for a long time. I just didn't know how to tell you."

Hope bloomed inside her chest as a flash of heat flared behind his dark eyes. When he remained stoically quiet, Nicki kissed him again.

She moved in deeper than before, letting the tip of her tongue meet the seam of his stunned mouth. Still, he made no move to reciprocate.

Come on, Ethan. Time to kiss me back.

Not ready to give up on the dream of becoming his, Nicki decided to give him another few seconds to come to grips with the bomb she'd just dropped. After that, she'd gather what little dignity she had left, and she'd walk away with her head held—

Ethan's primal male growl reverberated down her throat. In the very next heartbeat, his hands were on her hips, his tongue dancing feverishly with hers.

Holy crap!

It was finally happening! She was actually kissing Ethan McAllister! More importantly, he was kissing her *back!* And Lord have mercy...

The man sure knew what he was doing.

He tasted of beer and desire, the combination sending a rush of arousal straight to her core. From the steely bulge pressing against her belly, Nicki could tell he was every bit as turned on as she was.

A fact that sent her heart racing and her virgin body aching for more.

Several seconds passed. The longer they stood there, tasting each other for the very first time, the more convinced she became that this was right. That *he* was right. In short, Ethan was...

The one.

Having secretly loved him for pretty much forever, Nicki relished every single second in his arms. Every lick. Every taste. Every dig from his fingertips into the soft flesh of her hips.

Completely lost in the moment, she wasn't the least bit prepared for his next move. Or the heartbreaking words that followed.

"Wait." He pulled his mouth from hers. With a gentle grip on her shoulders, he put several inches of space between them.

"What's wrong?" She licked his taste from her swollen lips.

Horrified, Nicki watched as he used the back of his hand to wipe the remnants of their kiss away. With his gaze fixed on the concrete beneath their feet, Ethan rubbed the slight stubble covering his tense jaw.

"I'm sorry. I…" He shook his head. "Shit, Nic. I shouldn't have done that."

"You didn't. I was the one who—"

"But I kissed you back."

Yes, he had. Quite thoroughly, as a matter of fact.

So why won't he look at me?

Before, he'd been full of passion and heat, feasting on her as if he were a starving man. But now—seconds after their mind-blowing kiss had come to an end—all signs of that same passion were gone.

Destroyed by the regret pouring from his apologetic gaze.

"You're my best friend, Nic." Ethan ran a hand down his handsome face. "This…this can't happen."

No, no, no!

Hugging herself, Nicki lifted her chin and did her best not to sound as pathetically disheartened as she felt. "It can, if it's what we both want."

And he was most definitely something she wanted. More than anything in the entire world.

As for Ethan, well…she'd *felt* just how much he'd wanted her, too. Which was why his reaction had her both stunned and confused.

"Why?" He at least owed her that much.

For some reason, her question gave him pause.

Opening his mouth, Ethan started to answer but stopped himself short. He repeated the fish-out-of-water move two more times before speaking up again.

"It's like you said." His tone became flat and emotionless. Very un-Ethan like. "I'm leaving town tomorrow."

She had been the one to point that fact out a few minutes earlier, but only as motivation to finally do something about her burgeoning feelings toward him. Not as a reason to avoid them, altogether.

"You said you'd be back," she reminded him.

"Eventually." Ethan's sigh made her stomach churn. "But I have no idea when. BUD/S is a six-month commitment all on its own. And like you said, once I'm finished with that, they're going to assign me to one of the Teams. Sure, I'll come back home when I can, but I don't know how often that's going to be. Hell, I don't even know if I'll end up stationed on the east coast or the west."

"We're basically in the middle of the country." Nicki was quick to counter. "Either way, you'll only be a plane ride away."

"True, but you're leaving for art school in a month."

"So?"

The look of sympathy he wore tore her to shreds. "So, even if we wanted to pursue whatever it is you think you feel for me, we're both going to be too busy with our own things to even think about starting up something right now."

What I think *I feel? I love you, you big jerk.* That's *how I feel!*

Anger seeped into her veins. The longer she stared back at him, the more it fueled the hurt clawing away at her broken heart.

"Is this really about you going off to be a SEAL, or is it because it's me?" She had to know. "And please…be honest, Ethan."

He'd always, *always* been honest with her.

Sure, she'd felt his impressive erection when they'd been kissing. And the way he'd grabbed her and pulled her body flush with his had made her feel as though Ethan was as attracted to her as she was to him.

But as she stood there, waiting for him to answer her simple question, Nicki realized his physical reaction to kissing her didn't necessarily mean a thing. After all, he was a healthy twenty-four-year-old man. Of *course,* certain parts of his body would react...*that way.* Heck, every guy his age probably got hard after a kiss like the one they'd just shared.

And suddenly, it all became crystal freaking clear.

Ethan's erection wasn't the problem. It was his heart. Nicki's already belonged to him. Probably always would. But apparently his wasn't up for grabs.

Not for her, anyway.

"Why the hell would you think it's you?" The skin between his dark brows scrunched together with a deep scowl. His elevated voice nearly making her jump.

"Seriously?" She rolled her eyes. "I'm not blind, Ethan. I look nothing like the girls you've dated."

They'd all been tall. Skinny. Brunette. Basically, the complete *opposite* of her.

At barely five-three, Nicki was what her dad called "vertically challenged". She was also a natural blonde. And while she wasn't fat, she had more curves than most of the other girls in her class. So…. not Ethan's type.

Not. At. All.

"You're beautiful, Nic." His deep voice broke through her thoughts. "There's not a fucking thing wrong with you."

"If that were true, you wouldn't be shutting me down."

"I'm not shutting you—" Ethan blew out a frustrated breath. Raking his fingers through his short, black hair, he rolled his lips inward before starting again. "I don't want to hurt you. That's the last thing I *ever* want to do." Moving in, he lifted his hand toward her face and cupped one of her cheeks. "You're one of the most important people in my life, and I don't want to do anything to screw that up. And even if our friendship wasn't an issue, I could never ask you to wait for me while I'm—"

"Please don't." Nicki stepped back, forcing herself to pull herself free from his reach. "Don't use the Navy as an excuse. If you don't want to be more than friends, just say so."

One thing she learned early on about her friend Ethan... He went after what he wanted, and most of the time, he got it.

But he wasn't going after her.

He's pushing me away.

Something akin to pain flashed behind his troubled gaze, but it was gone as quickly as it appeared. With his shoulders back and his strong jaw fixed, Ethan looked her in the eyes and destroyed the only dream she'd ever truly had.

"I'm sorry, Nic. I-I don't know what else to say."

There wasn't anything more for him *to* say. Nicki had her answer. It wasn't the one she'd hoped for. Not even close. But at least now she knew...

Her love for Ethan wasn't reciprocated. Not in the way she'd prayed it would be.

Tears welled in her eyes, but by some miracle, she managed to hold them back. She wouldn't destroy what was left of her dissipating dignity by falling apart in front of him.

She would *not*.

"It's okay." With a forced smile, Nicki started to move past him. "You don't need to say anything."

She made it two full steps before Ethan's hand snaked out to stop her.

"Nicki, wait," he implored. "Don't leave. Not like this. You know I can't stand it when you're upset."

Ignoring the electric zing his innocent touch created, Nicki glanced back at him from over her shoulder. It took every ounce of strength she had, but she relaxed her features and allowed her smile to grow.

Because damn it. Even though he'd just crushed her, she couldn't bring herself to storm off with this hanging over his head. Despite her anger and heartache, the last thing Nicki wanted was for Ethan to go into BUD/S distracted because he thought she hated him.

Mustering her most genuine smile, she looked him square in the eyes and lied. "It's all good, Ethan. Really. Let's just forget this ever happened." She shrugged. "I already have."

"Nic, I—"

"Good luck with BUD/S." She pulled her wrist free from his gentle hold. "I know you'll do great. I'll...see you when you get back."

Unless I find a deep, dark hole to crawl into between now and then.

With her head held high, Nicki somehow managed to turn her back on him and walk away. Despite her silent prayers to the contrary, Ethan didn't call out for her again. The deafening silence another, final sign that this had all been a horrible, awful mistake.

And as she got into her car and drove away, she began to let go of her dreams—and the only man she'd ever truly wanted.

CHAPTER ONE

United States Embassy, Athens Greece
   Present day...

"ON BEHALF of His Majesty the King and my people, I would like to thank you and your men for assuring my safe arrival here in Greece."

Ethan "Apollo" McAllister stood to the side, watching as the man they'd spent the last sixteen hours protecting extended a hand to Digger, Ethan's team leader.

"Just doing our job, Mr. Ambassador." Digger returned the gesture.

Known to the rest of the world as Slade Garrison, Digger had been heading up Tac-Ops Team since the elite group was formed four years prior. A thirty-four-year-old former SEAL, the deadly man was known for his stoic personality, demolitions expertise, and all-around badassness.

"It's an honorable job, Mr. Garrison." Ambassador Ronald Baker released Digger's hand. The distinguished man's thick English accent was prominent as he spoke. "As I'm sure you are aware, my history with your boss is quite lengthy. Prior to our agreement to have Tac-Ops handle my security for this trip, Rafe filled me in on the kind of men you all are and what you do. That's how I know babysitting me is far beneath your team's level of skill and experience. I just hope you realize the job does not diminish the importance of your team's actions."

The 'Rafe' Ambassador Baker was referring to was Rafe Owens, creator of Tac-Ops, and Ethan's boss.

Tac-Ops—short for Tactical Operations—was the personal protection and hostage rescue team Ethan was damn proud to be a part of. Though the company was still relatively new to the world of security, there were already three teams stationed around the world, with more to come.

"Of course." Digger responded by giving Baker a polite nod.

"You know…" The British official spoke again. "Attending this meeting with Ambassador LaCroix is my last official duty before my retirement. It's been a wonderful ride, doing what I do, but I'd be lying if I said I wasn't looking forward to its end."

"What will you do once this conference is over?" Garrett "Falcon" Morgan, the team's sniper, asked from his place beside Ethan. "Our orders were to deliver you to the embassy here in Athens and then return to the States. I'm assuming you've already arranged for transportation back to England when you're finished here?"

"Actually, no," Baker responded with a shake of his head. "My resignation paperwork has been filed and approved, and my replacement is scheduled to take over my duties immediately following the conference's end. My wife is flying into Athens later this week, and from here, we're going to take a relaxing, long-overdue vacation."

"Good for you," Ethan offered sincerely. He and his teammates understood better than most how important a little downtime could be.

"Good for us *both*, Mr. McAllister." Baker turned his wise gaze in Ethan's direction. "You know, it really is true what they say about powerful men and the women who stand behind them. Without my Mabel, everything I've done with my life would be meaningless."

The man's affectionate words struck a sudden and unwelcomed chord with Ethan. Almost instantly, his mind conjured up the unsolicited image of a beautiful blonde with big blue eyes and dimples he longed to kiss.

A woman who used to know more about him than his own mother. The same woman Ethan had spent the last ten years trying to forget.

"Well, I suppose I should be going." The silver haired ambassador's voice tore Ethan away from his thoughts. "Wouldn't want to be late to the meeting. Besides, you have another long trip ahead of you. Thanks again, gentlemen. And safe travels to all of you." Baker gave the team a parting glance before disappearing through one of the embassy's guarded double-doors.

Looking down, Digger checked the time on his watch. "It's a little before eight here," he announced to the group. "We leave now, that puts us landing back home around seven tomorrow night."

"You're kidding right?" Bones looked at Digger as if he'd lost his damn mind. "We flew all the way to Greece just to drop this guy off and go back home?"

"You knew the assignment when we got it, Bones," Digger reminded the former Marine.

"Well, yeah, but...it's Greece, man." Bones—otherwise known as Beckett Stone—looked to the others for support. "I mean, the jet's not going anywhere without us, and we all slept on the flight over. Why not take a few hours to paint the town?"

Ethan arched a brow. "Paint the town?"

"Yeah, you know. Go sightseeing and shit." Reaching

down, Bones pulled his tablet free from its armored frame mounted on the front of his protective vest. Swiping his index finger across the small screen, the Texan started listing off all the places he apparently wanted to see. "We could go to the Acropolis and see the Parthenon. Oh, and then there's the Ruins of the Marketplace…"

"It *would* be cool to see the Parthenon," Falcon added.

With a what-the-hell shrug, Ethan decided to join in. "I heard the local food is pretty good."

Standing in the Embassy's elaborate entrance, the three teammates sounded a lot like brothers trying to talk their dad into taking them to an amusement park or someplace fun. But Digger wasn't having it.

"Owens was clear in his orders." Their leader shook his head. "We were to escort Ambassador Baker here, deliver him safely, and return home. He finds out we wasted company time gallivanting around Athens like a bunch of tourists, it'll be all our asses."

"I'm sorry, did you just say *gallivanting?*" Bones' expression turned serious. The former Marine's dark brows bunched with concern as he glanced at Ethan and the others. "Uh, oh, guys. I think the Brit may have rubbed off on our boy."

With a roll of his hazel eyes and a mumbled, "Fuck off," Digger turned and started down the building's concrete steps.

"Never mind! False alarm, everyone!" Bones put his hands up as if to settle down a non-existent crowd. "It was a close call, but I think our boy's gonna be okay. I repeat, the crisis has been averted."

Unable to hold back, Ethan, Falcon, and Bones all laughed together as they followed their leader down the steps and toward the secured parking area.

Squinting against the sun, Ethan slid his black tactical sunglasses down over his eyes while squelching the urge to shiver against the cool morning air. Spring was only a week away, but at barely forty degrees, the outside temperature felt more like winter.

Piling in the armored SUV their boss had arranged for them to use while in Athens, Ethan and Falcon chose the back seat while Digger and Bones sat up front. Clicking his seatbelt into place, Bones shifted in the passenger seat so he was facing Digger.

"Seriously, Dig." He continued to beg the man behind the wheel. "Can't we at least take a small detour? Just drive *by* some of the amazingly cool places that are here before we go back to the jet?"

"Straight home, Bones." Digger's tone left little room for argument. "Those were our orders, so that's what we're doing."

"Fine." Receding in his efforts to convince their team leader to change his mind, Bones settled back against his leather seat and stared longingly out the window. Under his breath, he added a grumbled, "Fun sucker."

Ethan caught himself smirking from his spot directly behind the disappointed operative. As the liveliest of the bunch, Bones was also the most emotional. The guy reigned it in, when necessary, but it was moments like this when his class-clown attitude shined through.

It was just one of the many things Ethan loved about being a part of this team. Each man brought to the table a special skillset, as well as a unique personality.

Together, they worked as an unbreakable, unbeatable force. And when it came down to the wire, there wasn't anyone Ethan would rather have in his corner.

Except her.

Shaking his head, he physically forced the frustrating thought away. It had been ten years, damn it. Ten. Years.

Time to move the hell on, don't you think?

Ethan ground his teeth together as he pretended to focus

intently on the historic scenery. It was the same mental reminder he'd given himself time and again. But this time...*this* time...he was finally going to listen.

Nicki was married to Trey, now. A man who, in another life, had been one of Ethan's closest friends.

The real kick in the nuts was that he couldn't even be pissed at the guy because Ethan had never admitted how he truly felt about her. Not to Trey. Not to anyone.

By the time he got his head out of his ass and decided to lay it all out for her, it was too late. Nicki was already with Trey, and last Ethan heard, the two were living the life he could only dream about.

And the only person he had to blame was himself.

Should've known better than to think you could have it all.

Yes, he should have. But as the voice in his head had so eloquently pointed out earlier, it was time to move the hell on. Starting now.

Glancing out the tinted window to his right, Ethan expected to feel lighter after finally making the choice to let go of something that would never be. But as he studied the scenery blurring past, all he felt was grief as he mourned what might have been.

"Think we can talk Owens into giving us a day off to recoup from this whirlwind trip?" Falcon asked no one in particular.

The question pulled Ethan back to the present. He blinked, surprised to see they'd already traveled several miles down the road.

From the front passenger seat, Bones shot Falcon a look from over his shoulder. "Dude. You just had like two weeks off for your honeymoon."

Falcon's expression turned incredulous. "*Dude.* That was like six months ago."

"Really?" Bones' brows furrowed a second before his

mouth turned upward into a cocky grin. "Guess time flies when you're kicking ass and saving the world."

Saving the world was a bit of an exaggeration. But the men of Tac-Ops did what they could to at least make it a little better.

"I bet if we ask nicely, Owens will give the green light for a couple extra vacation days," Falcon used the rearview mirror to glance at their driver. "What about you, Digger? Think Boss will let us—"

The ringing of Digger's phone cut off whatever else Falcon was about to say.

With it rested securely in the dashboard cradle, the name on the screen was visible to all. Digger tapped the screen and put the call on speaker.

"Hey, Shadow." He greeted the team's technical analyst. "The package has been delivered. You can let Owens know we're headed back to the jet, now."

Shadow—the only name by which Ethan and the others had ever known the mysterious woman—was an all-around tech goddess and hacker extraordinaire. Though they'd never seen her or met her in person, each man of Tac-Ops considered her a part of their team.

The woman was full of sass and could banter with the best of them, but she was also instrumental in the team's safety and success during their ops. Working overwatch from behind the scenes, Ethan and the others always felt secure knowing she had their back.

"No can do, big guy." Shadow's soft, feminine voice filled the SUV's interior. "I'm gonna need you to turn your handsome selves around and head back to the embassy."

"Turn around?" Ethan scooted forward so the woman could hear him more clearly. "Why are you sending us back?"

"Not me," Shadow clarified. "These orders came from the top."

"Okay, then why does *Owens* want us to return to the embassy?"

"Well, I'd tell you, Apollo"—the woman gave a dramatic pause—"but then I'd have to kill you." A moment of silence passed seconds before a small snort came through the phone's speakers. "Come on, guys. Really? That was funny. What's wrong, you forget to pack your sense of humor for this trip?"

"Shadow..." Digger warned, clearly not in the mood for Shadow's playful antics.

"Fine, fine, I'll get down to business." She released a long sigh of disappointment. "Okay, so here's the scoop. You're to return to the embassy, meet up with another team that should be arriving there as we speak, and assist them with a full evacuation of the property."

Not waiting for more information, Digger started to slow down. At the first break in traffic, he spun the SUV around and headed back in the opposite direction.

Tires squealed as the car directly behind them slammed on its breaks. Several other displeased drivers honked their horns in anger as they sped past, but the four men ignored them, their focus remaining solely on the sudden change of plans.

"What team are we meeting up with?" Ethan asked.

The vehicle made an abrupt swerve into the other lane, prompting Ethan to reach up and squeeze the edge of Bones' seat. At the same time, Bones grabbed the oh-shit handle, his knuckles turning white from their effort.

"And what exactly is it we're getting ourselves into?" Falcon piggybacked off of Ethan's question.

"Colonel Robinson just contacted Owens," Shadow explained. "If you'll remember, Robinson's the man in charge of the Delta Force team that assisted you with the hostage situation in the Dominican a few months back."

Hell yeah, Ethan remembered. How could he not? The

colonel's men were instrumental in the successful rescue of Falcon's now-wife, Avery, when she was kidnapped and held captive.

"Anyway…" Shadow spoke up again. "Robinson's team just arrived on scene after receiving intel from SecDef."

The colonel in charge of the fiercest Delta Force team in existence *and* the Secretary of Defense were involved? Whatever this thing was, it couldn't be good.

"Ghost and those guys are really here?" Falcon sounded as shocked as Ethan felt. "In *Athens?*"

Captain Keane "Ghost" Bryson and his Delta Force brothers had proven themselves to be a solid unit. They were men Ethan and the others had come to know well, and more importantly, they trusted them.

But why the hell were they in Athens, and what did it have to do with Tac-Ops?

Answering Ethan's unspoken question, Shadow explained further. "The Delta Force team arrived in the city less than an hour ago to meet with the mayor, as well as the head of local law enforcement, about a potential attack on the embassy. We're hoping it's all for not, but as you know, something like this can't be ignored."

"Attack?" Digger's deep voice rumbled as he swerved through traffic. "What exactly are we talking about here, Shadow?"

"SecDef's people intercepted chatter about a possible raid on the property. As a precaution, Ghost and his men were sent in to oversee the embassy's evacuation, including the annex next door. When SecDef learned you were in town, he contacted Owens and Owens had me call you."

"The Secretary of Defense called Owens directly?" Ethan's voice elevated to a slightly higher level.

That their boss was well-connected was no secret. But damn.

Ethan and Falcon shared a look before Falcon asked, "Where's the threat coming from?"

"*Possible* threat," Shadow reminded them. "And according to Secretary Bradford's intel, a sympathizer militant group known as The Dunamis is planning to take control of the property as a show of their revolt against the country's current leaders."

"The Dunamis…" Looking around at Ethan and the vehicle's other passengers, Bones frowned. "Never heard of them. What's their angle?"

"Dunamis means 'power' in Greek. From everything I've been able to find, these men want it and will kill anyone in order to get it."

"Shadow, we were literally *just* there," Bones reminded her. "Everything was fine."

"As I said, it's our hope that it will remain as such. For now, Owens wants you to get your sweet asses back to the embassy to offer the other team whatever assistance they need."

"Get out of the way, dumbass!" Digger's angry voice cut through the conversation. Slapping the palm of his hand against his horn, he shot a glare in the direction of an unaware pedestrian trying to jaywalk directly into their SUV's path. Startled, the man jumped back onto the sidewalk at the last second, then proceeded to flip them all the bird.

Shaking his head, Ethan blew out a breath. "Okay, so what's the plan once the evacuation is complete?"

"Assuming you don't meet an untimely end as a result of Digger's road rage?" Shadow teased. "You and the Delta team will escort Ambassadors Baker and LaCroix to a secured facility across town, along with any staff members present. You already have the property's floor plans and layout from the files I sent prior to the original assignment, as well as a list of those who should be present today. Use that information to ensure all spaces are cleared and every occupant is accounted for. Once you arrive at the secondary location, we will devise a plan based on the current situation. For now, your priority is getting those people out of there."

"Copy that," Digger acknowledged the order.

Ghost and his men had once put their lives on the line to help rescue Avery, who they all considered to be one of their own. As far as Ethan and the others were concerned, they'd help the kick ass Delta Force team do just about any damn thing they wanted.

"There's one more thing." Shadow's voice came through the speaker once more. "Bradford also asked Owens for a small favor."

"So, what exactly does this *favor* entail?" Digger spoke as he expertly maneuvered their SUV through heavy traffic.

"One of SecDef's people is on the property," Shadow explained. "A civilian artist on loan to the State Department. She's been overseeing the delivery and placement of the new art pieces that were procured as part of the embassy's recent renovations. Secretary Bradford wants your team to personally watch over her and ensure her safe arrival back to the States."

"This artist is coming home with us?" Ethan sincerely hoped he'd heard wrong.

Guarding a British Ambassador was one thing. Babysitting a hoity-toity artsy type, who'd probably throw a fit the second they interrupted her picture hanging, was altogether different.

"Affirmative," Shadow confirmed. "Once we know it's safe to move, she, Ambassador Baker, and Ambassador LaCroix will accompany you on the flight back to the States."

"So much for Baker's long-overdue vacation," Bones muttered low.

"That's all I know right now." Shadow began wrapping things up. "I'll be in touch as additional intel comes through. In the meantime, watch your asses out there. You've all been granted the same jurisdiction and privileges as Ghost's team, which will remain in effect for the duration of the op. Your orders are simple, gentlemen. Secure the property, escort all those on site to safety, and bring Baker, LaCroix, and the DoD employee home. Anyone who attempts to interfere with the implementation of these orders is to be considered a hostile threat, and you should respond accordingly. Any questions?"

"What about the local authorities?" Ethan rushed to ask before the brilliant woman could end the call. "They gonna be a problem?"

Given the positive relationship Greece currently had with the United States, he sure as hell hoped not.

"The Athenian government is aware of the situation and has offered their assistance, as well," Shadow put his mind at ease. "Not only are they expecting you, but they're also *glad* you're there. Trust me, no one involved wants this thing turning into another bloodbath like the one in Libya a few years back."

Several grumbled agreements filled the vehicle's closed space as the members of Tac-Ops One silently recalled that tragic day. Each of the four men had still been serving active duty when the embassy in Libya was overrun by militants.

Despite the years that had passed, Ethan's memories of that day were still as crystal fucking clear as if it were yesterday. And though none of them said it out loud, he and his team would do whatever it took to keep something like that from ever happening again.

"I'm switching off, now." Shadow brought the conversation to an end. "You all have my number. Use it if you need it. I'll be at my computer until I know you're in the air and on your way home."

"Copy that." Digger tapped the screen to end the call.

"Well, that was unexpected," Bones commented to no one in particular.

From over the back of the SUV's front passenger seat, Ethan gave the man's shoulder a tight squeeze. "Well, Beck. You wanted to stay in Greece a little longer. Looks like you got your way, after all."

Bones scoffed before responding with a dry, "Careful what you wish for, right?"

That's no shit.

While Digger concentrated on the road, the rest of the team began a habitual double-check of their weapons and coms. Not wanting to risk a jammed round or communications breakdown, it was a routine they followed faithfully.

A few short minutes later, they were pulling up to a group of police officers standing near two wooden A-framed barricades.

"Damn, they work fast." Ethan looked out the windshield at the small group of Athens' finest. They'd driven down this same road not long ago, yet the area already looked completely different.

From the seat beside him, Falcon followed Ethan's line of sight. "Let's hope Shadow's intel is right, and these guys don't put up a fight."

Bringing the SUV to a stop a few feet away, Digger rolled down his tinted window so the Athenian officials approaching them could see they were friendly.

With a thick Grecian accent, the young officer began to speak as he grew closer to their vehicle. "I'm sorry, sir, but this road has been temporarily closed."

Holding up the official government ID Tac-Ops used on occasions such as this, Digger quickly explained who they were and why they needed permission to continue. "We have orders to assist with the embassy's evacuation."

The officer eyed their protective vests and weapons closely before studying Digger's ID. Using the coms system attached to his own vest, the younger man relayed the situation, presumably to someone higher up the chain.

Whoever it was, they'd thankfully been brought up to speed. Without another word, the officer handed Digger back his ID before waving them forward.

Immediately, the barricade was opened, allowing them to drive through without incident. Two minutes later, the team was officially back on American soil and exiting their SUV.

Ethan eyed the two men headed in their direction. "Hey, isn't that Hollywood and…damn it. What's that other guy's name?"

"Blade," Bones reminded him as they rounded the front of the vehicle.

With a quick snap of his fingers, Ethan nodded. "Blade. That's right."

The two Delta Force operators strode toward them with the same level of confidence most special forces men held. Present company, included.

Dressed much like Ethan and his team, Hollywood and Blade wore sunglasses, long-sleeve t-shirts, jeans, combat boots, and tactical protective vests. In their hands were military-issued automatic rifles.

Standing right at six feet, Hollywood's dark hair was a bit too long, but the man had a face that probably melted women's panties at first sight. Luckily for Ethan and the rest of the single male population, Hollywood was happily married.

Blade, who was about three inches taller than his teammate, had thick, dark scruff and slightly crooked teeth. He wasn't quite as model-perfect as Hollywood, but Ethan was willing to bet the woman who'd put the ring on the man's left hand thought differently.

A familiar jealous ache did its damnedest to pry its way into Ethan's heart. There once was a time he believed true love and happily ever after wasn't in the cards for men like him. But just like Falcon and Avery, every man on Ghost's Delta team had found a way to make married life work.

So could you, if you'd get your head out of your ass and quit hanging onto something that's never going to happen.

"Ghost said you guys were in town." Hollywood's voice broke through Ethan's untimely thoughts.

"We were just about to fly out when we got orders to come back." Digger shook the other man's hand.

When the handshake had finished, Falcon pulled Hollywood in for a half-hug, patting the other man hard on the back. "Hey, man. Good to see you again."

"You too, brother." Hollywood grinned as he pulled away. "How's that pretty new wife of yours?"

Falcon's lips curved into the same affectionate smile he always wore whenever someone mentioned Avery. "She's good. Really good."

"Glad to hear it. Hey, you guys remember Blade…" Hollywood motioned toward his teammate.

"Of course." Falcon shook the man's hand. "How's it going?"

"Can't complain." Blade smirked before sliding his focus to Ethan. "Apollo, right?"

Ethan gave the man a quick nod. "That's me. And in case you've forgotten, this is—"

"Bones." Hollywood finished for him. "Good to see you, too, man."

"Right back atcha." Bones shook both Hollywood's and Blade's hands.

With the greetings complete, Digger got right down to business. "We're here to assist *you* this time, so just tell us where you want us."

"All right, then." Appreciation filled Hollywood's dark eyes. "Ghost, Fletch, Beatle, Coach, and Truck are already inside. While they apprise the ambassadors and staff of the situation, why don't you guys head on over to the annex." He pointed to Ethan's left, toward the smaller, two-story building located just south of the main building. "The embassy's head of security has been read in on the potential threat, so the staff there should already be gathering their things and preparing to leave. With any luck, this will be nothing more than a quick and easy transport job."

"Sounds good to me." Digger nodded.

"Speaking of transport," Bones interjected. He tilted his head toward a line of black, government-issued Suburbans parked in a line along the building's secured drive. "Those your rides out of here?"

"They are," Blade confirmed. "All gassed up with the keys in the ignitions. Since we've got a bigger team and more bodies to guard, we figured we'd take the first three. That leaves the last one for you, plus the one you drove here."

Pulling a folded piece of paper from one of his tactical vest pockets, Hollywood handed it to Digger. "That's an updated list of those currently inside the annex. Lucky for us, most of the staff was given the day off as soon as Ambassador LaCroix was made aware of the situation. Which is good, since the powers that be want this place cleared before the top of the hour."

Ethan glanced down at his tactical watch. "That leaves us a whole forty minutes to get everyone off the property."

"Guess we'd best get to it, then." Digger turned toward the embassy's annex positioned about thirty yards from where they stood.

Hollywood tipped his head in a solid nod. "I'll let Ghost know you're on it."

"Catch you boys on the flip side." Blade gave them all a half-salute.

With their objective clear, Digger tossed the keys to their SUV to Bones. "Park the car in line with the others then join us inside."

Snagging the keys with ease, Bones proceeded to follow orders as Ethan, Digger, and the others started across the perfectly manicured lawn separating the two buildings. The three men kept their heads on a constant swivel, their rifles held across their torsos as they moved.

"How many we lookin' at, Dig?" Ethan asked their leader as they made their way across the soft grass.

Digger gave the creased paper a quick scan. "Looks like ten, including the artist."

Artist.

The word sent Ethan's gut rolling. Against his will, he thought of another artist. One who had no idea she'd owned his heart for over a decade.

Goddamn it, McAllister. Knock that shit off!

The voice in his head was right. He was over Nicki. Or he would be, anyway. Because he was absolutely, one hundred percent done with the past. Not to mention, he needed to stay focused on the task at hand.

"Only ten?" Bones' Texas drawl broke through Ethan's thoughts. "I'm guessin' it won't be too hard to wrangle them up."

"Let's hope not." Digger started up the sidewalk leading to the annex's front door. He raised a hand to knock, but before he could make contact, a middle-aged man dressed in khakis and a blue button-up stepped outside.

"Gentlemen." The man greeted them with a friendly smile and a heavy Greek accent. "I'm Glenn Drakos, head of security for the annex."

Standing at about five feet, ten and probably weighing a buck forty soaking wet, the guy looked more like a museum curator than the man in charge of securing government property.

"Mr. Drakos, I'm Slade Garrison with Tactical Operations," Digger held up his ID. "My team and I have been sent here to—"

"Yes, of course." Mr. Drakos stepped to the side. "We've been expecting you. Please, come in."

With a mumbled "Thanks", Digger entered the premises, followed closely by Ethan, Bones, and Falcon.

A low whistle escaped between Bones' lips as he removed his sunglasses and glanced around the open entryway. "Wow!" He blinked. "This place is…"

"Spectacular, isn't it?" Drakos beamed with pride. "The renovations are nearly complete. I just pray whoever is behind the threat against us is bluffing. It would be a shame if someone were to destroy everything we've built here."

Sliding his own glasses to the top of his head, even Ethan couldn't help but to appreciate the building's welcoming feel.

Having already studied the intel Shadow had sent on both the embassy and the annex on the flight over, he *thought* he knew what to expect. But between the elaborate chandelier hanging over the entryway, marble floors, and comfortable seating area near the entrance, it felt more like he'd walked into a high-end hotel than a government facility.

"Mr. Drakos, not to be rude, but we're on a bit of a time crunch," Digger reminded the man. "We need everyone outside and ready to go ASAP."

The silver-haired man shook his head. "Forgive me. This situation took us all by surprise, so I'm a bit out of sorts. But please, tell me how I can help."

It was Ethan who spoke up next. "We'll need to clear all the rooms to ensure everyone gets out safely. Since you're more familiar with the building and staff, it will cut time if you'll help gather everyone and have them meet back here."

"Of course," Drakos agreed. "Let's see, there are four staff members finishing up in their offices upstairs. Our housekeepers, Darlene and Marcos, were cleaning the kitchen the last time I saw them. Two of my people are in the offices down the west hallway, securing those computers, and Ms. Castille is in the vault just down that hall. I'll start with the offices on the second floor while you gentlemen—"

"Hold up," Ethan cut the man off. "Did you say *Castille?*"

Confusion filtered through the man's eyes. "Yes. She's an American artist sent here by your government to ensure our newly acquired pieces were properly cared for in both their delivery and placement. Why? Is there some sort of problem?"

Ethan could feel the blood draining from his face as the man spoke. No way. No *fucking* way it was her.

"Nope, no problem," Digger's response barely registered as he began giving orders. "Falcon, go with Mr. Drakos and let Bones know where to meet you. Apollo and I will clear the main floor. I want everyone back out here, ready to go in ten."

"Sounds like a plan." Falcon dipped his chin.

Motioning to his left, Drakos spoke directly to Falcon. "The stairs are this way."

While Ethan stood there trying to convince himself the woman down the hallway *wasn't* the same Ms. Castille from his past, Falcon did as he was told and followed Drakos to the stairs. A loud ripping sound echoed off the freshly painted walls as Digger pulled at the Velcro top of his large vest pocket before yanking his own tablet free.

After a few taps of the screen, he pulled up the floor plans Shadow had sent earlier and gave them a quick glance. "You take the back three offices and the safe room, and I'll check the kitchen, two bathrooms, and the office at the far end of the west hall."

"Roger that," Ethan mumbled as he stared down the hallway in front of him. Belatedly he asked, "First, can I, uh... can I see that list for a second? I just want to check something."

Without question, Digger dug the list back out of his vest pocket and handed it over. Willing his gloved hands not to tremble, Ethan unfolded the paper and quickly scanned through the ten names.

His lungs froze, his entire world coming to a screeching halt when he saw it.

Nicolette Castille.

Ethan's eyes shot up from the paper, his shocked gaze flying to the open door at the end of the hall. It had to be a coincidence. It *had* to be. Except…

An American artist with the same name as Nic's? No way that shit's a coincidence.

"You good?"

Digger's question left Ethan blinking a little too forcefully. Tearing his focus away from that door, he re-folded the paper and handed it back to his team leader.

"Yeah," he lied. "Just want to make sure we don't miss anyone."

"We won't. But we do need to make it quick. I don't want to be here any longer than we have to."

Something about the way Digger spoke those words gave Ethan pause. "You think there's something wonky about all of this?" He knew as well as anyone that gut instincts were nothing to be ignored, but Digger simply blew off whatever had the man spooked.

"Probably just jet lag."

Ethan understood that, too. Between the jobs in Mexico and Turkey last month, and a couple high-end bodyguard gigs this past week, they'd all been hoping for a couple days off once they got back to the States.

He'd planned to use that time to kickstart his new lease on life. A life that didn't include obsessing over a gorgeous blonde with sexy-as-sin dimples and an ass that drove him insane with need. But now…

It's not her, dumbass. Which you'll see once you get your ass in gear and do your fucking job!

Once again, his subconscious was right. People from all over the world shared the same name. It didn't mean a thing.

Giving himself a mental reminder that he had a job to do,

Ethan headed down the hall while Digger took off to their left toward the kitchen. He wanted to go straight to that damn vault. To see for himself that the woman they'd been charged with protecting wasn't his Nicolette Castille.

She was never yours, dipshit.

No, she wasn't. The Nicki from his past, a woman who'd laid her heart on the line only to have him stomp all over it, had married his friend. Hell, her last name wouldn't even be Castille…it would be Ward. Which meant this little moment of panic was all for not.

And now it's over.

Putting the past out of his mind—hopefully for fucking good—Ethan stopped at the first room he came to. It was an office, and inside was a middle-aged African American woman who appeared to be frantically gathering her things.

She jumped when she saw him standing in the doorway. "Oh!" The startled woman put a hand to her chest. "Mercy, you scared me!"

"Sorry." His lips curved into an apologetic smile. "Didn't mean to."

"You're American," the southern woman drawled, her shoulders falling with a loud sigh of relief.

"Yes, ma'am. My team is here to escort you and the others off the property."

Sliding a laptop and a handful of files into her computer bag, she straightened her spine and said, "I'm ready to go."

You and me, both.

"We're asking everyone to meet in the entryway so we can do a quick head count before we leave."

"You don't have to tell me twice." The woman slung her bag over her shoulder and rushed across the room. "They don't pay me enough to stick around and wait for someone to start shootin' up the place."

No, he supposed they didn't.

Stepping aside, Ethan allowed her room to pass before

heading farther down the hallway to the only other office located in that part of the building. With a quick glance, he found the small space empty, leaving one final area to check.

His chest tightened as he stared at the open door at the end of the hall. In a lame attempt to distract himself, Ethan did a mental run-through of the safe room's layout. One he'd memorized from the file Shadow had sent the team earlier.

Minus two barred, bullet-resistant windows, the safe room's three outer walls were constructed from solid concrete. The private space contained a small seating area near a stone fireplace, as well as a bedroom and full bath for when Ambassador LaCroix needed to remain on property for an extended period.

On the west end of the room, he'd find two blast-resistant double-doors. In addition, a barred gate made of one-inch tubular steel had been installed behind those for added reinforcement designed to protect the fifteen-by-thirty space serving as the building's safe haven.

It all sounded very impressive, but as Ethan stepped through the ambassador's private quarters, he realized seeing was believing.

Damn.

The place looked like a palace made for a king, rather than the secured hideaway he knew it to be. With a quick scan, he could tell the main area and attached bathroom were both empty. But a shuffling sound coming from inside the secured vault to his right had him moving in that direction.

Despite his efforts against it, Ethan's breathing began to pick up. The closer he got to those damn doors, the harder his heart kicked against his ribs.

Nerves he shouldn't be feeling swirled low in his gut, and beneath the leather of his tactical gloves, he could feel sweat beginning to form on his palms.

Ethan barely resisted the urge to pull them off and wipe his hands on his thighs.

Jesus, man. You were a Navy SEAL, for Christ's sake. You've literally dodged bullets to rescue innocent hostages. Now buck the fuck up and relax because it's not her!

Taking a breath, Ethan pushed away the baggage he had no business carrying and composed himself.

He walked across the marble tile toward the large double-doors and barred gate. Stepping into the secured room, he'd just made it down three tiled steps before he spotted her.

When he did, Ethan froze mid-stride.

She was standing with her back to him, but that didn't matter. The body...the hair...the way she moved... It was all so deeply engrained in his memory that he didn't have to see the woman's face to know.

It's her. Holy shit, it's her!

Despite the pair of black dress boots she had on, Nicki still stood a full foot shorter than his six-four frame. Her blonde, wavy hair was pulled up into some sort of messy bun, and several stray curls had fallen around the nape of her delicate neck.

Ethan swallowed hard as his gaze traveled lower. Taking advantage of the fact that she hadn't spotted him yet, he soaked in the feminine curves of her tantalizing figure.

A very sexy, very *womanly* figure.

Yes, Nicki was all grown up, and damn if she wasn't a walking wet dream.

The tight black sweater she wore clung to a tiny waist, and tan dress pants hung loosely from her slightly rounded hips. They were the same hips he'd spent countless hours imagining himself gripping tightly as he moved in and out of her delectable body from behind.

The sudden hammering of a crate reminded Ethan of where he was and why he was here. Shoving the erotic image out of his sex-deprived brain, he watched with reverence as Nicki carefully placed a small sculpture into another wooden crate.

She was so intent on what she was doing, she had yet to spot him. A fact that sent his protective instincts into high gear.

You should really be more aware of your surroundings, sweetheart.

"I'm almost done." She surprised him by speaking without bothering to look up. "I just need to pack up a couple more paintings, and then I'll be ready to go."

His heart slammed against his ribs. Hearing her voice again was a shock to his system. That and the fact that she was aware of his presence, after all.

I stand corrected.

Opening his mouth, Ethan attempted to respond but found the words kept getting stuck at the base of his throat. Just seeing her again—hearing that sweet, angelic voice after all these years—sent a tingling rush racing down his spine.

And he had yet to lay eyes on her gorgeous face.

That voice, though...it still sounded soft and sweet, like when they were younger. But there was something else present. A note of strength and confidence that hadn't been there before.

And damn, if it wasn't sexy as hell.

"I promise I'm not trying to be a pain," Nicki spoke up again. "I get that you guys have a job to do, but so do I. These works of art are my responsibility. They're treasures, really, and I have to make sure they're repackaged and sealed before I leave."

For several long seconds, she went on, talking about the importance of her job while carefully wrapping and packing up the items she'd been hired to protect. Meanwhile, Ethan simply stood there, staring at her as if *she* were the long-lost treasure he'd been searching for.

When she finally turned to face him, his ability to breathe ended as his entire world came to a screeching halt.

Nicki was pretty as hell the last time he saw her. A beautiful, curvy young lady. But now? Now, she was fucking gorgeous.

A sharp intake of air seemed to fill the entire room, her wide-eyed gaze all the proof he needed that she recognized him, too. And when the woman standing before him said his name, the whispered sound was so sweet, so familiar, it was like a soothing balm to his damaged soul.

"Ethan?" Nicki stared up at him through a set of stylish glasses. Wide-eyes, her skin paled as if she were seeing a ghost.

"Oh, my God," she breathed. "Wha...what are you doing here?"

There were so many things he wanted to say. Words he'd mentally practiced more times than he cared to admit. Things that should've been said a long damn time ago.

Things like...

I'm sorry.

I made a mistake.

I never should've turned you down.

You shouldn't have married him.

I love you.

But as he stood there, staring into those gorgeous baby blues after all these years, all Ethan could think to say was, "Hey, Nic. How you been?"

CHAPTER TWO

How you been?

Minus a few awkward texts and emails, they hadn't spoken to each other in nearly ten years and *that's* all he had to say?

Nicki stared into those dark, soulful eyes while trying to hide her shock, anger, and…hell. She didn't really know *what* she was feeling.

She'd imagined this moment more times than she could count. So, *so* many nights Nicki had lain in bed, staring blankly at the ceiling as she thought about what she'd say to him if given the chance.

Some nights she *still* did that. Over and over again, Nicki would envision herself as this confident and self-assured woman with the ability to eloquently verbalize the many ways his leaving had affected her. But now that the moment was here, all Nicki could do was stare.

It didn't help that she'd made a complete and total fool of herself the last time she saw him. To this day, her single greatest regret in life was kissing him that night. It was the one moment in time she wished she could go back and redo.

Okay, so maybe marrying Trey was first on the list. But kissing Ethan was a damn close second.

It was her own fault, though. She never should've convinced herself that a guy like Ethan McAllister could fall for a girl like her. And if she'd just kept her big mouth shut—and off his—she wouldn't have lost the closest friend she'd ever had.

"You look good."

Nicki blinked. Her heart beat a hard staccato against her ribs as Ethan's male rasp brought her back to the present.

God, she'd always loved the sound of his voice. It was all deep and gravelly, like the steady rumble of a slow rolling thunder.

"Uh...thanks." She forced a smile. "You, too."

It was a bold-faced lie. He didn't look good. He looked freaking *fantastic*.

Standing a few feet away, the man looked like a super sexy G.I. Joe. Complete with a bullet-resistant vest and a very large gun. It shouldn't be such a turn-on, but her traitorous body felt otherwise.

Taller than she remembered, Ethan's short hair was still the color of coal. Even now, after all the pain and heartache she'd faced because of this man, Nicki found herself fighting the urge to run her fingers through that same hair. To trace the dark stubble lining the subtle curve of his lips.

Lips she'd once had the pleasure of tasting.

Yes, no matter how much she hated it, she couldn't help but acknowledge the fact that the years had been good to him. Damn good.

Asshole.

But it didn't matter what he looked like. Not to her.

Not anymore.

Of all the embassies in all the countries in all the world, he had to walk into mine.

Okay, so maybe it wasn't *hers*, but still. Nicki felt like the star of an old black and white movie. One where the woman's long-lost love appeared suddenly and without warning.

In those movies—the ones she'd seen, anyway—the man always pulled the woman into his arms and planted a swoon worthy kiss on her lips. The scene would fade to black with the promise of a happily ever after.

But this wasn't the movies, and Ethan most definitely was not pulling her into his arms. Not that Nicki wanted him to. Because she didn't.

Keep lying to yourself, Nic. That's worked so well for you in the past.

As a matter of fact, it *had* worked. Sort of. And that was exactly what she intended to do, now.

She'd been sent here to do a job, not relive the most embarrassing—and crushing—moment of her life with a man who'd made it crystal clear he had no romantic interest in her. Not only that, but Nicki was also trying hard not to freak out about the possible militia raid they were preparing for this very second.

It was all so…overwhelming. And incredibly frustrating.

"You okay?" Ethan's voice pulled her gaze back up to his.

Her chest tightened. Ignoring the question, she repeated her own. "What are you doing here?"

Not that the get-up he had on and the massive gun in his hands weren't a dead giveaway.

"My team and I were called in to assist with the evacuation."

Of course, you were.

Several awkward seconds passed before Nicki glanced down at the crate to her right. "Well, like I said, I'll be done in just a few minutes."

"We don't have a few minutes."

The ominous statement pulled her focus from the crate to the automatic rifle attached to a wide strap hanging securely over his shoulder. "I thought…" She licked her lips before continuing, a nervous habit she'd possessed since childhood. "They told us the evacuation was only a precaution."

"It is."

The tension in her muscles began to relax. "Okay, then. I just need five more minutes to—"

"Sorry, Nic, but we have to go. Now."

Nicki blinked at the abrupt interruption before drawing in a slow, calming breath. "You're not listening to me."

"I've heard every word you said, sweetheart."

Sweetheart?

The familiar sentiment left her battling the urge to growl. Taking a step toward him, she rested her hands on her hips and looked him square in the eyes. "My job is to ensure these pieces remain unscathed and intact."

"And *my* job"—Ethan towered over her—"is to protect you."

The words had Nicki's breath stuttering inside her chest. She knew he didn't mean *just* her, but that didn't keep the girly-girl inside her from feeling all sorts of swoony.

God, she hated that he could still affect her this way. She shouldn't care what he had to say. Not after all these years.

But the look in his eyes when he'd said that bit about protecting her *almost* made Nicki feel as though he still cared.

You know he doesn't.

Momentarily lost in her own thoughts, Nicki was hit with a slew of memories from years past…

The day they met. The countless nights she and Ethan stayed up late talking and laughing. The one and only kiss they'd shared.

Just like that, her heart sank as memories of their last night together came rushing back with a vengeance. She'd taken a leap of faith back then, confessing her feelings the way she had. And the very next morning, Ethan walked out of her life without ever looking back.

Something broke inside her that day. Something so fundamentally innate that she'd lost a piece of herself.

The girl who'd once been filled to the brim with optimism and hope had been transformed into the woman she was today. A borderline cynic who'd come to accept the fact that true love and happily ever after simply wasn't in her future. Not anymore.

Maybe it never was.

"Apollo, you in here?"

Shaking off whatever spell she'd fallen under, Nicki and Ethan both looked toward the safe room's entrance. A half-second later, another man dressed almost identical to Ethan —vest and gun, included—filled the opened space.

"Everyone's rounded up and ready to roll." The other man slid his gaze from Ethan, to Nicki, and back again. "Everything okay here?"

"Yep." Ethan nodded. "All good."

Hardly.

Looking as though he didn't quite believe the claim, the guy she assumed was Ethan's teammate tossed Ethan a set of keys. "Lock the gate and door behind you when you leave. We're rolling out in two."

"Right behind you." Ethan caught the keys with ease.

With a parting tip of his chin, the other man turned and left, leaving Nicki and Ethan alone once again.

"Apollo?" Nicki couldn't help but ask.

"My call sign. All the guys on the team have 'em." Ethan brought his steely gaze back to hers. "Look, Nic. I appreciate what you're trying to do."

"But?" Because a 'but' was definitely coming.

"But I've seen what groups like the one we're trying to protect you from"—he cleared his throat—"what the men we're trying to protect you *all* from can do. It's true; this is just a precaution. But on the off chance they do raid this place, I can promise you, those wooden crates aren't gonna do jack shit to keep whatever's inside them safe."

Nicki thought about past attacks on other embassies and consulates throughout the world. She remembered the devastating damage and loss she'd seen in reports and on the news.

As she stared up at the man who'd once owned her heart and soul, she also remembered that Ethan had always been the protector-hero type. It was one of the things she used to love most about him.

Because of this—and despite everything else—Nicki believed with all her heart that he was telling her the truth.

"Okay." She finally gave in. "I'll grab my things."

The heels of her black ankle boots clicked along the marble tile as she walked over to the corner of the room where she'd set her personal belongings. Putting on her denim jacket, she slid one strap of her backpack-style computer bag over a shoulder before lifting the extendable handle on her pink, hard-shell suitcase.

Rolling it behind her, she passed by Ethan without another word. Keeping her shoulders back and her eyes straight ahead, she heard the clanging of the gate as it was closed and locked, followed by the sound of the heavy metal door being secured.

Booted footfalls fell in line behind her, but Nicki didn't look back. Though she hated to admit it, she actually *did* feel safer knowing he was here.

Not that she'd ever admit that to him or anyone else.

"Ms. Castille!" Mr. Drakos, the building's head of security, smiled as she made her way down the hallway toward the main entrance. "I trust you were able to finish securing the pieces?"

"They're locked up tight as a drum," Ethan answered for her.

Nicki glanced over at him, but he'd already turned to discuss something with another man who looked to be on his team. She should probably be honest about the few pieces still needing to be crated but held her tongue.

Ethan was right. If there was an attack and the militia group somehow managed to breach the steel door and gate, a few slats of wood weren't going to keep the intruders from taking whatever they wanted.

"Excellent." Mr. Drakos smiled back at her. "When we get to where we're going, I'd like to get your input on—"

"All right, people. Listen up!" The same man who'd come to the safe room a few minutes earlier cut off whatever else Drakos had planned to say. "We're going to walk out those doors and across the grass in an orderly fashion. My team and I will position ourselves around you, so please stay inside the perimeter we set. There are five vehicles ready and waiting to take you and those in the other building to a separate, secured location. We'll be in the last two."

"What happens when we get to this other location, Mr. …?" Nicki's voice trailed off expectantly after speaking loud enough for the entire group to hear.

"Digger." The man in charge looked directly at her. "And you'll be given more information once we're there. In the meantime"—he addressed the group again—"please listen carefully and follow my team's directions without question or argument. You do that, chances are, you'll be out of there and home before dinner."

Several low mumbles rolled through the group, but no one argued or complained. Instead, they did as they were told, following the man out the annex's double doors and out onto the lawn.

As promised, Ethan's team stationed themselves protectively around the group. The man who'd called himself Digger led them across the grass while two others flanked the sides. Ethan took the rear, walking directly behind Nicki.

Careful not to let her thick heels dig into the soft earth, she held her suitcase with relative ease while keeping up with the group's steady pace. As she walked, Nicki could practically *feel* Ethan's gaze burning into her back. She didn't dare turn around, though, for fear she'd catch him checking her out while she walked.

If that happened, she might be compelled to do something monumentally stupid like forget about the way he'd annihilated her heart all those years ago.

I'll never forget.

Once they reached the convoy of cars, Ethan took her suitcase and put it into the back of the last one in line. Taking in the scene around her, Nicki nearly smiled as she watched the other embassy staff members and guests divide themselves up and begin climbing into the government-issued vehicles.

If she didn't know any better, she could almost convince herself that they were simply tourists preparing for a day of sightseeing. Except instead of cheery camp leaders wearing matching shirts and khaki shorts, she and the others were being escorted by a group of men with bullet-resistant vests and automatic rifles.

Go to Athens, they said. It'll be fun, they said.

"This one's ours." Ethan walked up beside her and opened the passenger door.

Okay, seriously. It was bad enough he looked even more scrumptious than she remembered. Did the man really have to sound like sex personified, too?

Barely resisting a childish foot stomp, Nicki ignored his outstretched hand and climbed into the Suburban's third row seat of her own accord. Sliding all the way to the driver's side window, she intentionally chose that spot with the hope that he'd sit up front...away from her.

So naturally, Ethan followed her right in, sitting so close their thighs were practically touching.

Just breathe, Nic. Deep breath in...slow breath out. It's one car ride. That's it. Just a quick, quiet ride through Athens, and then he'll be out of your life...again.

The voice in her head was right. She'd survived worse. Surely, she could handle something as simple and meaningless as this.

Once the five vehicles were filled, the caravan began to move. With tension so thick it would take a machete to slice through it, Nicki turned her head toward the window to her left and forced herself to focus on the tinted scenery outside, rather than the man next to her.

Though the drive wasn't quite as short as she'd hoped, Nicki was relieved when Ethan refrained from an attempt at small talk. The only thing worse than being forced into such close proximity to the man she'd spent years pining over would be if he filled the tense air with a conversation about the weather or some other meaningless topic.

A few miles—and several unwanted memories—later, the line of Suburbans turned down a narrow alley between two buildings at the edge of the city. As they pulled into a parking garage attached to the one on their left, Nicki and the two embassy staff members sitting in the middle seat waited patiently as the convoy came to a stop.

Sliding the gearshift into park, Digger unbuckled his seatbelt with a quick glance over his shoulder. "Get out but stay close and wait for further instructions."

The man in charge exited the driver's seat as both side doors opened. Following orders, the two embassy employees slid out of their seats. But when Nicki made a move to lower the back of the seat in front of her so she could follow, a strong hand wrapped gently around her right wrist to stop her.

"Not you."

She sucked in a breath, the unexpected contact creating a zing of electricity zipping through her veins. Spinning her head around, she shot Ethan a look of confusion. "What do you mean not me?"

"You're not going with them."

"I'm not?" She watched as the other passengers followed Digger toward the larger group of embassy employees and the men assigned to protect them.

"We're going to wait here while the rest of my men wrap up things with the other team, and then you're coming back to the States with us."

Other team? Back to the States? What the hell is he talking about?

"Uh, no. I'm not." Nicki pulled her wrist free. "I still have a job to do here, Ethan. Once this mess is all cleared up, I intend to finish it."

"Sorry, sweetheart." He didn't look it in the least. "My team and I have our orders."

"I have my orders, too. My boss—"

"Secretary Bradford?" He cut her off with an infuriating smirk. "Who do you think gave the orders?"

This gave Nicki pause. "My boss ordered you to bring me home?"

"Indirectly. Bradford called in a favor to the man who happens to be *my* boss, who in turn ordered us to assist the other team with the evacuation and safe transport here, and then fly you home. Feel free to call him if you don't believe me."

That last bit had her spine straightening. "Maybe I will," she retorted sharply.

"Good."

"Fine."

Ignoring the subtle twitching of his lips, Nicki dug her phone out of her backpack and tapped on her boss's name in her contact list. He answered on the second ring.

"Miss Castille?" Secretary Bradford's voice was deep and gravely with sleep.

Damn it. She'd been so intent on challenging Ethan's claim, she forgot all about the fact that Athens was seven hours ahead of D.C. Which meant she'd just woken the Secretary of Defense from what was probably a restful slumber.

Shit, shit, shit.

"Nicolette?" He spoke up again. "Is everything all right?"

"Yes, Sir," she rushed to answer one of the most powerful men in America. "Sorry to wake you, Sir, but I'm being told you want me to return home?"

Clearing the sleep from his throat, Secretary Bradford confirmed what Ethan had told her. "That's correct. You are to fly into Charlotte with Tac-Ops Team One. They have a private jet, so there won't be any hold-ups with customs and all that. Once you land, there will be a car waiting to take you home to Fredericksburg."

He expected her to be trapped on a plane with Ethan and a team of men she didn't know for twelve hours?

Don't forget Ambassador Baker.

Wanting to roll her eyes at the unhelpful thought, Nicki treaded carefully in her rebuttal of the unexpected order. "Respectfully, Sir, wouldn't it be better if I stayed here in case the threat turns out to be invalid? That way, I can still supervise the display as originally planned."

Please tell me to stay. Please, for the love of God, don't make me go home with Ethan! Just give the order to stay in Greece so I can say goodbye to him...again...and go on with my successful and borderline pathetic life.

"I've spoken with Secretary Biggs," Bradford informed her. "Given the uncertainty of the current situation, we both agreed it would be best to have you return to COTUS immediately."

COTUS was the acronym used by the government and military alike for the continental United States.

"But Sir—"

"The State Department appreciates your dedication to the job, as do I. Come home, Miss Castille. That's an order."

Damn it. "Yes, Sir."

The telltale click followed by silence told her the man had already ended the call.

"Well?" Ethan raised an arrogant brow.

With a relenting sigh, Nicki unzipped her bag and slid her phone back inside. Meeting Ethan's gaze once more, she kept her smile tight as she said, "Looks like we're sharing a ride back home."

CHAPTER THREE

Nicki. Fucking. Castille.

Sitting in his usual seat near the front of the private jet's cabin, Ethan kept his eyes forward, rather than looking toward the back of the plane...where Nicki was sitting.

He wanted to go back there. Had even planned to use the flight home to mend fences. But after several hours in the air, he had yet to go to her.

During the first part of the flight—after making sure their three guests were comfortable and had everything they needed—he and the team got busy typing up their official statements of the days' events.

Not a hard task since nothing nefarious actually happened.

After his statement was written and emailed to his boss, Ethan had gotten up with the ruse of needing to use the restroom. He'd hoped to maybe strike up a conversation with Nicki, but when he'd approached the rear of the plane, he'd found her sound asleep. Not wanting to disturb her, Ethan promptly used the facilities and returned to his seat.

That was several hours ago.

A few stolen glances told him she'd been awake for quite

ANNA BLAKELY

some time. They still had five more hours in the air, which meant plenty of time for them to talk. The only thing stopping Ethan from getting back up and going to her now, was the fact that he didn't know what he should say.

Bullshit. What's stopping you is the fact that you're afraid she'll give you exactly what you deserve... A big heaping order of cold shoulder with a giant side of "screw you".

His subconscious—the bastard—was spot on. Ethan knew he should go back there and apologize. Lord knows, he had plenty to atone for.

But like the chickenshit that he was, he kept his ass firmly planted in his seat while the girl...no, the *woman* who haunted his dreams sat several feet away. Alone.

"Jesus, Apollo. Would you just go talk to her, already?"

Turning to his left, Ethan met Bones' expectant stare. "What?"

"Come on, man. It's obvious you two know each other. Hell, the tension in the air was so damn thick in that SUV, it would've taken a freakin' chain saw to cut through it."

Noticed that, too, did ya?

"It's not what you think," Ethan explained. "Nicki and I.... we grew up together. We used to be—"

"High school sweethearts?" Bones waggled his brows.

"I was going to say *friends.*"

"Really?" The other man sounded surprised. "'Cause it sure seemed like there was a lot more goin' on there than just a couple of long-lost friends reconnecting."

After a long pause, Ethan admitted, "She wanted there to be more. But I..."

"What, you weren't into her like that? I mean, not that I can blame you."

His teammate's comment earned him an instant, angry glare. "What the fuck is that supposed to mean?"

So help me, you say a single, negative word about Nic, I swear to all that's holy, I'll—

54

"Nothing." Bones shrugged. "Just that she's smokin' hot, smart, successful...I mean, why on earth would you be interested in someone like *that?*"

When the former Marine smirked, Ethan realized the jackass was being sarcastic.

"Very funny, asshole." Ethan settled back into his seat. "And my not being into her wasn't the issue."

He'd been interested in Nicki back then. More than she or anyone else ever knew. But that hadn't been the problem.

"Okay, so what held you back? She have a boyfriend or something?"

Ethan shook his head. "No. No boyfriend. In fact, she uh...she actually kissed me once."

It felt strange sharing the details from that night aloud. Other than his mom, Ethan hadn't spoken to anyone else about it. Not ever. And he'd made her swear never to tell a soul.

Oh, his mom had done her best to talk him into pursuing a romantic relationship with Nicki. Both his parents had loved her nearly as much as he had. But as far as he knew, his mom never broke her promise and took his secret to her grave.

"Is that what did it?" Bones leaned an elbow on his armrest as he moved in closer. He lowered his voice to a soft whisper. "Was it bad? Like one of those kisses that's all tongue and spit and—"

"What? No!" Ethan shoved the guy back into his own space. Speaking with a hushed tone, he wasted no time setting that particular record straight. "It wasn't a bad kiss. Actually, it was really"—*fucking fantastic*—"nice."

"Nice?" Bones frowned. "Okay, so let me get this straight. She's gorgeous, clearly has more than a few working brain cells, *and* she can kiss? I must be missing something, brother, 'cause I don't see the problem."

"It's me." Ethan looked over at his friend. "I was the problem."

Taylor Swift, anyone?

"How's that?"

Releasing a long exhale, he gave Bones the same lame excuse he'd given Nicki all those years before. "Nic and I had been best friends since we were little, and I didn't want to screw that up. Plus, I was leaving for BUD/S the next day, and I couldn't ask her to live that sort of life."

His reasons for shutting her down sounded even more idiotic now than they had back then. He'd avoided moving things forward with her because he didn't want to hurt her or mess up their friendship.

But that was exactly what he'd done.

Wearing a knowing glance, Bones' lips lifted with a slight curve at the corners. "Let me guess... She wanted you, and you wanted her. But in all your worldly wisdom, you were convinced she'd be better off with someone who wasn't in the Service."

"Pretty much."

"Can't say I wouldn't have done the same thing back then." The team's medic blew out a breath. "But you do realize you're not with the Teams anymore, right? I mean, sure, Tac-Ops' schedule is still unpredictable. But we're home a hell of a lot more than when we were active duty."

"Doesn't matter." *Not anymore.*

"Why?" Bones scoffed. "Because you think she's still pissed at you?"

Ethan shook his head. "Because she's married."

"Oh!" The other man's brown eyebrows arched with a set of widening eyes. Almost as quickly, a look of sympathy fell over his fallen face. "Damn, brother. I'm sorry."

"It's all good," Ethan lied. "Like I said, it was a long time ago."

A stretch of silence filled the space between the two men

before Bones spoke up again. "You know, just because she's married doesn't mean you guys can't at least be friends. Unless, of course, her husband's one of those insecure control freaks who would lose his shit at the idea of his wife being friends with another dude."

"Nah." Ethan shook his head again. "Trey was never like that."

It took two full seconds for his comment to sink in. Shifting fully in his seat, Bones faced him head-on. "You *know* her husband?"

"Shh…" Ethan's head turned on a swivel to make sure no one else had heard the guy's blurted question. "Jesus, man. Keep your voice down. And yeah, I know her husband. Guy's name is Trey Ward. Nic, Trey, and I…we all used to run around together."

In another lifetime, the three of them were thick as thieves.

"All the more reason to go talk to her."

The tempting idea had Ethan risking another quick glance back over his shoulder. He couldn't decide if he was relieved or disappointed when he found Nicki's head tilted down, her eyes focused on the computer in her lap.

He turned back around. "It's not that simple."

"How do you know if you haven't tried?"

Hmm…how should he respond to that?

I just know because I broke her heart with my good intentions and misguided sense of honor. Because I can still see the unshed tears filling her shattered eyes as she turned and walked away. Because she's married to a guy who used to be my best friend, and I don't know if I'll ever get over that.

"Just talk to her," Bones repeated "I'm sure she's let all that go by now. Worst case, I'm wrong, and she tells you to go to hell. Either way, at least you'll know you tried."

Well, fuck. The man had a point.

On the one hand, there was a relatively good chance

Nicki would tell him to kick rocks. But on the other, he'd already spent the last decade tortured by all the what-ifs.

Did he really want to pile even more self-doubt on top of what already haunted him, simply because he was too much of a pussy to talk to a woman who'd once been his closest friend?

No. No, I don't.

Knowing full well he may be making another huge mistake, Ethan pushed himself to his feet and started for the back of the plane. As he walked, he heard Bones wish him a muttered, "Good luck."

The closer he got to Nicki's seat the more nervous Ethan became. He'd already screwed things up with her once before. He damn sure didn't want to do it again.

Slowing his footing, he came to a stop next to the empty seat across from where she sat. Throat suddenly dry as a fucking desert, Ethan swallowed back those fears as he shot up a silent prayer that he wasn't about to make a total ass out of himself.

Here goes nothing.

"Mind if I sit?"

Clearly startled by his sudden appearance, Nicki's big, round eyes flew up to his. Blinking quickly, she stammered, "Um...sure." She closed her laptop and motioned to the seat he was standing by. "I mean, it's your plane, right?"

Her sardonic attitude had Ethan's lips twitching as he settled back against the seat's plush leather. *Guess some things never change.*

Steeling himself for the ice-cold shoulder he deserved, he stared into a set of baby blues that stole his breath and said, "I was hoping we could talk."

CHAPTER FOUR

"You look worried." Nicki removed her glasses, her heart thumping a bit harder. "Is it the embassy? Did something happen?"

"What?" Ethan's dark brows scrunched together before smoothing themselves out. With a quick shake of his head, he put her mind at ease. "Oh, no. We haven't heard anything more on that front. In these types of situations, no news is good news. I just thought..." He shifted in his seat. "I mean, we still have a few hours before we land, and I thought maybe we could use some of that time to catch up."

The Ethan she knew never sounded anything less than confident when he spoke. Heck, back at the embassy, he'd all but oozed a sort of fearless self-assuredness. But sitting here now, the older, stronger, *sexier* Ethan looked and sounded almost...nervous.

Which in turn, made *her* nervous.

For the past several hours, Nicki had either been asleep, pretending to be asleep, or doing everything in her power to focus on work rather than the giant alpha male elephant in the room.

Or more accurately, the plane.

But despite her valiant efforts to evade this exact conversation, Ethan McAllister was inches away from where she sat. And he was looking back at her with the same intense stare she remembered.

Just get it over with, Nic. The faster you do the whole "What have you been up to?" bit, the faster he'll go back to his seat and leave you alone.

Glancing out the small, oval window to her left, Nicki studied the fluffy white clouds below. "What is it you'd like to know?"

"When did you start working for the DoD?"

She kept her eyes on those clouds. "I've been with them about four years, now."

"Really?"

Nicki *did* turn to him then. "You sound surprised."

"No, it's just…" Ethan paused. "I mean, yeah. I guess I am. You always said your dream was to own your own art gallery. I just assumed that's where you'd ended up."

Doing her best to ignore the fact that he'd just admitted to having thought about her at least once since the last time they spoke, Nicki forced a smile. "Well, you know what happens when you assume, right?"

Ethan's lips curved with a deep chuckle she felt in places she absolutely shouldn't. "Right. Sorry."

"No, it's fine." She kept the curve of her lips tight. "You're right. A gallery used to be a dream of mine."

"But it's not anymore?"

"I don't know. Maybe. But I like what I do, and I'm good at it, so…"

"And what exactly is it you do for the Department?"

The question shouldn't have bothered her. But it did.

There was a time when this man knew more about her than anyone else in the world. Now he didn't even know what she did for a living.

"I'm a civilian contractor for the DoD."

"Yeah, I got that part." The corner of his mouth curved into the same heart-stopping half-smile she remembered fondly. "I was thinking a bit more specific than that."

The stubborn part of her wanted to lie and tell him it was classified, even though it wasn't. But a guy like him would know that, so lying would prove futile.

Another part wanted to ask why his texts and phone calls had stopped. Why he hadn't bothered to check up on her throughout the years. Or how he could just up and leave to start a completely new life, leaving her behind.

And as she sat there, close enough to feel the heat radiating from his muscular form, Nicki wanted to *demand* Ethan explain why he hadn't cared enough to at least reach out now and then.

But she didn't ask any of those things…mainly because she already knew the answer.

He didn't care.

Of course, there was the other side to that story. The one Nicki so often seemed to forget…

You could've reached out to him.

"Nic?"

Startled away from her thoughts, Nicki lifted her gaze back to his. "I'm sorry, what?"

"I asked what it is that you do for the DoD."

"Right. Sorry." She exhaled. "I, uh…I construct 3D models of both man-made structures and specific terrain for special forces training and operational purposes."

She watched him closely. Knew the exact moment that information sank in.

"You build models of military targets?" Ethan sat up a little straighter. "How did you—?"

"Build them?"

"Well, that, too." He grinned. "But I was going to ask how did you get involved with something like that?"

Breaking eye contact again, she suddenly became hyperfocused on the closed computer resting in her lap. "Right after I finished art school, I got a job working at an upscale gallery in downtown Louisville. For a while, it was like a dream job come true."

"What changed?"

"I did, I guess." She looked back up at him. "I spent my days surrounded by these uber rich tourists who didn't so much as blink while writing a check for tens of thousands of dollars for a painting or sculpture, just so they could have bragging rights over their equally rich neighbors or country club friends. And I get that the whole point of owning a gallery is to make money, but I just..." Nicki sighed. "Don't get me wrong, I can absolutely appreciate the impact a quality piece of fine art can bring to a person. And like you said, being a part of that whole scene used to be my professional goal..."

"But?"

She licked her lips and gave him the rest. "But I woke up one morning and realized taking money from the rich wasn't as fulfilling as I'd always thought it would be. I wanted to make a difference. A *real* difference. I just wasn't sure how. Two nights later, the gallery hosted an invite-only show featuring works highlighting Louisville's history. About an hour into the show, a man approached me. He showed me his official government ID, told me he was impressed with the to-scale model of the Big Four Bridge I'd created, and he offered me a job right there on the spot. I put my two weeks' notice in that same night."

"Wow." Ethan settled back into his seat. "That's...wild."

"Wild?"

Pride and something else she couldn't quite name filtered behind his dark gaze as it slid back to hers. "When I was still with the SEALs, we used models like the ones you're talking about all the time. Used them to train and prep for infiltrations and hostage rescues. All sorts of missions, really." He stared back at her as though he were in awe. "Nicki, those models were instrumental in the success of each of those missions. Without them, all we would've had to go on would've been satellite images and asset information. And I can tell you from experience, those things are great, but sometimes you need a hell of a lot more to make it out of there alive."

The genuine appreciation relayed within his words sent a rush of unexpected emotions bubbling up inside her chest. But professional appreciation didn't make up for nearly a decade of silence, so Nicki pushed it aside with another forced smile.

"Yes, well...I started that job the same year you left the Teams, so the models you used weren't mine."

Ethan blinked. "How did you know when I got out of the Navy?"

"Um...what?" Even to her, Nicki's lame attempt to stall was obvious.

She just *knew* she had that deer-in-the-headlights look in her eyes as her mind spun to create a plausible explanation. Something other than the truth.

Chuckling, she went with the only thing she could come up with. "Oh, come on, Ethan. You know how Woodlyn Falls is. It's like Gossip Central. The way those people know everything about everyone...I mean, didn't I always say that town's a front for CIA housing or something?"

With a suspicious grin, Ethan nodded his handsome head. "Yeah. You uh...you did."

An uncomfortable silence followed, prompting a desperate Nicki to spin the focus onto him. "What about you? Looks like you've done well for yourself."

More than a little.

"I've done okay, I guess."

"You guess?" She shot an incredulous look toward the front of the plane, where the rest of his team was sitting. "We're on a state-of-the-art private jet owned by the company you work for, and we're flying with two ambassadors to the U.S. whom your super-elite private security and hostage rescue team has been charged with protecting until we're back on American soil." Nicki brought her gaze back to his, using air quotes to bring her point home. "I'd say that's better than 'okay'."

Ethan's broad shoulders shook with a soft, rumbling laugh. "Guilty as charged."

A stretch of silence filled their immediate space before she spoke up again. "Why did you leave the Navy?"

"It was time." A melancholy expression fell over his chiseled face. "The work I did as a SEAL was important, but it's not the kind of job a guy can do long-term."

"So, you leave one dangerous job for another?"

"What can I say?" He flashed a smile that made her heart ache for a simpler time. "I'm a glutton for punishment. Although this job keeps me home a lot more, so that's a plus."

"And where is home?" Nicki asked, even though she already knew the answer.

"Charlotte. But you've done well for yourself too. And what about Trey? How's he doing these days?"

Though it wasn't completely unexpected, the question threw her a bit off guard. Apparently, she wasn't the only one Ethan had lost track of.

Breaking eye contact, Nicki chose her words carefully. "Trey's, uh…" She cleared her throat. "Trey's good. He made partner at his law firm a few years ago."

"Partner? Wow." His brows arched high. "That's impressive. Good for him."

Yeah. Good for him.

"It's all he ever wanted." Nicki faked another smile.

"You know, I had full intentions of coming to the wedding. But my team got called up for an op overseas, and I couldn't make it back to the States in time."

He'd been sent an invitation to the wedding? And he'd actually planned on going?

Near panic—and a sudden onslaught of several other emotions—nearly had her running for the plane's tiny bathroom. Damn it, Trey had promised her he wouldn't invite Ethan.

Of course, they'd both broken plenty of promises during their short nuptials, so there was that. And the way Ethan was talking...

He doesn't know about me and Trey.

Feeling as though she should fess up to the fact that she and their mutual friend were no longer married, Nicki started to fill him in on...well...everything.

"Ethan, Trey and I aren't—" She stopped her confession short. There was no point in spilling her guts to a man who was going to vanish out of her life again the second his fancy jet landed. Amending her words, she tried again with, "You know what? It's not important. But I *am* really tired."

"Tired?" He frowned, concern flittering through his dark eyes. "You've been sleeping most of the trip."

Shoot. Of course, he would have noticed that.

"I just think my body's internal clock is out of whack from travelling through all the different time zones." That sounded plausible, right? "If you don't mind, I think I'll use the rest of the trip to catch up on my sleep."

As far as conversation enders went, it sucked. But it was the only thing she could think of to make him go away.

And she desperately, *desperately* needed him to go away.

Ethan stood, the slight smile curling his lips appearing suspiciously forced. "No problem. I'll be right up front if you need anything before we land."

Nicki used every ounce of strength she possessed to keep the relief she was feeling from showing on her face. "Thanks." She flashed a polite smile of her own before leaning her head against the small window and closing her eyes.

*Please, God...*please *let him go back to his own seat.*

Silent prayers answered, Nicki heard a set of soft footfalls sounding as Ethan walked back down the jet's carpeted aisle. Though she was tempted to sneak a peek, she didn't dare risk giving herself away.

Instead, she remained just like that. Head resting against the window, lids sealed tight. And finally, after what felt like an eternity, Nicki found herself falling into a deep, blissful slumber.

CHAPTER FIVE

Tactical Operations Headquarters
Charlotte, North Carolina
One month later...

"Gentlemen, meet your next assignment."

Ethan and his teammates turned their focus to the man standing at the front of the spacious conference room. A legend in his own right, Rafe Owens not only owned Tactical Operations, but the former British Intelligence officer also played a vital and active role in every op his teams took on.

Pressing a button on the sleek remote in his hand, Rafe activated the room's large smart screen mounted on the wall behind him. Within seconds, the picture of a bald man with a stone-cold expression and cold gray eyes appeared.

"Who is he?" Ethan studied the image that filled the giant electronic screen.

"His name is Dimitriy Kozlov." Rafe's thick British accent rasped through the air. "He's the head of a Russian criminal network based out of Riga, Latvia. According to my source in the CIA, Kozlov is suspected of running the most successful weapons trafficking and money-laundering empire in Europe."

Bones snorted, adding a sarcastic, "So what you're saying is, this Kozlov's an upstanding member of society."

"Hardly," Rafe countered.

Still locked on the picture of Kozlov, Ethan asked, "Who's he holding?"

Given that they were hostage rescue specialists, he figured it was a valid question.

But when Rafe's attention slid from Bones to him, their boss responded with, "More like *what*."

Glancing around the room, Bones frowned before swinging his confused stare back to their boss. "What do you mean, what?"

"The CIA and Homeland Security have both had Kozlov in their sights for the last few years," Rafe explained. "Unfortunately for us, the man didn't get to where he is by being stupid. Kozlov's smart, and his underboss is even better. We're talking genius-level good."

Rafe pressed another button and the image on the screen changed. Kozlov's image disappeared, replaced by several smaller images.

Several electronic bank statements and other scanned documents—all written in Russian—surrounded another man's photo. Ethan estimated the guy was in his thirties, which put him at least twenty years younger than Kozlov.

"This is Andrei Beñová. He's Kozlov's eyes, ears, and anything else the man needs him to be. In fact, Beñová is so deeply involved in the business, Kozlov moved him into his home so Beñová would be at his beck and call."

"So what you're saying"—Bones intervened—"is that this Beñová guy is Kozlov's bitch."

A rare smirk lifted one side of Rafe's bearded mouth. "Pretty much. But he's also incredibly brilliant when it comes to numbers and computers."

"A trait that no doubt comes in handy in the whole money laundering world," Digger muttered from his seat next to Ethan's.

"That it does." Rafe nodded his salt-and-pepper head as he clicked the remote again. "As does this."

The pictures on the screen faded away as a blurred photo replaced them. Ethan squinted to try to bring the image into focus. "Is that a flash drive?"

"Please tell me that's not the job," Digger added dryly.

The team looked to his boss for further explanation.

As usual, Rafe didn't disappoint. "I realize going after a piece of technology is not the kind of work we typically do."

"Well, since we're in the business of rescuing actual *hostages*"—Bones spoke up—"I'd have to agree with that astute assessment."

Ethan and Falcon both grinned. Rafe did not.

"The rumor currently making its way through the different alphabet agencies is that Kozlov's underboss designed a hard-drive cloning software system."

"Okaaay…" Bones let his voice trail off. "I mean, that's impressive, but it's not the first one in its existence. Hell, you can buy that kind of software online for less than a hundred bucks."

"Not like this, you can't." Rafe's expression never faltered. "According to the intel my CIA source acquired, this particular software isn't designed to clone the data from just any hard drive. It's specifically configured to break through the type of protective encryptions that most financial institutions use."

"You're talking banks." Digger's interest returned.

Their boss nodded. "From the chatter we've intercepted, in addition to our knowledge that there is some validity in the software's existence, it's the government's belief that Kozlov is planning a cyber heist. He'll either send a man in to gain access to the bank's server or make it an inside job.

Once the accounts have been breached, the software turns the funds into crypto currency, at which time they'll transfer those funds to a separate and virtually untraceable crypto account. All with the click of a button."

A low whistle filled the enclosed room as Bones looked around at each of his teammates. "You guys realize what this means, right? Something like that could financially destroy everyone who has an account with whatever bank they hit."

"It could do more than that." Ethan met the other man's worried stare. "If Kozlov really does have access to a system like that, he could bring down an entire country."

"Or count*ries*." Rafe nodded. "The problem is, we don't know when Kozlov is planning to strike or which bank he's going to hit first."

"It'd have to be local," Bones spoke to no one in particular. "Well, it wouldn't *have* to be, but that makes the most sense."

To the team's medic, Rafe instructed, "Go on."

Leaning forward, Bones rested his elbows on the table while linking his fingers together. "Think about it. You've got this breakthrough technology that, in theory, could potentially give you access to every bank account out there. You're gonna want to test it out first."

"He's right." Ethan nodded in agreement. "If this software has to be manually inserted into the server's mainframe system, there's no way for Kozlov to know whether it works until he actually tries it out. Easiest and quickest way to do that is to hit a local bank. Someplace where he'd already have connections."

"I agree." Falcon shot Ethan a quick glance. "But if that's Kozlov's plan, how do we know he hasn't already tried?"

"Because the CIA is already monitoring transactions through every banking system in Latvia and its surrounding countries," Rafe answered matter-of-factly.

"Jesus." Bones settled against the back of his chair and

rubbed his chin. "Remind me never to get on the Agency's bad side."

"Right?" Falcon agreed.

As usual, Digger got right down to business. "So, what's our next move?"

"Director Barnes wants us to breach Kozlov's mansion and retrieve the software." Their boss finally revealed the purpose of them being called in on such short notice. "Once the CIA has it in their possession, they'll be able to design a firewall to block it. When that's been completed, it will then be disbursed to every financial institution around the globe."

Barnes was the man in charge of the CIA.

"What's our timeframe?" Ethan wanted to know.

Not that he had a busy social calendar to rearrange.

"Director Barnes wants it done ASAP. Given what's at stake, I can't say I blame him."

"Why us?" Digger spoke up again. "Seems to me Barnes could send his own people in on this."

"Either that or a SEAL Team," Ethan muttered. Made sense, given that was the same kind of op his former team would've been tasked with. "Or hell, why not call in Ghost and Hollywood and those guys? We've seen them in action. They could handle this job as good as we can."

"I asked that very question." Rafe turned to Ethan. "Right before I suggested the CIA coordinate a joint op with one of the active spec ops teams."

"But…" He and the others waited.

"*But,* given the sensitive nature of the mission, and the fact that a Russian is involved, Barnes wants to keep the actual implementation of the op out of the government's hands. Which means no active-duty military involvement. They were very clear on that. And after a brief video conference with the White House, President Reynolds agrees. Officially, this will go on the books as a CIA op. Unofficially—"

"Tac-Ops will be the ones risking our lives while Barnes

and the rest of the Agency get all the credit," Bones finished for the man in charge.

Rafe flashed the other man a knowing grin. "Precisely."

No one in the room was surprised by the man's confirmation. From the moment they'd all signed on with Owens, Ethan and the others understood the job came without the glory or accolades others received.

And that was exactly how they wanted it.

Bones may have been quick to point out their lack of public acknowledgement, but every member of their team—Ethan included—was perfectly fine with that.

They didn't do what they did for a pat on the back or their five seconds of fame. The men of Tac-Ops did what they did to help rid the world of assholes like Dimitriy Kozlov.

"Okay, so we fly to Latvia, break into Kozlov's place, and get the goods." Bones turned to Ethan and shrugged. "Shouldn't be too hard, right?"

"I wouldn't be so sure about that." With an ominous expression, Rafe clicked the remote to change the photo on the screen once again. "This is a satellite image of Kozlov's property. It's located approximately twelve miles southwest of Riga."

Holy shit.

"Mansion, hell..." Digger studied the image intently. "Place looks like a full-on compound."

"Because it is," their boss confirmed. "And it won't be easy to breach." Rafe pulled up another photo. "The property is protected by an eight-foot concrete wall that spans the entire perimeter. There are armed guards stationed here, here, and here." He pointed to different spots on the screen. "In addition to Kozlov's main residence, there are four other buildings. CIA intel says these two are used for weapons storage" —Rafe motioned toward two of the smaller structures—"and these are for vehicles. All four buildings are kept under guard, as well."

"Damn." Ethan blew out a breath. "Guy sure likes to keep his toys protected."

Rafe's gaze slid to his. "Those obstacles aren't anything you guys haven't dealt with before. My main concern is Kozlov's residence. Thankfully my source within the CIA managed to obtain the home's schematics." Another click, and floor plans filled the screen. "These were drawn up using blueprints that were found, as well as ground and satellite imagery."

The floorplans were surprisingly detailed. Something that gave Ethan pause. "How do we know the details of the interior if the CIA hasn't actually been inside?"

"They have." Rafe surprised everyone in the room before giving them a slight shrug. "In a manner of speaking."

"Meaning?" Ethan pushed for more.

"Apparently the property used to belong to one of Riga's most successful businessmen. The Agency managed to track down the architect who designed the mansion, and they procured the home's original floorplans through him."

"What about the guy who used to live there?" Falcon directed his question to Rafe. "You say he was legit, but how do we know he isn't part of this whole scheme of Kozlov's?"

"Because that man is dead." Rafe didn't hesitate in his answer. "Shortly after the property's sale was finalized, he and his family met an untimely death at the hands of an unfortunate accident."

"Accident?" Bones arched a skeptical brow.

The look their boss gave the former Marine said he didn't buy that explanation, either. "The official report claims the group's private jet lost an engine over the Gulf of Riga. Authorities blamed mechanical error."

"And unofficially?" Ethan waited to hear what really happened.

Because if a guy like Kozlov was involved, chances were that plane crash wasn't really an accident.

With his next breath, Rafe confirmed the team's suspicions. "It's believed that Kozlov turned one of the owner's personal mechanics. Though we have no proof, and the mechanic in question has since disappeared, the working theory is that he purposely sabotaged the plane in order to make it crash."

"So Kozlov gets the mechanic to do something to the jet that would ensure engine failure, then the asshole makes that same mechanic disappear after the fact?" Ethan shifted in his seat. "This guy sounds like a real peach."

"Yeah, but why kill the property's previous owner?" Bones spoke up again.

Rafe shrugged his wide shoulders. "Who knows? Perhaps that gentleman knew things about the property Kozlov didn't want anyone else to know. Or it's possible the owner actually was in business with Kozlov. For the purpose of this op, it's not important. What matters is that the CIA was able to get the necessary floor plans. The *real* ones, not those filed with the city of Riga."

"So why let the architect live?" Ethan's curiosity got the better of him.

The man in charge smirked. "Believe it or not, that was pure luck on our part. Mr. Dougherty, the architect in question, heard the news of the plane crash and got spooked. He closed up shop and came to the States under a false identity. Dougherty covered his tracks as far as Kozlov went, but lucky for us…and Dougherty…the CIA has resources beyond Kozlov's reach."

"Okay, just so we're all up to speed"—Bones began a quick recap of the intel they'd been given—"Kozlov is a money-laundering son of a bitch who was willing to kill to keep the innerworkings of his home a secret, and now this Beñová guy, who also happens to work for Kozlov, has created the software program from hell that could potentially lead the financial ruin of every major country in existence. A program the CIA wants *us* to intercept and bring back to them. That about cover it?"

"That, it does, Mr. Stone." Rafe gave Bones a curt nod.

Silence filled the modern-style conference room as each man around the table processed what they'd just been told. After a handful of seconds, Falcon rejoined the conversation.

"The floor plans are great and all," the former Ranger commented. "But that place is what, at least five thousand square feet?" He glanced around the room. "How are we going to find something as small as a flash drive?"

"No shit," Ethan scoffed. "Talk about a needle in a haystack."

"Shouldn't be that hard," Digger countered Ethan's and Bones' skepticism. "We just need to find the room that's the most heavily guarded."

"Precisely." Their boss flashed a prideful grin in Digger's direction. "And we believe that room is here." Clicking the remote again, Rafe enlarged a portion of the floor plans. "This room was not part of the floor plans submitted to the city of Rigo. According to Mr. Dougherty, the reason for this was that the room was built as a safe room. Apparently, the original owner was paranoid about robbery attempts, given his wealth and status. So he paid Dougherty under the table to install this hidden room so his family would have someplace safe to hide in the case of such an event."

"And Kozlov doesn't want anyone knowing it's there, because that's where he keeps his most valuable possessions," Ethan surmised.

"So, when do we leave?" Falcon posed the question to Rafe after another collective pause.

"Once I can assure Director Barnes we're ready."

"Ready?" Bones' eyebrows bunched together. "I don't get

it. We know who we're after and why... What more do we need?"

"Practice, Bones." Rafe's tone was dead serious. "Like I said before, Kozlov's compound is heavily guarded, both inside and out. Given what's at stake, I don't want there to be any surprises going in." A quick, almost indiscernible glance in Ethan's direction left his gut tightening. "That's why I contacted SecDef. After I read Secretary Barnes in on the situation, he was more than happy to offer the assistance of one of his employees. She's someone I believe will help with this op's success."

Someone who works for the Secretary of Defense was coming here to help? And that employee is a she? Surely, he didn't mean—

"Ashley, will you please send Miss Castille back?" Rafe spoke to their vetted front desk receptionist through the intercom system mounted to the conference table.

What the fuck?

A sudden heaviness expanded inside Ethan's core, his stomach tightening from his boss's unexpected announcement. And he wasn't the only one shocked by the news.

Recognizing Nicki's name, Bones' widened gaze immediately flew to his. Leaning in closer, the other man whispered under his breath, "Did you know about this?"

"No." Ethan shook his head, his lips barely moving.

He had no fucking clue.

Of their own accord, his eyes became fixated on the room's closed door. Palms sweaty, he waited for Nicki to make her appearance. It had been four weeks since their initial—and unforeseen—reunion.

And it hadn't gone nearly as well as he would have liked.

After their awkward conversation on the jet, Ethan had gone back to his seat, where he'd stayed for the remainder of the flight. As soon as they'd landed on the DoD's private airstrip just outside of D.C., he and Nicki had parted ways with nothing more than a cordial goodbye.

He hadn't spoken to her since.

Ethan had damn sure thought about her, though. Every waking hour of every single day. And the nights…

Those were even worse.

Because it was at night when Ethan's unconscious mind created dreams he longed to make into reality. Dreams of him and Nicki together.

Smiling.

Laughing.

Making love.

They were dreams that left him feeling hungry and desperate with an uncontrollable longing to make them into reality. But then the dreams would fade, becoming overshadowed by the one *true* reality. One where Nicki was living her best life with someone else.

Someone other than him.

It was a torturous cycle that replayed itself over and over again. All Ethan could do was try his best to ignore it. To let go of the dream that only existed in his mind.

He'd almost convinced himself he was doing a bang-up job of it, too. But now…

That door opened, his breath stolen as Nicki stepped over the threshold and into the room.

Wearing red-rimmed glasses, her wavy blonde hair was gathered up into a curly, loose bun. She was dressed in a conservative white blouse, gray pencil skirt, and shiny black heels that made his sex-deprived mind think of all sorts of dirty things.

Things he wanted to do with her…and to her.

Between the glasses, heels, and the outfit, Ethan was struck with the impression of a sexy librarian. The combination proved to be positively mouthwatering.

Nicki's blue eyes found his almost immediately. Though Ethan was certain he'd imagined it, he could've sworn her pupils grew wide as their gazes met.

He greeted her with a tip of his head. "Nicki."

"Ethan." She smiled back. Beneath the flowy blouse, her breasts rose and fell with a soft inhale.

"I'm sure the rest of you remember Miss Castille," Rafe addressed the other men in the room.

"The artist." Falcon offered her a polite smile. "Good to see you again."

Nicki's gaze broke away from Ethan's as her lips curved into a professional grin. "It's nice to see all of you again, as well."

So polite and professional. Not exactly the wildcat I remember.

"As you know, Miss Castille is a civilian contractor working for the Department of Defense." Rafe regained control of the room. "She does things like supervising the acquisition and placement of artwork for numerous government agencies around the globe, which is what she was doing for our embassy in Athens when your team was sent in to assist the Delta Force team with the evacuation. What you might not be aware of is Miss Castille's other talent that caught SecDef's eye, prompting him to employ Miss Castille in the first place."

"Well don't keep us in suspense, Boss." Bones turned his charming smile in Nicki's direction. "Please, Miss Castille. Do tell."

Ethan's back teeth ground painfully together. Bones already knew exactly what Rafe was referring to, because when Ethan had returned to his seat on the plane that day, he'd filled the man in on Nicki's job building training models for various spec ops teams.

Jackass.

"Please, call me Nicki." The polite smile returned. "And what Mr. Owens is referring to is the main thing I do for the DoD, which is to build 3-D models of both natural terrain and man-made structures for special forces groups around the country."

"Sweet." Falcon grinned with approval.

"Miss Castille...Nicki...has been read in on the situation in Latvia. As such, she's agreed to construct a model of Kozlov's entire compound in order to help you prepare."

"What kind of time frame are we looking at?" Digger directed the question to Nicki.

Repositioning her glasses in the most adorable way, Nicki turned her focus to their team leader. "SecDef sent me the floor plans, which I studied on the flight here. Mr. Owens has already made arrangements for the supplies I need to be delivered here shortly. I'll get started on it as soon as they arrive. Barring any unforeseen complications, I should have the model completed by this time tomorrow."

"That fast?" Ethan blurted unintentionally.

Her baby blues slid across the table from Digger to him. "What can I say? I'm very good at what I do."

There she is.

With his eyes still locked on hers, Ethan felt his lips spread into a wide grin. Damn, he'd missed her.

"Mr. Owens?" Ashely's voice came through the intercom's speakers. "Sorry to interrupt, but that delivery you were expecting just arrived. Where would you like me to put it?"

"I think the conference room will suffice." Rafe looked at Nicki. "Do you agree?"

Giving the large, open space a quick once-over, she nodded. "This will be fine."

"Excellent." The man in charge returned his attention to the coms center. "Ashley, I'm sending the boys your way. They can haul everything back here."

"Thank you."

And with that, Ashely ended the call.

"All right, gentlemen. If you'll get the supplies from up front and bring them in here, Nicki can get started. Sooner she's done, the sooner we can take care of business."

"Speaking of business..." Slade spoke up. "What's the plan

for Kozlov and his genius sidekick? If we grab the software and leave, they'll just rebuild it."

"I'll have further instructions closer to go-time," Rafe responded cryptically.

In other words, they'd be given those particular orders before they left—and when Nicki wasn't within earshot.

She may work for the DoD, and Rafe may have had the go-ahead to read her in on what she needed to know to complete her given task, but that didn't mean she was cleared to know *every* aspect of Tac-Ops' newest orders.

And given what Rafe *wasn't* saying, those orders most likely included eliminating both Dimitriy Kozlov and Andrei Beñová.

Over the next few minutes, Ethan and his teammates helped Nicki carry the boxes and bags filled with top-of-the-line art supplies to one corner of the conference room. When they were finished, Rafe handed each of the men a folder containing vital intel on Kozlov and his organization with instructions to spend the evening studying the contents in depth.

Once they were free to go, the others wasted no time in heading out. Ethan, however, stayed behind.

Standing by the door, he leaned a shoulder against the wooden trim, watching as Nicki began pulling items from one of the boxes and placing them neatly on the large table.

"Didn't expect to see you again so soon."

"Same." She gave him a flicker of a smile before turning away to gather more of her things.

"I wanted to call you," he admitted. A purposeful move meant to feel her out. "But then I realized I didn't get your number before the team took off from D.C."

Could he have gotten it from Shadow? Yep. Did he consider asking their tech guru for Nicki's number? Only about a couple dozen times.

Should've called her, dickhead. A true friend would have.

A true friend would've done a lot of things differently. Then again, she'd come to mean so much more to him than that.

But then you waited too long to make your move, and she married another man. So there ya go, asshole. Case fucking closed.

"That's okay." Nicki's sweet voice brought him back to the present. "I've been pretty busy since we got back from Greece."

Ethan couldn't tell if it was a brush-off or the truth. And damn, if the distance that had grown between them over the years didn't gnaw at his gut.

A distance *he'd* personally created.

But she's here now. Play your cards right and you might at least get your friend back.

"Bet you didn't wake up this morning thinking you'd be spending your day here," he tried again.

"Nope." Nicki rolled out a generous piece of clear plastic before securing the edges to the table with clear tape.

Once that was finished, she went over to one of the bigger boxes and began pulling out several stacks of white chipboard identical to that used in the models Ethan and his former SEAL Team had used in the past.

"That for the scale model of Kozlov's home and surrounding buildings?"

Thank you, Captain Obvious. The second the idiotic question left his lips, Ethan wanted to pull the words back.

"Yep," Nicki uttered briefly as she went back to the box for more items.

Damn. He'd never proclaimed to be an expert in women, but even he knew one-word responses were never a good sign.

Feeling as though he'd forgotten how to talk to a woman —more specifically, *this* woman—Ethan drew in a cleansing breath and tried again.

"So, listen…" He shoved his hands into his pockets. "I

know you're going to be busy with this project for the next couple of days, but I was hoping we could get together while you're in town. Maybe grab a bite for dinner tonight or something?"

Her blue gaze turned to his. "Oh. Um...thanks, but I usually just order take-out or something when I'm working. That way I can get right back to it. And since your team needs this finished ASAP—"

"No, of course." Ethan pretended to not be disappointed. "I'll...leave you to it."

Turning to go, he had one foot out the door when he heard, a soft exhale followed by, "I guess it wouldn't hurt to go out for dinner."

Yes!

With a quick spin on his heels, he found a set of gorgeous, hesitant eyes staring back into his.

"As long as we don't take too long," she added belatedly.

"Not a problem. What time should I pick you up?"

Nicki glanced down at her watch, her lips rolling inward as she pondered his question. "How about...five? I know that's early, but it'll get us in and out before the dinner rush hits and still give me several hours of work time after the fact."

Though he tried, Ethan couldn't keep the smile from spreading across his face. "Sounds like a plan to me." A damn fine one, too. "I'm going to head home and spend the day trying to memorize whatever's in this." He held up the folder still clutched in his hand. "I'll be back here a little before five, and...actually..."

Ethan walked past her to the small desk located against the opposite wall. Grabbing a notepad and pen from the desk's only drawer, he quickly scribbled down his phone number before ripping the paper free from its pad.

"Here." He held it out for her. "This is my cell number. Put it in your phone, and that way you'll have it in case something comes up and you need to change plans."

She took the paper from his hand with a tiny sideways smirk. "Still bossy, I see."

A deep chuckle bubbled up from inside his chest as he pulled his hands free and leaned a shoulder against the door jam. "Sorry. Guess old habits die hard."

Smile growing slightly, Nicki pulled her own cell from her skirt pocket and added his name and number to her list of contacts. And though it probably shouldn't, the fact that he was saved in her phone made Ethan deliriously happy.

She's a married woman, dumbass. Don't forget that.

He wouldn't forget. No matter how much he wished he could.

"There." She looked back up at him. "Done."

"Okay, then. Unless I hear otherwise, I'll see you back here at five. I know a little pizza place not far from here. You'll like it." At least, he hoped she did.

"Guess I'd better get to work." Walking back to the table, she sat her phone down and began sorting the various sizes of chipboard.

Ethan started to leave, but as he crossed the conference room's threshold, her voice reached his ears once more.

"Hey, Ethan?"

"Yeah?" He glanced at her from over his shoulder.

Nicki rewarded him with a genuine smile. Looking as though she wanted to say more, she offered a soft, "I'll see you at five."

And this time, *this* time, that smile reached all the way to her eyes.

CHAPTER SIX

Nicki carefully placed the small white square onto the second layer of the model's walls. She aligned it just so before gently pressing it down onto the clear, industrial-strength adhesive covering the top edge of the connecting piece.

Leaning forward, she blew a gentle wave of a breath across the newly formed seam, securing the two pieces together. When she was confident it would hold, she straightened back up and glanced at the clock on the wall behind her.

Four forty-seven.

Her stomach tightened and began to churn. Ethan would be arriving any minute to take her to dinner.

"It's your own fault, you know," she mumbled to herself. "You had a steadfast plan to avoid him as much as possible while you're here, and what do you do? You go and agree to join him for a meal."

A move she'd regretted pretty much from the minute Ethan left.

All she had to do was keep her mouth shut and let him walk out that door, but *noooo.* Instead Nicki had allowed her repressed desire to bring him back into her life by accepting his sweet, albeit awkward, invitation.

Now here she was, counting down the seconds to his arrival, all the while, her traitorous mind continually bringing forth the endless list of things she wanted to say to him. Naturally that list was followed by all the things she still found herself wanting to *do* to him.

Smart, Nic. Really smart.

Releasing a low, frustrated growl, Nicki walked over to where her remaining supplies awaited. Bending over, she forced herself to focus on the work while rummaging through one of the larger boxes in search of the pieces she needed for the next stage in the model's build.

"Okay, so I'll take you…" She chose a small stack of brushes. "And…you." Nicki grabbed a box cutter and pair of scissors.

Caught up in her own head, she was still bent over with her ass to the door when she heard the low rumble of Ethan's deep voice.

"Lookin' good. I see you still talk to yourself while you work."

Not realizing he'd arrived, Nicki shot straight up and spun herself around. Disappointment she absolutely should *not* be feeling left her heart noticeably heavy when she found his soulful eyes glued to the partially built structure on the conference table rather than her.

He's looking at the model of Kozlov's compound, dummy. Not your ass.

Angry with herself for even entertaining the idea that Ethan might be interested in her after all these years, she swallowed back her misplaced dismay and offered him a polite smile. "Old habits die hard, I guess."

"That they do." The muttered comment was followed by a low, breathy whistle. "Damn, Nic. That's seriously impressive."

"Thanks." She gave him a genuine smile. "I've actually gotten a lot more done than I thought I would at this point. If things keep going as smoothly as they have been, I should be able to finish it before lunchtime tomorrow."

"Really?" Ethan shifted his surprised gaze toward hers. "I don't think any of us expected it to be done before tomorrow night, at the earliest, so anything before that is a bonus."

Setting the few pieces she'd collected from the box onto the table next to the model, Nicki breathed a silent sigh of relief. "Good. I know how important this mission is, so the sooner I can get this ready for your team, the better. Of course, I also want to make sure it's as accurate as possible, so I've been trying to rush without actually rushing. If that makes sense."

"It does." He flashed her a smile that made her insides tingle. Shoving his hands into the pockets of his jeans, Ethan began walking slowly around the table, leaning in to study her work with a closer eye. "That's how the guys and I always feel when we're training for a new op. From the minute we're read in on a situation, we want to be out there, getting boots on the ground so we can save those who need rescued. Or in this case, get our hands on a piece of technology before Kozlov can use it to cause a complete meltdown of the financial world." He straightened himself and looked back at her. "But we also understand the need for training and prep work. As much as we'd love to head out tonight to take this son of a bitch down, we know there are things that need to be done before that can happen. Things like using maps and 3D models built by a high-level government artist such as yourself. Which basically means we...rush without rushing."

His curling smirk drew her focus to a set of full, familiar lips surrounded by dark, neatly trimmed stubble that hadn't been there all those years ago. They were the same lips that had once given her the best kiss of her existence, and one she never could quite manage to forget.

A kiss that never should've happened.

Realizing she was just standing there, staring at Ethan's mouth, Nicki cleared her throat and glanced at the clock on the wall. "I suppose we should get going. The sooner we eat, the sooner I can get this thing finished. Like you said, then you and your team can get those boots of yours on the ground."

Something in her words caused his dark brows to twitch inward. But it was only for a second, and then that smile of his was back. "You're right. We should head out." He turned and started for the door. "We'll stop by Rafe's office on our way out and let him know we're leaving."

That was another reason Nicki wanted to be finished with this project. She wasn't used to working like this, with other people coming in and out of her space before her build was even complete.

Normally, back at the DoD, she'd lock herself in the room assigned to her for projects such as this one. No one, not even SecDef, himself, saw her work before it was finished.

Until now.

Until Ethan.

Grabbing her purse from one of the padded chairs, Nicki found Ethan studying the partially constructed design once more.

"It's funny." Those eyes of his slid away from the table in search of hers. "That whole time I was with the Teams, I never really thought about the work that went into making the models we used to prepare for our ops."

"Your focus was on the mission."

"I guess. Still, seeing what you've already built in only a few short hours is incredible." Their gazes remained locked as he added, "And in case I forget to say it later, thank you."

"No need to thank me, Ethan. I'm just doing my job."

A job that had yanked her from her perfectly content life

only to toss her straight into the past. *Except you're not content. Not really.*

"Shall we?" Breaking the intense connection they'd just shared, Ethan lifted one of his ridiculously defined arms and motioned to the door.

As planned, they stopped by his boss's office as they made their way down the hall. Nicki waited beside him as he peeked his head through the open doorway to let Mr. Owens know of their plans. After asking the powerful man if he'd like them to bring him back some food—an offer to which Owens politely declined—Ethan let the other man know they'd be back soon.

The elevator ride down to the building's lobby was as awkward as expected, their time spent in the enclosed space filled with silence, followed by a few sporadic bouts of small talk. As she stepped outside onto the sidewalk, Nicki squinted against the late afternoon sun.

"Man, it sure is bright out today." She stopped walking to dig around in her purse for her prescription sunglasses. Buried between a wallet, keys, a few pens, and some random receipts she'd haphazardly shoved in there in a rush, her sunglasses finally came into view. "Sorry." She quickly made the swap. "There. Much better."

"You good?" Ethan looked down at her.

"Yep." She folded her other glasses and carefully placed them in the interior zippered pocket. "So where are you taking me?"

"Two blocks that way." He pointed up the street. After a block and a half of shop talk, he jutted his chin toward an overhead sign that read *Geneo's*. "It's small and not super fancy, but I swear, their pizza's the best in town."

"I'm sure it'll be fine. I'm not a picky eater."

"I remember."

His words had her looking up at him as he opened the door and waited for her to pass. Stepping into the bustling establishment, a familiar heartache began to make its presence known. Despite the years she'd kept it locked tightly away with no intention of ever setting it free, Nicki could no longer ignore the fact that this man still carried an emotional hold over her.

And he had absolutely no idea.

Feigning interest in the restaurant's Italian décor, Nicki stopped a few feet inside the door so Ethan could take the lead. While she waited, she quickly made another swap with her glasses.

"We can sit wherever we want." He waited for her to choose. "You still prefer a booth to a table?"

Nicki nodded, hating that he remembered that about her, too.

Following him to a nearby booth, he stood at the table's edge while she slid onto the cushioned bench seat facing the restaurant's front windows.

"I was hoping you'd pick that side." He slid onto the seat across from her. "Hate sitting with my back to the crowd."

Before she could keep from saying it, Nicki heard herself admit, "I remember."

A slow, affectionate grin lifted the corners of his mouth. "God, I've missed you."

With her hands hidden beneath the wooden table, Nicki grabbed the seat's rounded edge, her fingernails digging into the cushion's smooth, faux-leather upholstery. She did her best to school her expression for fear he'd see just how much those four words meant to her.

I've missed you, too. So, so much.

They were the words she wanted to say back to him. Those and so many more. But she wasn't that same, naïve teenage girl who let her heart lead the way instead of her brain.

She'd tried that once before, and it hadn't worked out so well. Not for her, anyway.

Maybe if he knew the truth, things could be different. Maybe if you told him about you and Trey, the two of you might have a chance to—

"Hey, Ethan!" A pretty brunette with bouncing breasts walked across the wooden floor in their direction. With a white V-neck T that appeared to be two sizes too small and a toothy smile plastered across her flawless face, she kept her focus solely on Ethan while handing them each a menu. "Haven't seen you and your boys in here for a few weeks. That boss of yours keepin' you busy?"

"As always." Ethan returned the smile. "The guys and I have been out of town with work, but you know me...I can't stay away too long."

Nicki found herself wondering if that was because of the food...or the brunette? Either way, his tone wasn't flirty in the least. But the flushed skin on Stella's cheeks gave away the fact that *she* sure thought differently.

"Good thing, too." Stella batted her lashes. "This place gets awfully boring without you."

Oh, please.

Nicki was in the process of stopping a giant eye roll before it started when Ethan switched gears and introduced her to the other woman. "Stella, this is Nicki. She and I grew up together." He looked back over at her. "Stella's the best server Geneo's has. She always gets the order right and never lets your glass drop below half-full."

"Oh, you hush." Stella flirted shamelessly. "You keep talkin' so sweet you're gonna make me blush." Barely sparing Nicki a glance, those painted red lips of hers fell slightly with a less-than-genuine, "Nice to meet you."

Flashbacks from high school reared their ugly heads. All those busty brunettes Ethan used to date while Nicki hid away in her bedroom doodling her first name with his last and dreaming of the day he'd finally choose her.

But this wasn't high school, and Nicki was above playing those sophomoric games.

Forcing a smile she wasn't feeling in the least, she pushed away the unexpected wave of jealousy and offered the other woman a perfectly polite, "Nice to meet you, too."

It wasn't her place to feel such emotions. Not where Ethan McCallister was concerned.

"You want your usual?" The question was clearly meant for Ethan.

"That's fine." To Nicki, he asked, "Do you need more time, or do you know what you want?"

More time? She hadn't had any time to even open the menu, let alone read it.

"Could I have a couple more minutes, please?"

"Sure thing." Stella pulled out her ordering pad and a pen. "Can I get you two started with something to drink?"

"I'll have a sweet tea," Ethan answered without having to think about it first. "Nicki?"

"Water's fine for me."

"One sweet tea and a water comin' right up. I'll grab those and be back to finish your order."

"Thank you." Nicki smiled.

That time she truly was trying to be nice, but by the time she looked back up, Stella was already walking away.

"Sorry." She returned her focus to the menu in her hands. "Everything sounds so good, it's hard to decide."

Right on cue, her stomach growled so loudly she was afraid Ethan would be able to hear it.

Served her right. She'd been so nervous at the thought of coming here and seeing him again, she'd purposely skipped eating breakfast before her flight. After she'd landed in Charlotte, she'd taken a cab straight to the Travel Assurance building where the Tac-Ops office was located.

"Seriously, this all looks amazing," she told Ethan. Keeping her eyes on the menu, she asked, "Any suggestions?"

"I always get their barbeque pork flatbread pizza. Bones likes their Chicago-style meat lover's, Falcon usually orders the meatball sub, and Digger gets something different every time he comes. But really, you can't go wrong, no matter what you pick."

Nicki perused the options some more, and by the time Stella returned with their drinks, she'd decided on the personal sized thin-crust veggie lovers and a side salad with ranch.

"So." Ethan broke the uncomfortable silence that had fallen over their booth after Stella left to go put in their order. "You really think you'll have the model of Kozlov's compound finished by tomorrow?"

"Hopefully. I figure I'll work another few hours before calling it quits and then head to my hotel for the night." She took a sip of her water. "Mr. Owens said he'd stay as long as I felt like working, and honestly, I'd love to have most of it done before morning. But I also don't want to cause Mr. Owens to stay late on my account."

"I'll stay with you."

The offer left her heart racing. "I couldn't ask you to do that."

"You didn't." He shrugged. "I offered. Besides it's in both our best interests to let Rafe get a good night's sleep. Trust me."

Nicki smiled. "He get grumpy when he's tired?"

With a look that said it all, Ethan nodded. "You have no idea." After a slight pause, he chuckled. "I'm just messing with you. Rafe's a stand-up guy. But really, I don't mind hanging around the office while you work. It would give us more time to catch up, and I think it would be cool to finally get a chance to see you work your artistic magic."

And I think it would be torture knowing you're right there, watching my every move.

But even as the thought crossed through Nicki's mind, she heard herself asking, "You sure you don't have plans?"

Surely he had something better to do than watch over her while she glued a bunch of stuff together.

Before Ethan could answer, Stella returned with their food.

"Alrighty, here we are." The other woman set Ethan's food in front of him. "Barbeque flatbread for you, and a personal veggie with a salad with ranch for you."

"This smells delicious." Nicki smiled up at their server. "Thank you."

"Y'all need anything else?" Stella turned her entire focus onto Ethan.

Of course.

To his credit, Ethan didn't show a single inclination of interest in the voluptuous brunette. He also looked to her for the answer.

"Nicki?" His dark eyes took in the spread before her. "You got everything you need?"

Hardly.

The word damn near left her choking on the drink she'd just taken, but thankfully Nicki managed to pull herself together just in time. "No, I'm good. Thanks, though."

"You heard the lady." He moved his gaze to Stella's. "Looks like we're good to go for now."

With her eyes still glued on the enticing man before her, the other woman left them—or rather, him—with a parting grin. "You be sure to give me a holler if you think of anything else you need."

"We will." Again, Ethan made no move to reciprocate Stella's obvious flirtatious spirit. "Thanks."

Almost letting her disappointment show, their uber friendly server dipped her chin in response before turning and walking away. Picking up a square piece of pizza from his plate, Ethan dove right back into their previous conversation.

"To answer your earlier question, no." He held the cheesy pile of goodness in front of him. "I have no plans for tonight, other than going back over the intel Rafe gave us all earlier. Which I brought with me when I came back to the office to get you." He swallowed his first bite before continuing. "Figured I can either sit in there and work while you do your thing or keep you company. Whichever you prefer."

Whichever she preferred.

Nicki stared back at him, her inner thoughts warring as she thought about her choices. Her initial reaction was to tell him to stay in his office...and away from her.

But she really did miss talking to him. Missed staring into those dark, soulful eyes as he told her a story or some lame Dad joke that made no one else laugh but him. Nicki even missed his overprotective, big-brother routine that used to infuriate her to no end.

Oh, who was she kidding? She just missed *him.*

And was it really fair to hold a grudge against a man—against her former best friend—simply because he didn't share the same attraction for her as she felt toward him?

No.

The silent answer was immediate, slapping her in the face with the force of a Mack Truck.

Ethan did *not* deserve the cold-shoulder treatment she'd been dishing out. No matter what had transpired in the past, it was just that... The past.

Could he have handled the situation better back then, sure. But he wasn't the only one.

A tsunami of guilt assaulted Nicki as she sat across from a man she'd allowed to fall out of her life. All these years, she'd let herself off the hook by pretending he was the sole reason they'd drifted apart, when in reality, they were *both* to blame.

Yes, he'd rejected her advances that night at his going away party. But she was the one who'd walked away.

"It's okay, Nic." Ethan broke the awkward silence. "I can stay in my office when we get back. I just..." His shoulders fell with a sigh. "I just miss hanging out with you, that's all."

Her chest tightened, her heart longing to go back and redo that fateful night. Then it hit her...

She might not be able to travel back into the past, but he was here now. And something told Nicki if she didn't mend what was broken between them now, she would never get the chance again.

With a nervous lick of her lips, she forced herself to look him square in the eyes as she finally admitted, "I've missed you, too, Ethan. But before Athens, we hadn't seen or spoken to each other in almost ten years. So please, don't feel obligated to stay at the office. Not on my account."

"I don't feel obligated, sweetheart. I *want* to be there." He wiped his mouth with one of the white paper napkins Stella had been kind enough to leave on the table earlier. "As for our decade-long hiatus...that's on me."

A week ago—hell, five minutes ago—she would've been inclined to agree. But now, Nicki was beginning to realize it was time to let bygones be bygones.

"It's not all your fault, Ethan."

"Yeah, it is." His expression grew serious. "You laid your heart out on the line that night, and the way I reacted..." This time *he* was the one shaking his head. "Let's just say it definitely wasn't my best moment."

"You were just being honest with me." She was woman enough to admit that now. "And instead of accepting your feelings like I expected you to accept mine, I ran away like a spoiled child."

"You *were* a child, Nic."

"I was eighteen." Almost nineteen.

"Case in point."

The corners of Ethan's kissable lips curved upward, the crooked grin making her heart do a little flip.

"It was a long time ago, Ethan. We were both young and stupid." Well, she'd been stupid. "I do have one question, though."

"Shoot."

Nicki licked her lips again. With her eyes locked onto his and her heart beating wildly against her ribs, she bit the bullet and asked the one question that had been burning through her mind for the past ten years.

"Why didn't you ever come back?"

CHAPTER SEVEN

Ethan looked at the woman sitting across from him and knew what he needed to do.

You have to tell her the truth.

Food forgotten, he pushed his plate to the side—and the temptation to lie away—and rested his elbows on the table before him. After drawing in a steely breath, he did as his subconscious had instructed and told her the truth.

"I did come back, but I…" His chest tightened with fear of how she was going to react. "I didn't stay."

Nicki blinked, surprise flashing across her wide-eyed gaze. "You came back to Woodlyn Falls? When?" A flash of pain crossing over her beautiful, frowning face. "And how come you didn't come to see me?"

"A month after I finished BUD/S," he revealed. Seven months after he'd left for the most intense training of his military career. "And I did come to see you." Ethan swallowed the memory that was still surprisingly painful. "I drove straight to your house with full intentions of telling you, you were right."

"About what?"

"Us." He huffed out a breath. "About everything, really."

He knew the exact moment his revelation sank in. Looking more confused than ever, Nicki sat up a little straighter, her brow furrowing as those brilliant wheels of hers spun out of control.

"I-I don't understand." She stared back at him. "If you were coming there to tell me that, then why didn't you—"

"Trey." He just let the other man's name hang there, like an anvil dangling dangerously over its prey. "I saw the two of you walking out of your front door together, and it was obvious that you were...together."

Nicki's delicate lids fell a fraction of a second before she hung her head. When she glanced back up at him, those baby blues of her glistened with an onslaught of unshed tears.

"I had no idea." She had the same look of pain and regret he'd carried with him for what seemed like forever. "You should have stopped and talked to us. You should have—"

"Told you I was a fool to let you go?" Ethan said the words as if they were fact. Which they absolutely were. "I couldn't do that to you, Nic. Not to you or Trey."

"Why not?" She looked back at him as if he'd lost his damn mind.

Funny. There were a lot of days over the years where he felt as though he had.

He smiled sadly, remembering the gut-wrenching pain he'd felt seeing his two best friends kissing by her front door that day. Ethan could almost feel the rush of bile that had shot into his throat from realizing he was too late.

"You looked happy." He swallowed the unpleasant memory back down. "That's all I ever wanted, you know? To see that beautiful smile spread across your gorgeous face and to know you were happy. From what I saw from my car that day, you were both of those things, And, as much as it killed me to admit it, that was all thanks to Trey."

"Ethan, I—"

"It's okay." He raised a hand to stop her. "I mean, it makes sense that the two of you would end up together. Trey always had a thing for you, even before I was out of the picture. You knew that."

"Yes, but—"

"I missed my shot, Nic." His swallow was audible. "Trey knew what he wanted, and he wasn't afraid to say it." *Unlike me.* "No way was I going to be the one who messed things up for you. Not when I knew he could give you the kind of life you deserved. So I pulled behind a parked car and waited until you two drove away."

"And then you left."

It wasn't a question.

"And then I left." He gave her a solemn nod. "I got the wedding invitation in the mail a few months later."

A long stretch of silence passed between them as they both became lost in the past. Just when he was certain she would jump out of her seat and storm off, the woman who'd stolen his heart all those years ago surprised him with a bomb of her own.

"I haven't been totally honest with you, either." Nicki licked her lips in that adorably nervous way she used to do. "Ethan, Trey and I…we aren't married anymore." She kept her sights locked on his. "We haven't been for a really long time."

All the air that had been inside his lungs released with an audible *woosh.* She and Trey had gotten *divorced?*

Of their own accord, his eyes slid to the ring finger on her left hand. He'd noticed back in Athens that she wasn't wearing a ring on her left hand, just like she wasn't wearing one now. But given her line of work, he'd just assumed it was a precaution to keep it safe from the paint and glue and whatever other messy art supplies she used on a regular basis.

But now…

"Hold up." Ethan shifted in his seat, his muscles tensing

with the unexpected news. "You and Trey got divorced? When? W-why?"

"About two years after the wedding," she answered quietly. "As for the why, it's…complicated."

"Pretty sure I can keep up, Nic."

"I don't know. It wasn't one specific thing, really. I guess we both just finally faced the reality of the situation."

"Which was?"

"That we never should've gotten married in the first place."

Ethan waited for more. Because as sure as he was sitting in this booth, he knew there was more to the story. Much, much more.

"What happened, Nicolette?" He used her full name hoping she'd see how badly he needed to know. When she hesitated to answer, another thought struck suddenly. One that had his fists instinctually balling atop the table. "Did Trey hurt you? So help me, if he laid a hand on you, I swear to Christ, I'll—"

"What? No!" Nicki rushed to bring him down off that particular cliff. "Trey would never act violently toward me. Or *any* woman, for that matter."

Relieved as fuck, Ethan glanced down in time to see the color returning to his relaxing knuckles. "Then what was it? 'Cause there's something you're not saying."

"Guess you didn't outgrow your old habits either, huh?" She gave him a tiny, melencholy smile. "You always could read me better than anyone else I knew."

"I can, which is how I know you're holding back."

She's also trying to change the subject.

"It's nothing, really. And it doesn't even matter because it's all in the past, anyway. Bottom line, Trey and I got together out of convenience, really. You left, and he was—"

"There."

With a chagrined expression, Nicki gave him a slight nod.

"I realize now how stupid it all sounds. But I was really hurting after you left, and Trey was a shoulder for me to cry on. Before I knew it, we were spending nearly every night together. It was perfectly innocent at first. We'd go to the movies or out to dinner. Sometimes it was a group of us, but most of the time, it was just me and him. As *friends*." She emphasized that part. "But then, out of the blue one night, Trey leaned over and kissed me. Things just sort of happened after that."

"Did you love him?"

"Yes." She answered instantly. "I still do. Just not the way a wife should love her husband."

"You loved him, but you weren't *in* love with him." Just so he was clear about what she meant.

Thankfully, Nicki nodded her pretty head. "Exactly."

Ethan remained quiet for a bit, giving himself time to process what she'd just shared. When he didn't respond right away, Nicki kept the conversation going.

"I should have told you the truth back about me and Trey back in Athens. But between the shock of seeing you there and the craziness of the embassy's evacuation, I guess I just…" She sighed. "I don't know. I guess I figured it didn't really matter. Not anymore."

"Didn't matter?" He frowned. "Nicki, minus my folks, you and Trey were the two most important people in my life back then. Of course, it matters to me." Taking a chance, he reached across the table and covered one of her hands with his. "*You* still matter to me."

She glanced down at where their hands were joined. With a pained expression, she slowly flipped hers over, her fingers curling around his palm and giving it a light squeeze.

It was the most meaningful physical connection he'd had since their kiss.

"You still matter to me, too, Ethan." Her thumb caressed his calloused skin. "You always have."

Ethan stared at the way their hands fit so perfectly together, letting her words sink in, the relief and gratitude her words created filling his aching soul.

Too soon, Nicki gently pulled herself free. Sitting back against the cushioned seat, she tried to swipe away a tear that had escaped her own eye without him noticing.

He noticed, anyway.

"Hey," he whispered softly. When she continued to avoid his gaze, he tried again. "Sweetheart, look at me."

"What?" A set of watery eyes met his, the regret and grief he found staring back at him ripping a hole down the middle of his heart.

"Why are you crying?"

He'd always hated seeing her cry.

"Oh, I don't know." She blinked more tears away, her tone saturated in sarcasm. "Maybe because I just found out the man I was crazy about liked me back, after all. But he couldn't tell me as much because I was stupid and fell into a relationship with the wrong man for all the wrong reasons." She sniffed. "Or maybe I'm sad because I lost both of my best friends, and I have no one else to blame for that but myself."

Ah, Nic. "What happened between us wasn't your fault."

"Uh...yeah, it was," she countered. "If I hadn't kissed you that night, then we'd still be friends, and I—"

"That kiss got me through the worst parts of BUD/S."

Shit. He hadn't meant to just blurt that shit out like that. But that didn't make it any less true.

"I don't believe you." Nicki shook her head in denial.

"It's true." Ethan's voice lowered, his next words succinct and unwavering. "That training was pure hell. There were stretches of days when I didn't know whether or not I'd make it to sundown. But every time I thought about ringing that damn bell, I'd close my eyes, and there you'd be. Staring up at me with those big blue eyes and those adorable dimples. I remember how incredible it was to finally taste you, and I'd hear your voice pushing me to keep going. And it wasn't just during my SEAL training. I did the same thing countless times out in the field. So don't you think for one second that kissing me that night was a mistake, because it wasn't. The only mistake from that night was mine and mine alone" He ended the soul-cleansing confession. "And that was when I let you walk away."

Feeling emotionally drained, Ethan sat back in his seat, wishing like hell he could go back and change damn near everything about that night all those years ago. Especially the way it had ended.

"I know I'm probably too little, too late with all this," he shifted the conversation. "But if nothing else, I'd really like it if we could at least be friends again."

Ethan held his breath and waited. After what felt like an eternity, Nicki nodded her pretty blonde head.

"I'd like that." She swallowed. "I'd like that a lot, actually."

The relief those few simple words brought with them was damn near overwhelming.

Clearing his throat, Ethan felt a hundred pounds lighter as he sat up straight and smiled wide. "Now that that's settled, what do you say we finish our food so we can get you back to work?"

"Sounds like a plan to me."

Best fucking plan ever.

There was still a whole lot more they needed to delve into, but the most important thing was that Ethan had his friend back. What that meant for their future was anyone's guess.

For Ethan, however, their reconciliation was only the beginning.

CHAPTER EIGHT

The following day...

"HOLY SHIT."

Nicki stood to the side of the Tac-Ops conference room, unable to keep the smile from forming at Bones' reaction to seeing the completed model of Dimitriy Kozlov's compound.

Dressed in a pair of well-worn jeans and a light gray V-neck that showcased his magnificent muscles, Ethan winked, flashing her a panty-dropping smile of his own. "Told ya."

Heart skipping a beat, she responded with a perfectly professional, "Thank you."

Inside, though…inside she was jumping up and down and cheering like a nerdy schoolgirl. Not so much because Ethan's team approved, but because *he* did.

Ten years she'd lived with the embarrassment and regret from her decision to share her feelings with him. At first, she'd been angry. So, so angry. And hurt.

That's where Trey had come into the picture. He'd always been there, of course. But not like Ethan.

With Ethan, things were different. Better, even. Until they weren't. But now…

After a decade filled with guilt, regret, hope, and prayers that had gone unanswered, Nicki and Ethan were on their way to repairing all that had been broken.

When he'd told her about how deeply their one shared kiss had affected him, she'd found herself completely and utterly speechless. Everything she thought she knew—about Ethan, the kiss, how he felt about her…

It all went right out the proverbial window with that blindsiding confession.

Sitting with him in the booth, she'd tried to decide if she should be mad he hadn't said something sooner or happy he'd actually enjoyed their one and only kiss. In the end, as she'd considered the implications of such an astounding admission, the one thing that continually found itself at the forefront of her mind was…

He thought of me.

When the going got tough and he considered bowing out of BUD/S, he'd thought of her. *Her!* And that surprising admission held more power than he'd ever know.

The power to heal, and with any luck, the power to grow. And if she played her cards right, maybe the power to love.

Baby steps, Nic. Baby. Steps.

"You've really outdone yourself, Miss Castille."

Snapping herself out of her own head, Nicki realized the glowing acknowledgement came from Ethan's boss.

"Thank you, Mr. Owens."

"Please, call me Rafe."

"Rafe." She returned the man's smile. "Got it."

"Bones is right," Falcon joined in. Carefully leaning over the table, he studied the open interior of Kozlov's mansion closely. "This is great."

"Thank you," Nicki said again. "I just hope it helps."

"It will."

She turned to find Ethan looking straight at her, his confidence in her work touching. Though she dreaded the idea of flying back home so soon, she had other responsibilities she needed tending to, and Tac-Ops One had a mission to complete.

Deciding it was best to get the goodbyes out of the way now before it became even harder, she turned to the man in charge. "Is there anything else you need from me before I go?"

"I believe this is it. Thanks again, Nicki." He held out one of his large hands. "I'll have Ashley ship the remaining supplies to your office in D.C., and I'll be sure to let Secretary Bradford know what an asset you've been."

"Thank you, Sir." She returned the handshake. "And if you ever need my assistance again, I'd be happy to help."

"I'll keep that in mind."

With her hand back to her side, Nicki turned to Ethan. "Do you have time to walk me to the elevator?"

Ethan turned to his boss, who didn't hesitate to wave them both away. "Take your time."

Stretching his hand toward the door, Ethan allowed her to take the lead. Nicki stopped to grab her purse and small wheeled suitcase, and with a quick wave and a sincere "Good luck" to the rest of the team, she stepped across the threshold and into the hallway.

"Do you think you and the guys will be able to stop Kozlov?" she asked as they walked side-by-side.

He blew out a breath and gave a slight shake of his head. "Sure as hell hope so."

So do I.

Nicki thought about the mission, her gut churning from the danger he and the others would be running head-first into. "How long do you think you'll be gone?"

"Hard to say." Ethan lifted one of his broad shoulders and let it fall. "With any luck, it'll be a quick in and out job.

Though there's no guarantee, of course. But if everything goes as planned, we'll leave tomorrow night and be back home before the weekend."

The weekend, huh?

An idea began to form, but given her track record with this man, she was hesitant to pursue it. Exiting the office's main reception area, Nicki followed him to the secured elevator a few yards away.

"I guess this is it." Her pulse raced anxiously.

"Guess so."

Ethan glanced at the electric panel on the wall beside him but made no move to push the elevator's button. Shoving his hands into his pockets, he seemed almost nervous as he continued speaking.

"So listen, I was thinking…" He licked those enticing lips. "Would you maybe want to plan a time to get together after I'm back? We could do it this coming Saturday, in fact. Assuming we're back in time, that is. I'll even fly to D.C. so you don't have to make the trip back down here." He grinned and her heart melted. "We could make it a movie night like the old days."

When they were younger, Nicki, Ethan, and Trey would have monthly movie nights. They'd take turns going to each other's homes, and whoever was hosting got to pick the movie and the menu.

"I'd like that." She smiled up at him. "But I have this thing Saturday night. Actually, I was going to see if maybe you'd want to be my plus one? As friends, of course," she rushed to add. "And only if you're back and you want to."

"I'd love to be your plus one." He smiled. "What's the thing?"

"The annual Department of Defense dinner."

Ethan blinked. "That the same DoD dinner the White House hosts every year?"

"That's the one." Nicki smirked. "Apparently Secretary

Bradford had an opening at his one of the department's tables, and for whatever reason, he chose to invite me and a guest to join him."

"That reason's probably because you're an invaluable member of his team."

"Oh, I don't know about that." She laughed the compliment off.

"Well, I do." Ethan took a step closer. "The proof is sitting right back there on that table."

With heat flooding her cheeks, Nicki stared up into the same set of eyes that captured her heart a lifetime ago. "Thank you."

"Just speaking the truth, sweetheart."

Sweetheart.

There it was again. That sense of pure joy that only *this* man could provide.

"I should probably go," she whispered softly. Even though leaving was suddenly the very last thing she wanted to do.

"Yeah, I need to get back in there. Sooner we take care of business, the sooner you and I can have that date." When Nicki opened her mouth—to correct him or confirm, she wasn't exactly sure—Ethan cut her off at the pass. "Sorry, our *platonic* date."

"Right." A nervous chuckle escaped. "Because we're friends again."

"Hell yeah, we are." Ethan grinned. "Always."

Tears pricked the corners of her eyes, but she managed to blink them away. Seconds from an embarrassing breakdown, Nicki released the suitcase handle and closed the distance between them.

"I'll send you the details on the dinner. If you don't make it back in time, I understand. Just promise me one thing?"

"What's that?"

Swallowing the painful knot of emotions blocking her throat, she hesitated only briefly before wrapping her arms

ANNA BLAKELY

around his solid form and pulling him in for a hug. "Be careful out there."

Warmth from Ethan's strong embrace enveloped her as he returned the gesture. "Trust me." He held her close. "I'll keep my ass safe if for no other reason than to make it back home to see you again."

And just like that, all the crap that had come between them vanished, leaving behind a mended heart that was finally beginning to feel whole.

CHAPTER NINE

Dimitriy Kozlov's private compound
  Twelve miles southwest of Riga, Latvia

STANDING near their acquired operational vehicle, Ethan kept his eyes glued to the lenses of his field binoculars. Like his teammates, he was dressed head-to-toe in their go-to combat gear.

Camouflage shirt and cargo pants, protective vest, boots, and a helmet equipped with an internal communication system, night vision goggles, a small, mounted flashlight.

Topping off this season's latest in the find-the-asshole-Russian-fashion lineup was his custom desert camo M4 CASV carbine rifle, extra mags, a KA-BAR knife, a canister of tear gas, a smoke bomb, and a shit ton of other stuff designed with only one purpose in mind…

To protect the innocent and take out the bad guys.

God, I love my job.

The thought nearly had him grinning, mostly because it was true. What he did for a living—what they *all* did—was dangerous as hell. But there wasn't another job on the planet he'd rather do. He only hoped this really was a quick in-and-out so he could make it to D.C. in time for that banquet.

Just like that, Nicki's beautiful face filled his mind's eye. Ethan did grin then as he remembered how surprised—and fucking relieved—he'd felt when she'd pulled him into her arms for a hug goodbye.

Having her in his arms again—even as nothing more than an innocent hug between friends—had felt more satisfying to him than any one of the sexual encounters he'd had in his thirty-four years.

"Okay, my merry band of badasses." Shadow sounded almost cheery despite the seriousness of the situation. "You ready to get this party started?"

As usual, their brilliant and mysterious guardian angel was watching their six as they prepared for go-time.

"Affirmative," Digger confirmed from his spot next to Ethan. "Tac-Ops Team One is good to go. I repeat, we are good to go."

"Copy that, One." Shadow switched gears, her tone becoming more serious as the sound of her fingers clicking across her keyboard reached their ears. "Current satellite imagery shows pretty much what we expected. The perimeter's protected by the eight-foot-high concrete wall. I see two guards manning the gated entrance at the front. There are two more at the mansion's main entrance, and one at the back. From what I can tell, the guard at the back walks the home's perimeter every thirty minutes."

"That's a hard copy." Digger let the woman know he'd heard the intel clearly and understood. With his own night vision binos pressed against his eyes, he told their guardian angel, "I see the two tangos at the gate, as well as the front of the house. There are also men keeping watch at each of the four side buildings. Anything we need to know about them?"

"Good question, Dig." Bones leaned against the back of

the vehicle. "This op's gonna be hairy enough. Last thing we need are surprises."

"Well don't get your party hats and blowers out just yet, Bones," Shadow teased. "As far as I can see, everything is exactly as we planned for."

From Ethan's vantage point, he had to agree. The only problem was things seldom went exactly as planned.

"Falcon, you good for position?"

Falcon, who'd also been leaning against the banged-up van they'd procured for the mission, pushed himself off the vehicle and adjusted the set of NV goggles mounted to the front of his helmet. "Ready when you are."

"Excellent. I'm sending you the coordinates now." More clicks. "You should be able to get a clear shot of just about any spot on the property, minus the backs of the buildings. Your orders are to cover the team as they make the trek downhill, and then join them once they're in a secured location."

"Copy." Falcon pulled his tablet free from his protective vest. Tapping the screen, he silently read the numbers. "Checking coordinates now."

Ethan and the others waited as the former Marine studied the data closely. Returning the tablet to its rightful place against his chest, Falcon then used his NV binos to get a real-time view of the spot Shadow had carefully chosen for him.

"Location looks good," he relayed to both the team and overwatch as he shoved the field binoculars into a side pocket of his pants. "Show Falcon on the move."

"Message clear, showing Falcon moving toward the given location," Shadow confirmed she'd heard the order. "Once you're in position, the team has the green light to initiate entry."

Sliding his NV goggles down over his eyes, Falcon made a slight adjustment to their settings before grabbing hold of the gun draped across his chest. The man's field weapon of choice: a desert tech SRS-A20 Covert sniper rifle.

Known to be the shortest sniper rifle in the world, the deadly firearm's overall length was a mere twenty-seven inches, making it easier to carry and conceal without giving up any of the traditional sniper rifle's power or accuracy.

Of course, with Falcon behind the trigger, accuracy was never a concern.

"Alrighty, boys." The former Marine gave them a two-finger salute as he walked past. "See you on the flip side."

"Stay safe, brother," Ethan reminded his friend. "We've got your back."

"And I've got yours."

It was the foundation of Tac-Ops' success. No matter the mission objective, their goal was to always come home together. As a team.

The remaining three stood at the ready, their guns up and their eyes on alert for any possible threat that could get their boy—or any of them—hurt. A few short minutes later, Falcon was in position, and the team was ready to roll.

"Shadow, this is Tac-Ops One. Falcon is in position, and we are on the move."

"Copy, Tac-Ops One. Your pathway is clear. Proceed with caution."

Meaning the guards were still in their original position, and there are no obvious outliers. But they'd all been around long enough to know that didn't mean they weren't there.

"Okay, gentlemen." Digger addressed Ethan and Bones. "Just like we practiced. The three of us will take position at the bottom of the hill behind that cluster of bushes." He pointed to a cluster of thick foliage they'd already mapped out for cover. "Once we're there, we'll make our way through that section of trees and to the front gate. At that time, Falcon will take out the first two tangos. After that, he'll rejoin us, and that's when we'll breach. Any questions?"

Making their way past the front gate was only step one of the plan…and the easiest. Because the second the front guards are down and the team made entry, all hell would no doubt break loose.

"I have a question." Bones raised his hand half-way. "If we do find Kozlov, can I be the one to shoot him? Please? With a cherry on top?"

Ethan snickered at the other man's joke, even knowing Bones was probably only half-kidding. Not that he could blame the guy.

Dimitriy Kozlov was a narcissistic asshole who thought nothing of destroying an entire society by robbing its people of their hard-earned cash. Between the terrifying technology he and his buddy Beñová had created and the weapons sales and money-laundering bullshit, Ethan couldn't wait to get his hands on either one of the bastards.

Ignoring their teammate's antics, Digger set in motion part one of their plan.

"Let's move."

Falling in line behind their leader, Ethan and Bones kept their weapons up and their heads on a swivel as they began the trek down the rugged mountain. Dust and dirt kicked up beneath their booted feet, and Ethan was grateful for the area's unusually warm weather as of late.

Digger motioned to an area in front of them, and Ethan and Bones shifted directions to follow. Taking a previously chosen path that would avoid crossing a wide-open space, the three teammates used a moderately treed section of ground. Before long, Digger was using hand signals a second time to point to the spot where he wanted them to wait.

"Shadow, this is Team One. We passed the trees and are stationed at our second checkpoint now."

"Hard copy, Team One," Shadow responded immediately. "Be advised, a third guard has just joined the other two at the gate."

Shit.

"Any reason to think we've been made?" Ethan spoke low through the comms.

"Negative, Apollo. They appear to be lighting up cigarettes and carrying on a casual conversation."

"Copy that." Ethan turned to Digger who was crouched down at his left. Keeping his voice hushed, he told his team leader, "Sounds like the perfect time to strike."

"I agree." Digger nodded. "Falcon?" He spoke directly to their highly trained sniper. "You good to go?"

Falcon replied almost instantly. "Affirmative. Targets are in sight, and I've got a clear shot on all three."

"Gonna have to make it quick." Bones chimed in. "Any of those guys get off a shot before you can take 'em out, we'll have a hell of a time making it through that gate."

"He's right." Ethan looked to Digger. "If Falcon misses even one of his shots, this is going to get real ugly, real fast."

"He'll make the shots." Digger looked as confident in their brother as he sounded.

Probably because Falcon almost never missed.

"Get ready." The sniper in question gave them a heads up. "Taking the first shot in three...two..."

Crouched safely behind the evergreen bushes, Ethan watched through the spikey green needles as the three guards fell where they stood. First one, then the other. And then the other.

"Hot damn." Bones pushed himself to his feet. "Looks like that old ball and chain Falcon's been dragging around this past year hasn't slowed our boy down one bit."

"Hey, now." Falcon grunted as he presumably stood from his sniping position to join them. "Pretty sure Avery would kick your ass for calling her that."

"I didn't mean *she* was the ball and chain," Bones rushed to explain. "Just that you *had* a ball and chain. Get it? Because you're married?"

"I think he gets it just fine, dumbass." Ethan also stood.

"Sure hope so, 'cause I'd never say anything bad about Avery. She's my girl."

"Correction, asshat." Falcon popped over a nearby hill. "She's *my* girl. But you're right. For reasons I'll never understand, my wife loves you. Hell"—the man chuckled— "Aves loves all you guys."

With his arms outstretched in dramatic fashion, Bones looked at their teammate and said, "Well yeah. I mean, what's not to love?"

Several low, breathy chuckles filled their immediate area, but for Ethan, the conversation brought forth that same sort of coveted need he'd felt before. It was different this time around. More of a sense of longing, rather than a blatant jealousy.

Nicki had done that. She was the reason for the shift.

Though the thought was always there, hidden somewhere deep in the back of his mind, seeing Nicki again made Ethan realize he wanted the same sort of deep, lifelong commitment Falcon had found with Avery.

Yes, at thirty-four, he was past the stage in his life where the occasional hook-up or a casual fling sufficed. Ethan wanted more. He wanted forever. And he wanted it with her.

He just hoped that ship hadn't already sailed.

"Shadow, this is Team One," Digger's verbal report to their overwatch cut through Ethan's wandering thoughts. "First three tangos are down, and we are heading for the compound's entrance now."

Focus, McAllister. Stay on task and get the job done. Sooner that happens, the sooner you can see her again.

"Copy Team One." Shadow acknowledged Digger's most recent transmission. "No new movement outside the target building or the surrounding structures. You're clear to breach."

With his head back where it belonged, Ethan and the

team proceeded across the dirt road to the compound's concrete wall. Using it and the night sky as cover, they silently made their way to the property's front gate where the lifeless bodies of the three fallen tangos lay.

As he'd done several times in the past, Ethan got his phone out to take verification pictures of the men Falcon had eliminated. Meanwhile, Digger slid his rifle over his shoulder and got to work disabling the electronic system connected to the iron gate.

Less than a minute later, the locking system was no longer an issue.

"Team One is entering the property now."

"Copy Team One. Be advised, the tango behind the target building is on the move."

"Think he knows we're here?"

"Negative, Apollo. His movements aren't rushed. It appears he's simply starting his routine check."

"That's a hard copy, Shadow." Digger turned and addressed the team as a whole. "All right, gentlemen. This is what we trained for. Falcon, you and Bones clear the two buildings on the right, and Apollo and I will take the ones on the left. After that, we hit the house."

As always, Bones failed to hide his enthusiasm. "Let's light 'em up, boys!"

"Remember the mission objective," the man in charge reminded them. "There's a lot riding on this one so stay focused and alive."

Without further discussion, the team positioned themselves accordingly. Making sure each man was ready for launch, all four brought their respective targets into their crosshairs and waited for the signal.

The second they saw Digger give them the sign to fire, Ethan and the others pulled their triggers. Almost simultaneously, their targets crumpled to the ground, paving a clear pathway to Kozlov's private residence.

One good thing about nighttime missions...most of the time, their targets never saw them until it was too late.

"Six down," Bones announced as the team approached the first two buildings. "Who knows how many more we have to go."

"You do know how you eat an elephant, don't ya, Bones?" Shadow's tone was lighthearted.

"Yeah, yeah, I know," the other man drawled. "One bite at a time."

"Exactly."

"Plan the dive, and dive the plan," Digger chimed back in. "We know what we need to do, so let's get our asses in there and do it."

Both Shadow and Digger were spot fucking on in their assessments. Each member of Tac-Ops knew to approach every op the same. No matter how many enemies they faced, the four-man team worked as one to achieve the mission objectives, one step at a time.

Splitting up as discussed, Falcon and Bones went right while Ethan and Digger went left. The first building Ethan and his team leader cleared, housed two heavily armored vehicles, as well as a four-wheel-drive pickup and a high-end side-by-side.

Finished there, Digger communicated their findings to Shadow, followed by Falcon. Both men reported the same: The north buildings were clear, and they were good to move south.

On Digger's count, the team swiftly and efficiently cleared the remaining buildings. Each a treasure trove of weapons and ammo.

"Shadow, this is Team One. Outer buildings are secure."

"Copy Team One."

"Guess we know where we can go if we need more bullets," Ethan joked as the group gathered beside the southeast structure.

"No shit." Bones adjusted the strap keeping his automatic rifle in place. "Only thing this guy's missing are a couple of tanks."

"Probably has those stashed out back," Falcon joined in.

Taking charge once more, Digger addressed the group as a whole. "Less talk, more work. We've had it easy so far, but you all know as well as I do this shit can turn on a dime. Our focus needs to be on finding Kozlov and the software, and then destroy any electronics that could be used to rebuild it."

"That brings up a good point, Dig." Bones turned to their team lead. "How do we know they don't already have another flash drive out there somewhere? Or that Kozlov and Beňová didn't email themselves a billion copies of the plans?"

"If you don't mind, Dig, I'll take that one," Shadow joined their conversation.

"Be my guest."

The intriguing woman quickly explained Bones' concern away. "The asset we've been using is confident there is only one copy. A prototype built to test the program's performance. As the intel you were given prior to arrival stated, the software, as well as the notes used in its design, are being kept under lock and key in Kozlov's private office located in the northwest corner of the first floor. There's a safe hidden behind a painting on the northeast wall near the fireplace. You get inside that safe, you'll have everything you need for mission success."

"Minus Kozlov and Beňová," Falcon pointed out.

"Yes, well...I assumed that part of the plan was a given." A soft, breathy sigh filled Ethan's and the others' ears as Shadow paused before finishing up. "That same asset also confirmed Kozlov and Beňová's plan to do a dry run at a local bank in downtown Riga soon. The exact date is unknown at this time; however, our guy was certain it would be within the next few days."

"Hence the urgency to get our asses here," Ethan surmised.

"Precisely."

Regaining control of the conversation, Digger's hushed voice carried through the night air. "Any other questions, or are we ready to take this bastard down?"

"Take down a couple of wanna-be domestic terrorists?" Bones smiled wide. "Can't think of a better way to spend a Friday night." But then the corners of his lips fell, his dark brows furrowed as he turned to Ethan. "It is Friday, right? Or is it Saturday here? I can never keep the whole time zone space continuum BS straight."

"Time zone space continuum?" Ethan shook his head, chuckling as he set his brother straight. "Okay, follow me on this. Time wise, we're seven hours ahead of Charlotte, which means it's Friday morning there, but it's Friday *night* here."

With any luck, they'd complete the op and be on the jet back to the States before sundown. Upon landing, they'd be free to go home for the night, but the team would then go back into the office the next morning for their official debriefing first thing tomorrow morning.

Barring any major hiccups with the op, the debriefing shouldn't take more than a couple of hours. Of course, this *was* the U.S. government they were dealing with, and Ethan learned a very long time ago that the players in that particular game often ran things on their own personal timetables.

"A Friday night fight." Bones gave an approving nod. "I like it."

Patience clearly wearing thin, Digger recentered the conversation around the mission at hand. "We set?'

Ethan looked to his brothers-in-arms, each of the men sharing a solemn look that spoke volumes before returning their focus back to the man in charge.

"We're good, Dig," he assured their leader. "Let's do this."

Giving him and the others a curt nod, Digger relayed the

ANNA BLAKELY

initiation of the final part of the plan. "Team One approaching target building. You still have sights on the back guard?"

"Affirmative, Team One." The tech goddess's reply was immediate. "He's returning to his assigned station now."

"Hard Copy, Shadow," the former SEAL acknowledged the shared intel. "Starting for the residence now."

For the next several minutes, Ethan and the others remained silent as they followed Digger to a previously designated area serving as a blind spot for the two men standing guard at the home's front entrance.

In position, Digger used hand signals to relay his next orders to the others, letting each man know exactly where they needed to be in order to successfully take out the two men guarding the front doors and breach the residence.

Falcon and Bones moved forward, both men crouching down and positioning their weapons. As they brought their targets into their sights, both Ethan and Digger remained standing behind them, readying their rifles to keep their brothers safe.

On Digger's signal—a hand to Falcon's shoulder—the former Marine slid his finger to his trigger. Following his lead, Ethan gave Bones a light tap letting him know to do the same. They waited while each man steadied their guns and prepared themselves to take a human life.

It was an unfortunate task for men like them. One they'd all experienced more times than they cared to admit.

In an ideal world, they'd never be in a situation such as this. But the members of Tac-Ops knew better than most that the world they lived in was hell and far away from ideal.

As if they were one, Falcon and Bones both drew in a steadying breath before releasing the air in their lungs slowly. They were halfway through a long exhale when each man pulled their trigger.

Ethan watched as his teammates' bullets penetrated their

targets' foreheads. Like the previous six tangos they'd already eliminated, Kozlov's men fell dead where they stood.

"Front targets down." Digger gave Shadow a whispered SITREP, or situation report. "Making entry in sixty seconds."

Not waiting for a response, he rounded Falcon and Bones, taking the lead as the team made their way to the building's entrance. Just as they'd trained, Digger went straight for the door. Squatting down, he dropped the backpack he'd been carrying and got busy pulling out his go-to roll of chargeable tape.

Ethan and the others kept their eyes peeled for any possible threats, their heads and weapons in constant movement as they protected their leader whose job it was to gain entry.

Swiftly unrolling a generous strip, Digger ripped it off with his teeth and pressed it against the wood near the door's hinges. Repeating the move, he did the same with a second strip, this one placed next to the heavy, metal knob.

Next, the lethal man set about connecting the charging wires to both strips. When he was finished, Digger slid his backpack over one shoulder and pushed himself to his feet. With Ethan and the others watching his back, he took several hurried steps backward, unwinding the electrical wires as he went.

Following his cue, Ethan motioned to Bones and Falcon, the three men dividing up and taking shelter several yards on either side of the door. With their backs to the impending explosion, he and the other two men bent at the waist and covered their heads.

And then they waited.

CHAPTER TEN

Right on cue, Digger worked his demolitions magic and ignited the charge. Seconds later, the door blew straight off its hinges, a plume of dust and debris filling the space where the team had just been standing.

Knowing the explosion would have almost certainly alerted those inside of their presence, the team wasted no time making entry. Going low and to the left, Digger swept his immediate area while Ethan did the same to his right.

Keeping their weapons at the ready, the group of deadly operators cleared the initial area with ease before making their way further into Kozlov's home.

From the outside, Kozlov's mansion was large, but simplistic in its design. The inside, however...

Marble tiled floors had been laid throughout. From his peripheral, Ethan glanced past several framed paintings lining the walls. An open seating area was to their right, the space decorated to the nines with expensive—and in Ethan's opinion, gaudy as hell—furnishings.

Of course, a man like Kozlov would need a place to entertain wealthy guests. Assholes who probably refused to do business with anyone willing to settle for less.

Though this was their first time in the home, Ethan once again found himself in awe of Nicki's model. The blueprints were one thing but seeing the structure in 3D beforehand solidified the home's layout in his mind.

Seating area to their right, and though he couldn't see it from where he stood, Ethan knew down the hall to his left was a chef's kitchen, full bath, and industrial-sized pantry.

Straight ahead was a wide hallway leading to the back patio and luxury pool. Positioned off-center to the right was an elegant staircase leading to the home's second level, complete with a solid wood banister and decorative, wrought iron balusters.

Movement reached their ears from above, causing Digger to stop dead in his tracks. Raising his fist in the air, he signaled the others to do the same.

Ethan tilted his head to the side, but as he attempted to pinpoint the sound's origin, Shadow's feminine voice filtered through the comms.

"Team One, you have movement heading your way. Three tangos, including the guard from the back. And they appear to be heavily armed.

"On it." Ethan took the lead. With Bones by his side, he rushed with hurried steps head-first into danger.

Appearing several yards away, the first target yelled something in Russian as he pointed his gun in Ethan and Bones' direction. Letting his training take over, Ethan's finger was pulling the trigger before his brain even registered the act.

A double tap to the chest and one to the head took care of the initial threat, but almost immediately, the other two enemies came into view.

They fired their weapons, Ethan and Bones ducking for cover on opposite sides of the hall to avoid being hit. At the first respite in the barrage of bullets sweeping past, Ethan lifted his rifle and took the shot. Releasing his own stream of deadly projectiles, he dropped the tango closest to him while Bones took care of the third.

Start to finish, the entire interaction took less than thirty seconds.

Knowing the mission was far from over, the team split up as planned and began clearing the rooms on the main floor. Digger and Falcon covered the kitchen, pantry, and bathroom while Ethan and Bones took care of the rooms lining the hallway.

Once those areas were clear, they made their way back to the base of the staircase, at which time, Digger motioned for Falcon and Bones to head upstairs. Per the plan, those two were tasked with eliminating any threats on that level, which hopefully would include Kozlov and Beňová.

The two men made it halfway up the impressive staircase when gunfire erupted from somewhere up above.

"Shit!" Falcon dropped to the steps, narrowly avoiding an incoming bullet. "Bastards definitely know we're here!"

"You think?" Bones drew the tango in his sight and fired.

Joining the fight, Ethan and Digger lit up the area where the shots were coming from, giving Falcon and Bones a chance to safely cover more ground. By the time his teammates reached the top of the stairs, the firing had stopped, and the men trying to kill them were dead.

There'd be more, though. There always was.

"Team One, be advised I'm reading three heat signatures upstairs. They're gathered in the northeast corner inside the fourth room on the right.

Ethan pulled from his memory bank to envision Nicki's model. Upstairs, fourth room on the right…

"Kozlov's bedroom." He looked to Digger. "That has to be him."

"Him, Beňová, and a guard." Digger nodded. "Either that or Kozlov and two guards."

Either way, Ethan had full faith that Falcon and Bones would do what needed to be done.

"Find Kozlov!" Digger shouted up the stairs. Turning to Ethan, he then pointed to a set of wide double doors positioned on the living room's south wall.

Kozlov's office.

Spinning on his heels, Ethan crossed the space between him and their target room, confident his team leader was watching his six. His steps were nearly silent, the soles of his boots falling deaf as they pressed against the tile's slick surface.

Ethan reached for the doorknob, not surprised in the least to find it locked. Stepping to the side, he gave Digger room to work. Within seconds, the lock had been blown away, and both men were entering Kozlov's personal space.

"Shadow said the safe is behind a painting near the fireplace," Digger recalled aloud.

Turning to his right, Ethan spotted said painting almost immediately. Crossing the room, he lifted the heavy frame from the wall and set it to the side. As promised, mounted inside the drywall was a state-of-the-art wall safe.

Constructed of top-of-the-line carbonized steel, the door was secured by two external bolt hinges and an electronic keypad. Since they didn't have the code, and there wasn't a chance in hell Kozlov was going to give it to them, it was up to Digger to make entry.

Lucky for them, the former SEAL always came prepared.

Ethan stood guard. With his back to the wall and his eyes glued to their surroundings, he covered his teammate while he got to work.

Dropping his backpack to the floor, Digger bent down and shoved his hand into the main zippered section. When he pulled his hand free, there was a small black box clutched tightly in his fist.

"You sure that thing's gonna get us in?" Ethan spared the device a quick glance.

"That's the plan." The other man peeled a thin protective sheet from the back exposing a flat, sticky surface before pressing the little black box to the safe's door.

Once it was securely mounted, Digger pressed a button and a small rectangular screen lit up across its front. Soon, a series of bright green digital numbers appeared, and in his next breath, those numbers began to rapidly change.

"That it?"

"That's it." Digger nodded. "This little guy right here is a computer in and of itself. Once it's connected to the safe lock's internal software, we can reset the code and gain access without damaging whatever's inside."

Made sense that the man would choose to break into the safe this way, as opposed to his usual go-to of blowing shit to smithereens. Their orders were to retrieve the jump drive containing the hacking software intact so the powers that be could use it to develop a high-tech firewall system that could then be distributed to every financial institution in the world.

Given the delicate nature of the flash drive, a mound of C4 would probably destroy it—and their chances for mission success.

Several gunshots sounded from the second floor, making Ethan's chest tighten with concern for his friends. But no sooner had they heard the shots—and subsequent shouting—when Falcon's voice came over the comms.

"Target One is down. I repeat, Target One is down."

For the purpose of this op, Target One was Dimitriy Kozlov. Which meant Falcon and Bones got the bastard.

Yes!

"Hard copy on the elimination of Target One," Shadow responded immediately. "Any sign of Target Two?"

Meaning they didn't have eyes on Beñová.

This time, it was Bones who answered. "Negative, over-watch. No sign of Target Two on property."

"Keep searching. I'm not picking up any other heat signals apart from the team's, but you never know. It's a big house with a lot of hiding places, and if he's behind brick or concrete, I won't be able to see him."

"Copy that. Clearing the remaining rooms now."

Turning her attention to Digger, Shadow asked, "How's it going with the safe?"

"Just waiting on the reader to make a match."

"Excellent. Let me know when you're in, and you have the package."

Ethan and Digger watched and waited as the little black box did its thing. Right about the time he began to get antsy, the device beeped, and the newest series of numbers froze on the tiny screen.

"We're in."

They were?

Ethan brought his gaze to Digger's. The man had no more said the words when a loud click broke through the tense air. With an arched brow and a told you so smirk, his teammate reached up, turned the safe's knob, and opened the door.

"Nice." Ethan grinned.

Before they could celebrate too much, Shadow spoke up again. "You see the jump drive?"

"Give me a second." Digger grabbed his pocket flashlight and looked inside. "There you are." Reaching in, he pulled out the small black rectangle.

"Hard to believe something this small could cause world-wide financial ruin."

"Believe it," Shadow countered. "Gather everything from the safe and run a search of Kozlov's office. Take whatever you can carry and photos of what you can't. Then follow siege protocol, particularly in that office."

"What about the other rooms?" Ethan needed to be sure on his orders.

"All the intel we've gotten thus far tells us the planning, designing, and building of the target software took place in the room you're currently standing in. So do what needs to be done and then get your asses out of there before someone else decides to join the party."

Siege protocol consisted of following steps to destroy any weapons or intel that could later be used against the U.S. or its allies should they find themselves under attack. There was no current threat to the team at present, but the special incidence protocol also covered Tac-Ops' tracks, preventing possible identification of its members by enemy forces.

Ethan and Digger went straight to work doing just that.

Over the next twenty minutes, the two highly trained operatives did a quick but thorough search of Kozlov's office. They gathered what they could and took pictures of what had to be left behind.

While they were busy with that, a separate jump drive Digger had inserted into Kozlov's laptop prior to the search was copying the data stored on the son of a bitch's hard drive. A back-up plan should the computer suffer irreparable damage during the team's departure.

"Team One, what's your exfil ETA?"

Shadow's question reminded the entire team that their time on the property was limited. It didn't matter that it was the middle of the night. With men like Dimitriy Kozlov, you never knew when a deal was scheduled to go down.

"Team One is exiting the target building in ten. Falcon, Bones, do you copy?"

"Hard copy on exfil," Bones replied for both men. "And that's a big giant negative on locating Beñová."

"Bones is right," Falcon confirmed. "We've checked everywhere. The asshole's not here."

"Copy that, Team One. Marking down the missing target and showing you off property and heading for exfil in ten."

Picking up the pace, Ethan raced back to Kozlov's desk. A quick scan of the computer screen told him the cloning upload was complete, so he pulled the flash drive free and secured it in one of his vest's zippered pockets.

Across the room, Digger went to his bag and began pulling out several small metal canisters. Splitting them up between himself and Ethan, the two teammates worked like a well-oiled machine, strategically placing them around the office to ensure complete and total destruction to the other electronics they were placed on or nearby.

More than ready to get the hell out of there, Ethan slammed Kozlov's computer shut before sliding it and the mound of documents they'd collected into Digger's bag.

"That's it." Digger returned to his bag, zipping it closed. "We'll activate the thermite and burn it down as we leave."

Ethan gave the other man a nod of understanding. "Copy that."

Thermite was the main component of their portable incendiary devices. A composition of metal powder and metal oxide, thermite is highly flammable, making it the perfect substance for the task at hand.

When ignited, it undergoes a reaction that creates bursts of heat and high temperatures, which combines to create fire. But it does so in small areas, which allows the user to pinpoint exactly what will be burned, and what won't.

In this case, only the things they needed to keep out of enemy hands would be burned.

The house, the bodies...those could stay. After all, it wasn't the dead they had to worry about. It was the living.

"You two ready to roll out of this joint?"

Ethan looked up to see Bones entering the office, followed closely by Falcon. "Igniting the thermite now," he informed the former SEAL. "Why don't you two give us a hand?"

"Buddy, I'll give you my left nut if it means getting the hell out of here."

Grabbing one of the canisters, Ethan held down the thin lever on the side and slid his middle finger through the cap's metal ring. "Got two of my own, but thanks for the offer." He shot Bones a wink. To Digger, he gave one final check before launch. "You ready?"

A set of dark gray eyes lasered in on his. "Burn it."

Don't have to tell me twice.

Pulling the ring free, Ethan carefully set the canister down next to a desktop and three monitors at the opposite corner of the room. A bright white flash appeared, followed by a burst of sparks, the loud sizzling sound letting them know ignition was a go.

Each member of the team repeated the move, setting various items in the office—and a few other places in Kozlov's home—on fire. When they were finished, the group met back at the home's entryway and headed out the door.

"Shadow, this is Team One," Digger gave their guardian an update. "Siege protocol complete; we're headed for exfil."

"Copy that, Team One. The jet is fueled and ready for takeoff. As always, another team is en route for clean-up. Proceed with caution and don't forget to give a final check once you're on the road."

"Copy that."

"Oh, and guys?" A slight pause. "Great job out there. Have a safe flight home."

Home.

"Shit. What time is it?" Ethan shoved up his sleeve to get a look at his watch as they headed back to their awaiting vehicle.

"Why?" Bones walked beside him. "You got a hot date?"

"Something like that."

"Woah, really?" The other man wore a goofy grin. "Who's the lucky lady? Oh, wait. Don't tell me…you and your high school sweetie kiss and make up while she was in town?"

"There was no kissing." Ethan pulled his shirt sleeve back down and continued walking. "But yeah, I think we got all that other shit worked out."

"I knew it. Hang on, though…didn't you say she was married?"

"She was." A fact that still burned his ass, but only because the thought of Nicki being with another man made him want to kill. "They got divorced eight years ago."

"And she never remarried?"

"Apparently not."

"Huh." Bones considered this. "So she's single…you're single…and you both like each other. Please tell me you've learned from your mistakes, and you're gonna see this thing through to the end this time."

"I have learned from my mistakes, and not that it's any of your business, but no. I have no intentions of letting her go again."

"That's my boy!" Bones slapped him on the back.

Shrugging his friend's hand free, Ethan gave the other man a playful push as the team continued, covering the half-mile hike back to where they started.

"Why do you even care? It's not like you know Nicki or anything."

"True, but I know *you*." Bones kept up the swift pace. "And for as long as you and I have been on this team, I have never seen you look at a woman the way you look at Nicki. It's been kinda nice seeing you walk around with a smile instead of that permanent scowl you've usually got going on."

He'd been smiling? Since when?

The answer to that question seemed pretty clear.

Since her.

"Oh, and in case you're wondering," Bones broke through

his thoughts again. "The way you look at Nicki..." The man huffed out a low chuckle. "Brother, it's carbon copy of the way she looks at you."

Ethan swung his head around, his disbelieving gaze falling on his friend. "Bullshit."

"No BS, man. I'm tellin' ya. That woman is totally into you. Only question is what are you planning to do about it?"

I'll be damned.

Ethan thought about what his friend had just revealed. If what Bones said was true, that meant Nicki still had feelings for him, just as he did for her. And *that* meant he still had a chance.

Excitement pulsed, racing through his veins. Filled with a sudden burst of energy, he almost felt lighter as his boots carried him the remaining few yards to their van.

He'd have to be careful, though. The last thing he wanted was to scare her off by coming on too strong too quickly.

It's been ten years, dipshit. Pretty sure you've waited long enough.

He had waited long enough. Wasted too damn many years not going after what he wanted. What they both wanted, according to Bones. So yeah, he needed a plan of action.

But where should he start?

Ethan checked the time again and smiled. The first thing he needed to do was get his ass home to the States—and to that banquet. After that, he'd play it by ear.

He'd already put himself out there when he admitted to having gone back to Woodlyn Falls with the intent of telling her he was wrong, and that he *did* want to be more than friends. And he'd taken an even bigger chance by admitting that the worst mistake of his life was letting her leave the way she had the night of his going away party.

Even so, their renewed friendship was in its infancy. So yeah, he needed to take things nice and slow. Give Nicki time into the idea of them as a couple.

But not too much.

They'd already lost an entire decade. In that time, they could've dated and gotten engaged. Been married and started a family. Instead, they'd both let their pride and pain decide for them.

Fuck that.

They belonged together. Any doubts he may have had about that over the years were squashed the moment he saw her in that damn embassy.

He'd just been too damn scared of what would happen if he told her.

I'm not scared now.

No. No, he wasn't.

Bullets, bombs, crazed men willing to die for a man willing to take down entire countries for his own greed… Not a single one of those things scared him. In fact, there was only one thing in this world that had the power to fill his veins with fear.

And that was the thought of losing Nicki all over again because he didn't have the balls to go after what he wanted. What he needed.

So no, Ethan wasn't wasting another fucking second where Nicki was concerned. He let her go once before, and it was the single biggest mistake of his entire life.

But not this time. This time, Ethan was going to do whatever it took to make her see the truth.

She belonged to him, and he was hers. And he'd be damned if he let her walk away again.

CHAPTER ELEVEN

Annual Department of Defense Banquet
   1600 Pennsylvania Avenue
   Washington D.C.

NICKI LIFTED her glass of champagne to her lips, using the move as a distraction while she gave her watch another surreptitious peak. Disappointment befell her when she realized it was only a few minutes before eight.

He's not coming.

She sat her glass down and pretended to listen intently as yet another important political figure spoke at the podium in front of the room. And not just any room, mind you...but the *East Room*.

As in, the East Room of the White House.

Round tables covered in stark white cloth had been strategically placed around the elaborate space, their chairs filled with men and women who were much more important than her. Giant floral arrangements adorned their centers, and there was a long, rectangular table at the front of the room for the President, First Lady, the Vice President and his wife, Secretary Bradford, and those invited to speak at tonight's event.

The dinner had literally had six courses, the food much more sophisticated than her simple palate was used to. She'd taken a few bites of everything offered, not wanting to come off as rude or uneasy to please, the whole time thinking of the pizza delivery menu currently tacked to the front of her refrigerator.

Definitely making that order as soon as I get home.

Despite the lack of sustenance in her stomach, Nicki couldn't help but be in awe of the company she was in. Her boss had introduced her to President Reynolds and his wife earlier before the banquet began.

He'd even agreed to use her phone to take a picture of her with the powerful couple. An image she planned to print and frame the first chance she got.

The Deputy Secretary of Defense, who was second-in-line to her boss, Chairman of the Joint Cheifs of Staff, and the Vice Chairman of the Joint Chiefs, and their guests filled her table's seats.

And then there was her.

For Nicki, being invited to an event such as this—meeting the President of the United States, among others—was the opportunity of a lifetime.

Yet, here she was, sitting in the company of the most powerful men and women in the country, dressed in the most expensive gown she'd ever owned—wedding dress, included—and rather than soaking up the experience, she kept bouncing back and forth between stealing glimpses of her watch and checking the door.

She'd tried not to worry while he was away this past week and kept herself busy by putting in extra hours at work and at the gym. And when those things no longer worked, Nicki had given the house she rented a serious deep clean—closets and all.

But at night, when she'd lay her head on her pillow and settled down under the covers, her mind would become filled with worry. No matter how hard she fought against it, all sorts of worst-case-scenarios would start playing frame-by-frame, like some sort of terrifying spy-games movie.

It had gotten so bad the last couple of days Nicki had already decided to ask her boss if he could find a way to check in on them. No specifics. Just confirmation that Ethan and the others were okay.

Thankfully Nicki had woken up this morning to a text from Ethan, and just like that, the worry vanished. The text had been sent late last night, while she'd been asleep. It was short and sweet, but long enough to let her know he and the team had made it back to Charlotte in one piece.

It was the best news she'd heard in a very long time.

The text also said he and the guys would be in the office the first part of the day today to write up their official after-action reports and complete their official debriefing, but that he still planned to make it to tonight's banquet.

So she'd taken extra time getting ready for the event. Not because she was coming to the White House. Not even because she was going to get to meet the President of the United States, as well as other incredible political figures.

No, Nicki had given herself an entire day of pampering and preparation because the only man to ever steal her heart said he'd be here.

When Ethan didn't show, those same, deep-seated doubts and insecurities threatened to claw their way back to the surface. And sadly, thanks to years of regret and too many mistakes to count, they didn't have very far to go.

You should've known better than to get your hopes up.

That was where her thoughts initially went. She'd known there was a good chance he wouldn't make it. Not because he didn't want to be here, but because of the mission.

Even so, Nicki told herself not to get her hopes up, just in case. And she'd gone and done it anyway.

It wasn't for lack of trying, mind you. She'd tried to keep herself grounded about the possibility of his absence. She really, *really* had. But while her efforts had been valiant in nature, in the end, they'd all been for not.

I'd really hoped he'd be here.

Maybe this was the universe paying her back for messing things up between them in the first place. If her dad was here, he'd probably crack some joke about tables turning or some other fitting metaphor. And the most annoying part of it all is that he'd be right.

Only the tables hadn't just turned. Her entire *world* had been turned onto its side.

For years, Nicki had carried a cache of regrets and what-ifs on her shoulders. So many nights she'd lain awake wishing she could go back and fix what was broken.

Dating Trey…*marrying* him… Those had been some really big errors on her part. Even so, until last week, that kiss she'd shared with Ethan had still topped the list.

Because that was the commencement of every event and every decision that followed.

But after seeing Ethan again—after talking and most importantly, really *listening* to him during their shared lunch —Nicki finally realized the biggest mistake of all had been turning her back on Ethan that night so long ago.

Another apperception she'd come to was that, while the initial chink in their friendship armor might have been her fault, his fade-to-black vanishing act after BUD/S wasn't. They'd *both* made mistakes where the other was concerned.

Hers was pretty damn obvious at this point. But his…

The only mistake from that night was mine and mine alone. And that was when I let you walk away.

Unlike Nicki's adolescent—albeit life-altering—blunder,

Ethan's error in judgement had stemmed from his innate need to protect her.

Growing up, he'd always seen it as his job to keep her safe. When they were young, that meant putting himself between her and kids at school who thought it was fun to pick on her. His protective genes of his came back into play a few short years later, when those same boys decided they wanted to *date* her.

Nicki had accepted that part of him a long time ago. But now, knowing he'd walked away because he felt he couldn't give her the life she deserved?

Oh, Ethan.

The crowd erupted in applause as the President introduced the final guest speaker of the evening. Nicki blindly joined in, but she wasn't listening to a word the woman was saying. She was too busy replaying the other precious words Ethan had spoken while they'd waited for the elevator outside his team's office.

Every time I thought about ringing that damn bell, I'd close my eyes, and there you'd be. Staring up at me with those big blue eyes and those adorable dimples. I remember how incredible it was to finally taste you.

Those weren't platitudes tossed her way for the sake of making her feel all warm and fuzzy inside. She'd seen the emotion on in his eyes when he'd spoken those beautiful, wonderful things. Nicki could actually *feel* the truth behind every uttered word.

And she really thought maybe, just maybe, tonight would be the start of something more than two friends reconnecting. Nicki was hoping for—

"This seat taken?"

Her gaze shot up to find a set of dark, soulful eyes staring back at her as if she were the only one in the room.

"Ethan?" Nicki blurted a little too loudly. Glancing at her

tablemates, she rushed to offer a silent apology only to find their attention still glued to the front of the room.

Sitting in the empty chair reserved especially for him, Ethan placed a hand on the back of her own chair and leaned in close. His hot breath feathering across her ear as he whispered, "Sorry I'm late."

Before she could respond, he pulled back slowly; the look in his eyes stealing away her very next breath.

Intense, unmistakable heat darkened the browns in his eyes as they stared back at her. The hand that was still resting casually over the corner of her chair shifted slightly, and before she realized his intent, Ethan lifted his thumb to her bare shoulder, its pad caressing her there.

"You look beautiful."

He hadn't spoken the words aloud, but Nicki still heard them. They were there, in the way his lips formed the silent compliment, the truth behind him staring back at her from his hypnotic gaze.

Nicki wanted to say something. She *needed* to say something. But just like the last time she'd seen him, the man had once again rendered her speechless.

Her heart gave a hard thump against her ribs, the sensation kickstarting her lungs and restoring her ability to speak. Praying he couldn't hear how hard the dang thing was beating, Nicki mouthed back, "So do you."

And boy, did he ever. It was the first time in her life she'd understood the true meaning of *suit porn*.

Only Ethan wasn't wearing just *any* suit. The man was dressed in what appeared to be a custom-tailored black tuxedo with a white shirt and long, sleek black tie. The appearance made him look like the best versions of James Bond, G.I. Joe, and that guy from those erotic books her co-workers feverishly passed around the office a few years ago.

Nicki swallowed, her mouth suddenly desert dry, and it was all she could do not to embarrass herself—and her boss

—by grabbing those perfectly pressed lapels and pulling his mouth to hers.

Another round of applause broke the spell they'd both been under, and Nicki was stunned to see the banquet had come to an end.

No!

Disappointment returned ten-fold, this time because their evening was over before it ever had a chance to begin.

Following the crowd's cue, they both stood and continued clapping for a speech neither had heard. When the clapping died down and she knew he'd be able to hear her, Nicki turned to him with apologetic eyes.

"I'm sorry you wasted a trip here."

There wasn't so much as a hint of regret anywhere on his handsome face. "Are you kidding? Seeing you in that dress was worth the jet fuel it took to get me here."

Heat crawled into her cheeks, and Nicki inwardly cursed her pale skin. There was no way to hide her body's reaction to Ethan's sweet words or the blatant desire flickering in his stare.

She wanted to ask him about the mission and Kozlov, but given the classified nature of the op, Nicki knew better than to bring that up in the middle of a crowd.

Your house isn't crowded.

Nicki had never been more appreciative of that annoying voice in her head as she was in that moment. Desperate for more time with him, she took a risk and ran with the genius idea.

"Do you have to go back to Charlotte tonight?"

They hadn't discussed the after-banquet plans before, and she was more relieved than she had the right to be when Ethan shook his head and smiled. "Nope. Owens let me use the jet for the night."

"Wow." Nicki blinked. "That was awfully generous of him."

"He knew how much I wanted to be here."

The words gave her pause, and Nicki tried—and failed—to get a bead on their intent. If there was one.

He's here. Does the why really matter?

No, she didn't suppose it did. Her friend had put on a tux and flown his boss's private jet, despite knowing he was going to be superbly late. That was enough...for now.

"I was planning to go home, throw on some sweats, and watch a movie." She licked her lips, doing her best to sound casual when she added, "You're welcome to come over if you want." And then, remembering the poor man hadn't had dinner, she added, "We can order pizza."

Right on cue, Ethan's stomach let out a low rumble. Slapping a palm to his flat abs, he chuckled. "Pizza sounds fu... uh..." He looked at their present company before amending what he was about to say. "Pizza sounds great."

Hiding her giggle with one of her hands, Nicki tried hard not to let him see how deliriously happy she was that he'd accepted the impromptu invite to her place.

There was no hidden agenda. She genuinely wanted to spend time with him. And though nothing ever truly could, Nicki desperately wanted to try to make up for some of the time they'd lost.

One pizza and movie at a time.

"You ready to go, or do you need to—"

"Well, Miss Castille." Secretary Bradford appeared beside them. "What did you think of your first DoD Banquet?"

"It was lovely." Nicki flashed her boss a smile. "Thanks again for inviting me here."

"Of course." He leaned in closer to prevent those around them from hearing his next words. "Between you and me, I dread coming to these kinds of things. Too many politicians in one room for my taste."

Shoulders shaking from soft laughter, Nicki motioned to the sexy man standing next to her boss. "Sir, this is Ethan

McCallister. He and I grew up together and recently reconnected."

"McCallister." Her boss faced Ethan with an outstretched hand. "You're one of Owens' men, yes?"

"Yes, Sir." Ethan took the man's hand in his and gave it a solid shake. "It's nice to finally meet you in person."

"Likewise." The other man withdrew his hand and let his drop to his side. "I should congratulate you. I hear your latest op was a success."

"Sir?"

"It's okay. Director Barnes read me and the rest of the Joint Chiefs in on the situation in Riga. I know we can't talk about it here but know your team's work has not gone unnoticed by this administration."

"Thank you, sir. Although, if you've been read in, you're aware the op was only a partial success."

Partial?

Nicki looked to her boss, who's expression gave away nothing.

"I'm aware." Bradford nodded. "The most important task was completed. But rest assured, Mr. McCallister. The other is being worked on as we speak."

With a stone-cold expression, Ethan gave a curt nod and a solid, "Good to know."

Still confused, her gaze bounced back and forth between the two men who shared a look that spoke volumes. Like before, she didn't dare ask questions.

"Secretary Bradford! There you are." A woman who looked really important—but whom Nicki didn't recognize —waved at Bradford from several feet away. "Come. I have someone I want to introduce you to."

"Duty calls." Bradford smiled. "Ethan"—he held his hand out again—"It was great meeting you. Tell that boss of yours he still owes me a tee time."

"I'll tell him."

When their departing handshake ended, Bradford offered her a softer, gentler version of the same. "Nicki. I'll see you at the office on Monday? We have that meeting to discuss plans for the next Embassy renovation, don't forget."

"Eight o'clock sharp." She gave his hand a tight squeeze. "I have it on my calendar."

"Excellent."

"Secretary Bradford!" the impatient woman hollered for him again.

With what appeared to be a carefully controlled expression, Nicki's boss parted with a passing, "See you bright and early Monday."

"Anyone else you need to say goodbye to, or are you free to leave?"

Nicki returned her attention to the sexiest man in the room. "I can leave. I'll need to stop at the coat check on our way out."

"Did you drive here?"

She shook her head. "The Department sent over a car."

"Wow. Look at you, hobnobbing with the rich and powerful."

"And yet, I still prefer a pair of comfy sweats and my couch."

Ethan laughed, the familiar sound like music to her ears. "Come on. Let's get your coat and get out of here."

"I take it we'll need to call a cab?"

"Nope." He shook his handsome head. "When Owens told me I could fly the jet here, he also made arrangements for me while I'm in town. Had a car waiting for me at the airstrip when I landed."

Something about the way he said it had Nicki stopping in her tracks. "Wait. When you say your boss let you fly the jet, you don't mean you actually...you know...*flew* it. Right?"

"That surprise you?"

Holy crap. "You know how to fly a jet?"

Ethan's broad shoulders shook with a deep chuckle. "Guess we do have a lot to catch up on, don't we?" Gentleman that he was, he offered her his arm. "Shall we start with pizza and a movie?"

Nicki slid her hand into the crook of his bent elbow, the heat from his arm weaving itself through the tux's smooth fabric as she curled her fingers around him. Of its own accord, her mind wandered to the sinewy muscles flexing beneath her touch, and suddenly, she wanted nothing more than to see him out of said tux.

Baby steps, remember?

Baby steps. Right. Those probably didn't include attacking him and stripping him down the second they were alone.

No, Nic. As much as you want to, you can't attack the poor man. Stick with being friends and work up to the other.

She wanted to growl but refrained for fear he'd hear her and start asking questions. And that was definitely not a conversation she was ready to have. Not yet, anyway. But the second he made his interest known—if that ever happened, and God, she hoped it did—all bets were off.

Nicki was done. Done waiting for happiness to find her. Done letting the past control her future.

Life was short…and getting shorter with every breath she took. And she'd be damned if she let her second chance at love slip through her fingers again.

CHAPTER TWELVE

Ethan stood in the small entryway of Nicki's home. Looking around, he took a minute to study the personal haven she'd created for herself and smiled.

It's so...her.

Less than two-thousand square feet, the quaint brick house was located in Riggs Park, a residential neighborhood in D.C.

Decorated in a combination of neutral tones, Nicki's artistic side shone in the colorful paintings hanging on her walls, throw pillows on an otherwise bland cream couch, and several other places he could see.

The open floor plan showed hardwood floors throughout. Looking straight ahead through the living room, Ethan could see a sleek, well-kept kitchen with dark, ceramic tiled floors.

About six feet from where he stood was a break in the wall on his right. An entry into a hallway that, he assumed, led to the home's bedrooms.

Thoughts of bedrooms led to thoughts of beds. And thinking about beds while standing less than a foot from Nicki Castille conjured up all sorts of dirty thoughts.

Nicki's nude body beneath his as he drove himself into her delectable body. His hands on that luscious ass of hers. His mouth between her legs.

"It's not very big, but it's just me, so…"

Nicki's trailing voice had Ethan blinking the erotic images away. "Sorry, what?"

Pay attention, asshole!

"I was just saying, it's not much, but the rent is really good for this location. Plus it's just me here, so I didn't really need anything bigger."

"It's great." He gave the place another once-over and grinned. "It's you."

"I think so, too." Nicki smiled, her dimples caving in deep.

Ethan could imagine the tip of his tongue dipping into them as he planted slow, sensual kisses on her cheeks. Her mouth. Her neck. Her…

"Ethan?" "What?"

Nicki chuckled. "Are you okay?" Then, as if it just occurred to her, she added a rambled, "Oh, my gosh. I didn't even think. You're probably exhausted. I mean, you just got back from Latvia last night, and then you had that meeting all day today…" Her shoulders fell, her expression softening. "We don't have to do the whole pizza and movie thing tonight. If you want, we can plan for another—"

"I'm not tired."

He *had* been earlier, but then he'd walked into the East Room and had seen her. She'd been sitting at that table with men who spoke to the President on a regular basis, looking like she fit right in with them and the rest of the crowd.

No, that wasn't true. With her blonde locks piled high in a curly, formal-type do, her makeup fixed just so, and her naturally stunning beauty, the woman he longed to have had shined like a beacon in the night.

One designed to show him the way home.

And then there was the dress…

Holy. Hell.

Long, black, and sparkly, the sequined gown showcased a set of perfect, voluptuous breasts—and the cleavage that separated them. Hugging her narrow waist and toned curves below, the fabric was divided by a slit that began mid-thigh and ran the entire length of her leg.

Between that and the strappy fuck-me heels she had on, it had been all he could do to keep his hands to himself on the drive here.

So yeah. Ethan was feeling a whole lot of things at the moment—namely the massive hard-on hidden behind his jacket—but tired wasn't one of them.

"Why don't you go change?" He suggested for purely selfish reasons. Sweats typically didn't offer tempting cleavage and thigh-exposing slits.

And right now, Ethan was way the hell past tempted.

"Okay." She agreed without giving it much thought. "You want to order the pizza, or should I?"

"I can do it. You have a certain place in mind?"

"There's a menu on the fridge and..." She reached for something behind him, the scent of raspberries and vanilla filling his nostrils.

Fighting the urge to draw in a deep inhale—which would be creepy as fuck—he locked his muscles down and waited for her to get whatever it was she was after. From his peripheral, Ethan could see the small purse she'd just pulled from a hook mounted on the wall next to the door,

Nicki reached in and grabbed her wallet. Flipping open the flap, she slid one of her credit cards out of its protective sheath.

"Here." She held it out for him. "Use this to pay. And get whatever you want. You know me. I'm not—"

"Picky," Ethan finished for her with a grin. *Damn, she's adorable.* "I'll make the order, Nic, but I'm not letting you pay for it."

ANNA BLAKELY

"You're my guest." She jutted the card toward him insistently. "You covered lunch last week. It's my turn to pay."

Not wanting to waste the time he had with her by arguing over who was going to pick up the dinner tab, Ethan took the card without any intentions of using it. "Thank you."

"You're welcome. Um..." Nicki turned and walked to her coffee table. "The remote's there, and there's beer and a fresh pitcher of iced tea in the fridge. Make yourself at home. I won't be long."

"Take your time."

Her baby blues remained on his a beat, their hues darkening with what he could swear was desire. But then she blinked and turned to walk toward the hallway.

With free reign to do so, Ethan took advantage of the opportunity to enjoy the view. His mouth watered as his gaze fell over every angle and curve, and the way the dress hugged her ass...

Lord have mercy!

Nicki vanished around the corner, and he let out the breath he didn't realize he was holding. Knowing he was alone in the room, he quickly reached down and adjusted himself. Not that it helped.

He was so fucking hard his dick ached with the need to slide into her hot, wet heat. It was the same way the last two times he was around her.

Better get used to it.

Ethan nearly laughed at himself, mainly because it was true. Every time he saw her, he wanted. *Needed.*

You're not here for a booty call, jackass. Now go order the pizza before she comes back and finds you still standing here like an idiot.

Feeling as though he was precariously close to failing some sort of cosmic test, he cleared his throat and mind and slid his jacket from his shoulders. Hanging it on one of the empty hooks behind him, Ethan loosened his tie before

154

yanking it up over his head and placing it on the same hook as his jacket.

As he made his way to the kitchen, Ethan pulled the hem of his shirt loose from his waistband. *Ah...much better.* Spotting the menu Nicki had mentioned, he rounded the room's granite-topped island and went to the fridge.

Deciding to help himself to the beer she'd offered, Ethan opened the heavy door and smiled.

She drinks my favorite beer.

Grabbing one of the amber colored bottles, Ethan twisted off the top and put the bottle's rim to his lips. The cool, carbonated liquid felt refreshing as hell as it made its way down his throat and into his empty stomach.

Still thirsty, he started to lift the bottle but stopped when he heard Nicki's sweet voice.

"So, this is embarrassing, but do you think you can help me get this thing unstuck?"

This thing?

"Sure. What is it you need help getting un—" Ethan turned his head, his words seizing the second he saw her.

Nicki stood just outside the kitchen's entrance. The updo she'd wore for the dinner was gone, replaced by a waterfall of golden, wavy locks. But she was still wearing the dress...sort of.

She was still covered—damn his bad luck—but the top portion of the dress was loose enough Nicki was using both hands to keep the shimmering material from falling.

"The zipper got stuck when I was trying to pull it down," she quickly explained. "I tried, but the waist is too tight to pull up or down." An adorable blush filled her cheeks as she gave her lips a nervous lick. "Do you mind?"

Definitely being tested.

Cursing his overactive and seriously deprived libido, Ethan set the bottle down onto the island and went to her.

"Turn around," he ordered softly.

"Thanks." Using the balls of her heeled feet, Nicki spun on the hardwood floor with ease, and...

Jesus.

Her entire back was bare. No bra. Nothing. Just a blank canvas of toned muscles and smooth, flawless skin.

Ethan's fingers twitched with the urge to touch her. To run the tips of his fingers down the length of her spine, letting them dip beneath the zipper until—

Shit. You're supposed to be fixing her zipper, remember?

With a mental slap, Ethan reached for the problem area, damn near gasping when the backs of his fingers accidentally brushed against her cool skin. Nicki's muscles tensed, her breath hitching slightly from the contact.

Glad to see I'm not the only one.

A smug smirk lifted his lips as he focused on the task to which he'd been assigned. "Some of the lining got stuck," he told her. "I'm trying to get it out without ripping the dress."

Nicki looked at him from over her shoulder. "Not exactly the way you expected your evening to go, huh? First you miss dinner, and now you're standing in my kitchen helping me out of a dress that cost more than my rent."

"Oh, I don't know." He gave the silky lining a gentle tug, pleased when it started to pull loose without damaging the fabric. "I could think of worse ways to spend my night."

"Speaking of...what happened with Kozlov? If you can tell me, that is."

"I can tell you we retrieved the software and all the plans that went with it."

"And Kozlov?"

Ethan remained silent as he freed the last of the pinched material. "He's been handled."

"Handled..." her voice trailed, her head still turned to face him.

Lifting his gaze to hers, Ethan said nothing as he stared up into the most beautiful eyes he'd ever seen. Hearing the unspoken answer in his silence, Nicki's expression softened as she gave him an understanding nod.

"Good."

Her answer made him smile. That was his Nic. She'd fight to the death for the good guys, but someone like Kozlov?

She'd be the first one in line with the torch.

With his gaze still locked on hers, Ethan stood. "Zipper's fixed." Without thinking, he let his thumb brush softly her skin as he moved.

Nicki's pupils widened, the blues in her eyes darkening with arousal.

Well, fuck me.

He wasn't upset that she wanted him. God, no. But tonight wasn't supposed to be about that. They were just supposed to be hanging out as friends.

And damn it…he was *trying* to be good.

Nicki turned slowly, not stopping until she was facing him fully. She was standing so close Ethan could feel the soft whisps of her breath on his chin.

With one hand securing the dress to her front, she lifted the other, pressing her palm against his chest. "I've missed you so much."

"Me, too, sweetheart." So fucking much.

They'd already said those words but saying them now—like this—somehow felt…different. Intimate.

She moved in closer, erasing the inches between them.

"Nicki…" Her name was a breath. Released not a warning, this time, but a promise.

On the flight here, he'd had some time to really think about everything. What he wanted, and what he prayed *she* wanted.

And then he'd made a solemn vow to keep his needy hands to himself. Not forever. Just for tonight. But now…

If she wanted this, if she wanted *him*…

I'll never say no again.

"I thought I was over you," Nicki whispered softly. "I'd convinced myself that I didn't care where you were or what you were doing. Or who you were with." The tip of her tongue ran the length of her lips. "I convinced myself so much I agreed to marry someone I didn't love. But seeing you again, knowing the truth about everything that happened back then, I...I have to know."

"Know what?"

Breaking eye contact, Nicki pulled her bottom lip between her teeth. The move was innocent, but damn if it didn't nearly drop him to his knees.

"Nic?" he prompted when she remained silent. "What is it you need to know?"

"I still want you, Ethan." She brought her gaze back to his. "I always have. But if you don't want this, if you don't want *me*, then I need to know. Because I can't; I *won't*, waste another minute hoping for something that's never going to happen.

Oh, it's going to happen, sweetheart. Don't you worry.

Standing in almost the exact same position they had when she'd first confessed her feelings for him all those years ago, Ethan stared down into Nicki's eyes and told her everything he should've said back then but didn't.

"I've never wanted a woman more than I want you." There, he finally said it. "I've compared every woman I've ever dated to you, which is probably why none of my relationships ever lasted. Back in high school, I purposely dated brunettes because I thought it would help me get over the incessant need I felt to be with you. But it didn't work. If anything, it made me want you more."

"Ethan..." She huffed out a shocked breath.

"I don't want to be your friend, Nic," he continued. "Well, I do, but that's not all I want."

"Tell me." Ever so slowly, she began caressing the area over his wildly beating heart. "Tell me what you want."

Reaching up, Ethan wrapped his fingers around her wrist and gently pulled her body flush with his. With the swells of her breasts pressing against his chest, he told her the truth.

"You." He brought his free hand to her face, cupping her cheek as gently as if she were made of delicate glass. "*You're all I want, Nic. Only you.*"

With tears welling in her eyes, Nicki whispered the most precious gift he'd ever been given.

"I'm yours, Ethan." She rose onto her tiptoes and brushed her lips against his. "Only yours."

There was more he wanted to say. Thoughtful, meaningful words he'd practiced over and over on the short flight from Charlotte to D.C. But after holding Nicki in his arms, finally hearing her say the one thing he'd spent a decade hoping to hear, suddenly talking was the very last thing on his mind.

"You're sure?" He needed to know.

Giving him a light kiss to his lips, Nicki licked her lips slowly and nodded. "Oh, I'm sure."

It was all he needed to hear.

Pizza order forgotten, Ethan framed both sides of her face with his hands and slammed his mouth to hers. He didn't go slow or explore. There'd be time for that later.

He parted his lips, teasing her with the tip of his tongue. Understanding the sensual request, Nicki opened herself to him.

That's my girl.

She tasted minty, and he suspected she'd brushed her teeth before the whole dress fiasco. The thought nearly had him smiling, but he swallowed the tiniest of moans, and...

He. Was. Lost.

Lowering his hands to her hips, Ethan lifted her into his arms with ease. With her hands keeping her steady on his shoulders, she wrapped her legs around his waist in one, swift move.

Ethan growled, his tongue sparring with hers in the best of ways. Needing to be closer—so much closer—he spun them around and sat her on the island's smooth granite.

"God, Nic." He feasted on her mouth. "Need you."

"You have me, Ethan." She bit him playfully. "Always."

Easing back, Nicki shocked the hell out of him when she lifted the hand holding her dress in place. The loosened material fell, gathering around her waist and exposing the most perfect breasts in existence.

Full. Perky. Two dusty rose nipples begging for his touch, just as he'd always imagined. She looked like every single fantasy he'd ever had and every man's wet dream.

"Jesus."

"I take it you approve?"

"Approve?" He reached for her, filling his palms with the globes. "You're the most beautiful thing I've ever seen." Leaning in, Ethan took one of her rock-hard nipples between his lips.

"Oh!" Nicki gasped, her body arching beneath his touch.

Ethan moved to the other breast. After giving it the same up-close-and-personal attention, he released her and brought his mouth back to hers.

"Taste so good." He spoke between frantic kisses. "Need...more."

Nicki's tight grip on the front of his dress shirt was the only warning he had. Buttons flew, the tiny plastic discs flying in every direction before bouncing loudly against the cabinets, countertops, and floor.

Helping her out, Ethan pulled the ruined shirt from his shoulders, yanking it from his arms and tossing it to the floor. The white undershirt was the next thing to go.

Big ocean eyes stared back at him, their focus moving slowly, starting at the top and working their way down.

"I take it you approve?" He repeated the same question she'd asked him.

Rather than answer with words, Nicki lifted both hands and pressed them just below his collar bone. Moving at a torturously slow pace, she began to trace every crease and crevice his sculpted body had to offer.

"You're so strong," she whispered. "So beautiful."

"No, baby." Ethan brushed some hair from her eyes. "You're the one who's beautiful."

Nicki chuckled nervously. "I'm a mess."

Disheveled hair, flushed skin, swollen lips...

Yeah, she was a mess. A gorgeous, sexy as sin mess. And the best part of all...

We're just getting started.

CHAPTER THIRTEEN

Nicki didn't know what had come over her. She wasn't this bold, confident woman. Not when it came to sex.

It's him. He's the reason.

The voice in the back of her head was right. Ethan gave her strength she never knew she had. He always had.

All I want is you, Nic. Only you.

They were the words she'd always dreamed of hearing but thought she never would. Speaking of dreams…

Ethan's tongue swiped against hers. He tasted of beer and pleasure, and Nicki decided right then that it was her most favorite flavor in the whole world.

Note to self: Always have a twelve-pack on hand.

Breaking the kiss, Ethan began a trail of hot, wet kisses across her cheek, along her chin, and down the length of her neck.

Nicki tilted her head to the side to give him better access. She moaned shamelessly when he licked and then lightly bit the place where her neck and shoulders met.

God, he's good at this.

She'd barely finished the thought when Ethan brought his mouth around to the front, dropping a kiss in the dip at the base of her throat and lower. Guiding her backward, he kept a protective hold to prevent her from falling as she laid down on her extra-wide island.

Tracing an imaginary line with the very tip of his tongue, Ethan worked his way down the center of her torso, not stopping until he reached the sparkly black material. With his hands pressed against the counter on either side of her hips, he pushed himself up.

Nicki watched and waited, confused when she found his heated gaze filled with awe.

"So fucking beautiful," Ethan rasped low.

When he looked at her like that, Nicki felt like the most beautiful woman in the world.

Keeping his eyes on hers. Ethan leaned in and slid his hands between her back and the hard stone countertop. Sensing his intent, she lifted her pelvis to allow him room to work.

An appreciative smile spread across his salacious lips as he worked the zipper over the curve of her rear, not stopping until he reached the end. Raising himself back up, Ethan fisted some of the material on either side of her hips, gently pushing it over her hips and rear and down her legs.

He let the dress drop to the floor next to him.

Lying before him in nothing but a black thong and heels, Nicki was more exposed than she'd ever been to this man. And she didn't care.

She *wanted* him to see her. To look and touch to his heart's content. If he wanted her…

He can have all of me.

"Make love to me, Ethan." Nicki ran a heeled foot up the side of his panted leg. "Please."

Ethan didn't speak. He simply brought his hands to his belt and pulled the black leather strap free. Mesmerized by the muscles in his chest, arms, and abs, she almost missed the unveiling.

He unbuttoned his pants. Still silent, he moved at a snail's pace, lowering his hands to the zipper's clasp. Nicki's pulse raced, the anticipation almost too much for her pounding heart to take.

He knows exactly what he's doing to me.

A rush of arousal went straight to her core, causing her innermost muscles to ache with need. Nicki shifted her body in an attempt to find relief, nearly groaning when she found none.

There was only one thing that would ease the burning need building higher and higher with each beat of her frantic heart. Only one man.

Ethan.

Slowly, he began lowering his zipper. Nicki's fists tightened at her sides from the urge to reach for him, but she forced herself to wait.

He'd better hurry. Otherwise, I cannot be held responsible for my actions.

The tux pants fell from Ethan's hips, exposing a pair of black boxer briefs. And in the center was a massively impressive bulge.

Holy mother of...

Nicki *did* reach for him, then. Sitting up, she dipped the tips of her fingers beneath the boxers' elastic waistband. When he made no move to stop her, she pushed them down his powerful legs until they fell out of reach.

Ethan's erection jutted out from between his thighs, and she had to physically keep her jaw from dropping.

She'd only ever been with one other man, and that was Trey. Sex with him had been okay, but nothing like she'd read about. There was no hunger. No urgency or raw, animal need.

Not like she felt with Ethan. With him, everything was different.

Nicki took him in her fist, the velvety-steel rod hot

beneath her palm. He sucked in a breath, his eight-pack tensing when she began moving her fist up and down the length of his shaft.

Once, twice....

"Jesus, Nic." His eyes burned into hers.

A tiny drop of moisture hit her thumb, letting her know he liked what she was doing.

Bet he's gonna like this a whole lot more.

Licking her lips, Nicki made her intentions clear. Dropping her head, she couldn't wait to take him into her mouth.

A deep, throaty moan sounded from up above as she wrapped her lips around him. Taking her time, she took more of him in, a little at a time.

"Ah, god," Ethan panted. "Baby, you don't have to—"

She erased whatever else he was going to say by taking him in deeper, as far back as he could physically go. He moaned again, and for the next several minutes, Nicki used his sounds and movements as a guide to giving him the ultimate pleasure.

Given her lack of sexual history, she wasn't the most experienced of women. Not by a long shot. But she'd read articles on techniques and so forth on the off chance she found herself in the position to need them.

Like now.

Ethan placed a hand on the back of her head, his fingers giving her hair a slight pull when she flicked the tip of her tongue along his swollen crown. Filling her mouth again, she began pumping him in and out at a slow, steady pace.

She added a fist, moving it and her mouth in tandem. Ethan's breathing picked up, his muscles becoming more and more tense with each stroke. Feeling empowered, Nicki picked up the pace.

She moved faster. Harder. Soon, her rhythm had moved to an almost frantic staccato. And just when she was sure he was about to come, Ethan jerked himself free.

"Wha…what are you—"

"My turn."

Before she could comprehend the growled declaration, Ethan was pushing her back onto the island and spreading apart her legs.

My turn.

Oooh. He means he wants to—

Sliding the tiny scrap of material out of the way, Ethan put his mouth on her. His lips and tongue began working her as if he'd been studying her body for years.

"Ah!" Nicki cried out, the intense pleasure sending her eyes rolling to the back of her head.

He ran his tongue along her slit, and she could feel her body weeping for more. Taking his time, Ethan spent her in the most magnificent way.

"Oh, Ethan," she crooned his name. "God, that feels so good."

For the next several minutes, the generous man took his time making love to her with his mouth. And just as she'd done with him, he listened to her body's cues.

She squirmed beneath him, another cue that she needed more. Smart man that he was, Ethan lifted his mouth higher, his lips finding her clit swollen and begging for attention.

Nicki cried out again, the sensation almost enough to push her over the edge.

Continuing to lick and tease her aching bundle of nerves, Ethan brought a hand between her legs and pressed a finger into her greedy core. She moaned, the addition a welcome intrusion.

In and out, Ethan thrust his finger along the walls of her most sensitive muscles. Adding a second finger, he kept the same, languid pace from before as he stretched her body in preparation of what was to come.

She was embarrassingly wet, but she couldn't help it. The

man affected her in ways no one else had. And the need she felt for him now…

"Not yet," he rumbled, his fingers a piston moving through her soaked core as he seemingly read her mind.

"Please," Nicki begged. "I need you."

"I've got you, sweetheart." Ethan's hot breath blanketed her clit. "Just need you ready first."

If she was anymore ready, she'd be unconscious.

But when Ethan began to add more pressure with his tongue while also moving his hand faster, she understood what he meant.

He wants me to come first.

More than willing to oblige, Nicki closed her eyes and gave herself over to him. Mind filled to the brim with the most intense pleasure she'd ever experienced, she did nothing but *feel.*

His mouth. His tongue. His fingers.

His love.

A familiar tingling began to build in her lower belly and back. As Ethan continued playing her body as if it were made especially for him, Nicki found herself being drawn closer and closer to the edge.

"I'm close," she panted. "God, I'm so close"

"I've got you," Ethan promised.

And there was no doubt in her mind that he did.

He moved faster. Licked her clit a little harder.

There…right there…exactly like that…just a little… bit…longer…

"Ethan!"

Nicki's hips flew off the counter as a powerful current shot through her. Spreading from her core to every nerve ending in her body, her senses were overrun with electricity as her orgasm rolled over her in waves.

When those same waves changed to a calming breeze, Ethan lifted his head and pulled his hand free.

"Holy shit." She worked to control her breathing. "That was…I don't even…"

She had no idea what to say.

The man had just given her the best orgasm of her existence. How did you thank someone for that?

I can think of a way.

Pushing herself back into a seated position, Nicki waited while he finished taking off his shoes and socks. Pulling his pants free, tossing them somewhere to the side.

He straightened his spine and flashed her a wicked grin. But when she started to reach for Ethan's angry-looking cock, he stopped her by stepping just out of her reach.

What the…

"What's wrong?" she frowned.

"Trust me, sweetheart." One corner of his lips curved upward. "There ain't a damn thing wrong."

"Then why did you pull away like that?"

"Because." He slid his hands beneath her arms and lifted her into his arms once more. "I want to be inside you, and our first time isn't going to be on some hard-as-fuck kitchen counter."

Nicki laughed. "My bedroom is down the hall, last door on the left."

Careful not to poke him with her heels, she wrapped her legs around his waist and linked her arms behind his back. His steely bulge pressed against her sensitive flesh as he carried her through the living room and down the hall.

Despite the coma-inducing climax she'd just experienced, Nicki found herself longing to feel him buried inside her.

Soon, Nic. Very, very soon.

Entering her bedroom, Ethan made a bee line for the bed. Laying her in the center, he made quick work of the thong before joining her. But when he started to slide his hand between their bodies, she stopped him.

"Wait!" she blurted loudly. "There's something you should know."

With an unreadable expression, Ethan said, "Okay…"

She drew in calming breath and let it out slowly. "I've only ever been with one man."

There. Embarrassment over.

Surprise widened his dark eyes. "Really?"

"Really."

"I thought you said you and Trey divorced a couple years after you were married."

"We did."

"But that was how long ago?"

"Seven and a half years ago."

She knew the second his mind caught up to what that meant.

"You haven't had sex in seven in seven and a half *years?*"

Nicki shook her head, her hair swishing against the soft comforter.

"You're serious."

"Yes."

She took care of things, of course. When the needs arose, she'd either use her own hand or one of the few toys she'd had the nerve to buy. But there'd been no one since Trey.

Until now.

"Holy shit." He ran a hand over his face. "I wish you had told me."

"Why? So you could change your mind?"

"What?" Ethan scowled. "Hell no, I wouldn't change my mind. I just wouldn't have been so rough with you, that's all. If I'd known, I would have taken things a little slower. Eased you into this instead of attacking you in the middle of your kitchen."

Oh. In that case…

"I don't want gentle, Ethan." She let her legs fall open. "I want you to fuck me."

Something she could only call primal male desire ignited behind his heated gaze. Without a word, Ethan pushed himself higher, aligning his body to hers.

He looked down at her and paused. "I can't say it's been seven and a half years, but it has been nearly a year. And the team is required to get tested every quarter. We just had our last run a couple of months ago. I'm clean, Nic. You don't have anything to worry about with me. But if you want to stop—"

Nicki grabbed his arms to keep him from getting up. "It's okay."

"You sure?"

She nodded. "I trust you."

As crazy as it seemed—given the years that had come between them—she did.

Ethan's muscles relaxed beneath her touch. Repositioning himself, he locked his gaze with hers and pushed his hips forward.

Because it had been a while, and her toys weren't all that big, it took several gentle attempts for him to become fully seated inside her. But when that happened, when their bodies joined together for the very first time, Nicki finally felt like she was where she belonged.

I belong with him. I belong with Ethan.

"You feel that?" Ethan rumbled. "We fit together perfectly. Like we were made for each other."

Her heart swelled, her body instinctively moving beneath his. If she wasn't already in love with the guy, that right there would have done it.

And he was right. They *were* a perfect match. Two halves of a whole who'd finally found their way back to one another.

I never want to let him go.

Ethan began to move, the sensation pulling her back into

the moment. He kept things slow at first, giving her body time to adjust.

The feel of his swollen cock sliding in and out of her body was almost indescribable. The connection they still shared after all this time was nothing short of magical.

Speaking of magic...

He thrust his hips forward, filling her to the brim. "God, you feel so good." Another slow thrust.

Nicki tried to respond, to tell he was the best thing she'd ever felt, but all she managed to choke out was a greedy moan.

Presumably taking it as a hint, Ethan began to move faster. His hips a piston between her thighs, his sensual rhythm bringing her closer and closer to Heaven.

She moved her body in time with his, meeting him thrust for thrust. Before long, Nicki felt the same electrifying warning from before, her lower body trembling with her impending release.

"Oh, Ethan," she breathed his name loudly. "I think I'm going to...oh, god!"

"Come on, baby." His movements became almost frenzied, his strangled words forming between each new penetrating thrust. "Need you...there.... Need you to...let...go. Now, Nic. Just let it all...*go!*"

As if waiting for his order, Nicki began to fly. Though the second climax wasn't quite as powerful as the first, she still found herself lost in euphoric sea of primal satisfaction.

Almost at the exact same moment in time, Ethan's entire body stiffened, his movements becoming jerky and uneven as he used her willing body to find his own release.

When it was over, when they were both sated beyond words, the two of them lay together in a tangled web of heaving breaths and limp, unmoving limbs.

"Wow." Nicki finally managed to formulate a complete

thought. "That was…" Though she tried, she couldn't find a word worthy of what they'd just shared.

Carefully pulling himself free from her sensitive core, Ethan fell beside her. Chest heaving, he turned his head to look at her…and smiled.

"Hell yeah, it was."

She laughed, her naked breasts bouncing with the breathy sound. "I had no idea it could be like that." And now that she'd experienced such an astonishing level of satisfaction, Nicki realized he'd just ruined her for every other man on the planet.

Not that it mattered. There was only one man she wanted to have in her bed, and he was already here.

Several minutes later, after Ethan had so graciously—and gently—cleaned them both up, the two of them settled under the covers, snuggling closely together. With him spooning her from behind and his arm hanging sweetly over her midsection, Nicki felt more at peace than she had in…forever.

She closed her eyes, the tendrils of sleep wasting no time pulling her under. Somewhere in her euphoric state, Nicki thought she felt Ethan's lips pressing sweetly against her temple.

And just before she fell under the Sandman's spell, she could have sworn she heard him whisper…

"I love you."

CHAPTER FOURTEEN

Undisclosed location
  Riga, Latvia...

"SON OF A *BITCH!*" Shards of crystal exploded as the glass Andrei Beňová had just been drinking from smashed against the stone wall.

Everything was ruined. His software was gone, the plan he and Dimitriy had so carefully constructed systematically destroyed by the goddamn Americans.

And now here he was, hiding out in this shithole of an abandoned building because his face was being passed around every one of their government's agencies.

I have to make them pay. I need to find a way to get my software plans back from the Americans and make them pay for what they've done.

He picked up the remote and hit pause. The grainy image frozen on the screen showing four heavily armed men laying siege to Dimitriy's home.

A place that had also come to be *his* home.

The need for revenge had never weighed as heavily on his

shoulders as it did now. From the moment he'd arrived home to find all of Dimitriy's men dead and the once-powerful man's own lifeless body lying in a pool of blood, Andrei had begun to plan.

By the time he got there, the killers were already long gone. With no other choice but to protect himself, Andrei had grabbed those things that meant the most to him and ran.

Leaving his friend and trusted mentor behind like that had felt wrong. Dishonorable, even. But Andrei had to believe it is what Dimitriy would have wanted.

He had to continue the fight. To bring the plan they'd constructed to fruition. It was the one thing he could give back to his fallen friend. A legacy that would follow them both for centuries to come.

Having worked by Dimitriy's side for the last several years, Andrei had made plenty of connections. Over the past week, he'd made numerous calls, putting out feelers within his and Dimitriy's tight circle.

Men with more money and power than God.

But in the end, there was only one person he trusted to get the job done...

Himself.

So here he was, holed up in an abandoned granary that hadn't been used by anyone in years. The place was dark and dank, the floors made of dirt and every window in the place long-ago destroyed. And there was no electricity or running water.

While it was worlds away from the luxurious lifestyle Andrei had become accustomed to, he wasn't above doing whatever it took to survive.

Food and water could be brought in, and there was an endless span of vacant land for when he needed to relieve himself.

A gas-powered generator created enough power to give

him some light, as well as providing power for his computer and phone.

Using the skills he'd been born with, as well as the knowledge he'd picked up along the way, Andrei had also managed to connect to the satellite controlling a server used by an industrial site located a mile away.

You should have made a copy of your plans, Andrei. You should have ignored Dimitriy's orders and cloned the software.

He'd argued with Dimitriy about this very thing, but the stubborn man had been very clear in his orders. He was to make one prototype of the software and no others. Period.

Though he hadn't necessarily agreed with the decision at the time, Andrei had understood Kozlov's concern. The more copies they had, the greater the risk of it falling into the wrong hands.

Because Andrei both respected and feared the other man more than he did his own father, he had gone against his natural instincts and obeyed the order without fault.

I tried to tell you, my friend. You should have listened to me.

Unwilling to waste more time and energy on things he could not change, Andrei walked over to the makeshift workstation he'd set up in the corner of the large, pillared space and turned his opened laptop to face him. Fingers flying over the keyboard, he initiated the facial recognition program he'd designed the previous year to better help Dimitriy combat his enemies.

Enemies that were now his own.

The Americans had struck Dimitriy down like an animal —in his own home, no less—but Andrei was still here. It was his duty to bring honor and justice to his friend and mentor. To avenge his death in the most magnificent way he knew how...

By bringing the most powerful country in the world to its knees.

As if given approval by the gods, his computer chose that

exact moment to ding, notifying him of a possible match. When he looked, Andrei realized that was an incorrect assessment.

There wasn't a single match. There were *three* faces filling his computer screen. Below each one read a different name:

Slade Garrison.

Beckett Stone.

Ethan McCallister.

Below those names were possible dates of birth listed for each of the men.

A slow, satisfied smile began to form. "And the Americans think *they're* the smart ones."

From a young age, he knew he was different from the other kids. While they ran around kicking balls in the dirt, laughing, and screaming, Andrei would be in his room, devouring every book he could get his hands on.

When he was deemed old enough, his father had gotten him his first computer. By the time he was thirteen, Andrei was efficiently writing code.

So no, the Americans were no threat to him. They may have stolen what belonged to him, but he would not stop until he found a way to get it back.

As smart as they believed themselves to be—and despite only having a few names and faces to go off of—there wasn't a single man on the team that took out Dimitriy that was as smart as him.

Of that, Andrei was certain.

If they were, they would've realized their murderous, thieving actions were being recorded by the multitude of hidden cameras he'd personally installed in and around his friend's compound.

Father was right. No one is smarter than me.

Feeling more like his confident self, he studied the numbers next to each of the names on his screen, pleased to find the probability of each match well over ninety-five percent.

Excellent.

Opening a different program—also of his own design—Andrei clicked several keys on his keyboard to initiate a thorough electronic search on each of the three men.

Names and birthdays were not enough. He needed to know everything there was to find.

If there was one thing he'd learned during his years spent serving beside a man like Dimitriy Kozlov, it was that everyone had a weakness. Whether it be money or power... honor or even love...everyone had something they were willing to fall on their sword to protect.

Using the security footage as fuel for his cause, Andrei watched the infuriating scene again.

He still couldn't believe his old friend was gone, but it wasn't lost on him that if he hadn't been late getting out of that meeting...

I'd be gone, too.

Fury stirred and deep in his gut as he watched the team of American operatives take over the one place where he and Dimitriy had felt safe. Andrei rewound the recording and played it again. And again.

And again.

The more times he watched it, the angrier he got. He needed a solid plan, and he needed it fast.

Right on cue, his computer dinged with the results of his search. Scanning what should have been a detailed background report on each of the three men, Andrei was vastly disappointed when the program wasn't able to find the specifics he'd hoped for.

There were no phone numbers listed under their names, no physical addresses. The search didn't even produce so much as an old electric bill or high school transcript.

I've underestimated them.

It was a mistake he didn't make often.

There was one thing the report did manage to find. A picture that gave him hope, just when he was beginning to think there was none left to be had.

It was recent, only a few days old in fact, but the information it revealed was even better than he could've hoped for.

Andrei studied the photo that had been posted on every major social media platform by none other than the Associated Press. In it, there was a crowd of finely-dressed men and women, some in ribbon-adorned military uniforms, others in dresses and tuxedos.

But there was only one person in the digital image who mattered to him.

Despite his change in appearance, his program had easily identified Ethan McCallister—Former Navy SEAL, current Travel Assurance employee, and one of the three men captured on the footage from Dimitriy's home.

Showcasing a recent White House dinner hosted by none other than the Department of Defense, McCallister could be seen talking with a man Andrei recognized as Secretary Bradford.

The man in charge of the DoD.

While that definitely piqued his interest, it was the woman standing *next* to McCallister who first caught Andrei's eye.

Blonde hair. Blue eyes. Tits he could spend days getting lost in.

He estimated her to be in her mid-to-late twenties. In the photo, she was staring up at McCallister, her gaze locked solely on him.

And the look on her face said she thought he hung the moon.

It's her. She's the key.

Not one to jump to conclusions or assume, Andrei went straight to work trying to identify the buxom blonde.

Using the same facial rec program from before, it didn't take long for him to pinpoint her image and run it for a match.

It was the same process he'd gone through to identify McCallister and the others. And just like before, it took less than a minute for the program to get a hit.

"Well, hello there, Miss Castille," he spoke to the woman on his screen.

Nicolette Castille.

Unlike the three mercenaries he couldn't wait to kill, the woman's whole life was readily available. Birth certificate, high school diploma, college graduation photos, a wedding photo that, surprisingly showed her married to a man other than her hero SEAL.

But there was another image, one from long, long ago. It was a picture that appeared to have been taken for the Castille woman's high school yearbook.

In it, a younger version of the voluptuous blonde was standing between two teenage boys. The one on her left appeared to be the same man she'd married. The other...

Ethan McCallister.

Not only that, but a quick skim of the intel detailing her adult life revealed another interesting fact. One that was every bit as intriguing as her connection to the American asshole.

One of the documents Andrei's program discovered was a tax form submitted by the pretty artist. And the name listed in the section marked *employee*...

The United States Department of Defense.

His pulse spiked with excitement, a renewed sense of purpose and drive racing through his menacing veins.

There it was. The definitive connection he'd been looking for.

Not only did the Castille woman have a history with one of the three identifiable targets, she also worked for the very government responsible for murdering his friend and stealing his life's work.

Hours later, Andrei found himself sitting back in his chair, the next step in his plan solidified the moment he found Miss Castille's home address. *Washington D.C.*

How serendipitous it was that the key to his cause could be found in the heart of the nation he was planning to destroy.

Staring at the information that would bring him back into a position of power—as opposed to hiding out in this shithole like a disease-ridden rat—he knew exactly what he needed to do.

He stared at the pretty blonde once more and smiled.

Shouldn't be so careless, my pretty Nicolette. You never know who might be trying to find you.

CHAPTER FIFTEEN

Two weeks later...

NICKI BOUNCED AROUND HER APARTMENT, putting away the last of her weekly laundry haul. Normally she dreaded the necessary chore, but even the thought of pairing socks and steaming blouses did nothing to tamper the ridiculous smile permanently etched across her face.

It was the same smile she'd worn every day since the night of the DoD banquet.

Memories from the most incredible night of her existence made their presence known, making her lower belly tighten in response. More flashes followed, images from Ethan's surprising morning-after wake-up-call—how she wished she could wake up every morning from now on—still fresh in her mind.

It had been hard saying goodbye to him that same afternoon, but he'd returned to D.C. that very next weekend. They'd spent two full days alternating between mind-blowing sex, pizza deliveries, and OG movies that made her laugh so hard, she'd had tears streaming down her cheeks.

You feel that? We fit together perfectly. Like we were made for each other.

They *were* made for each other. Nicki was certain of it. In fact, she'd never been more sure of anything in her entire life. And not just because of the amazing sex, although that certainly didn't hurt.

No, it was all the other things—the *little* things—that solidified the idea of a future with Ethan. The random texts he'd send just to say hi and that he missed her. The phone calls at night to ask about her day and share what he could about his.

Minus the physical distance between their two cities, there wasn't a single thing Nicki would change about the way things between them had transpired. It was much different than the relationship her teenage mind had created, and that was okay.

The past was the past, and every decision they'd both made had brought them here, to this place. To a time when they were old enough to appreciate what a precious gift a second chance at happiness truly was but still young enough to build a life together. A *real* life.

One filled with joy and laughter. Passion and, maybe someday down the road, even marriage and kids.

So for now, Nicki was content knowing he was back in her life again...and finally, *finally* in her bed.

Speaking of beds...

A large, unladylike yawn struck as she set her empty laundry basket in its designated spot at the back of her walk-in closet. Checking the digital clock illuminating from her bedside table, she saw that it was already after nine.

Not super late by her normal standards, but she had a flight to catch in the morning, and she was *not* going to be late.

Nicki smiled to herself as she went to the bathroom to finish up her bedtime routine. Once her teeth were brushed and she'd changed into her satiny shorts and tank sleep set, she made her way back into her bedroom and climbed beneath the covers.

Double checking her alarm was set—multiple ones, in fact—she laid her phone on its magnetic charging station and turned off the bedside lamp. Her head hit the pillow right as her phone began to ring.

Her lips curved, recognizing the personalized ringtone she'd set especially for Ethan. It was the theme song to the original Superman movie and had started out as a joke. Nicki decided to keep it, however, because it was so very fitting.

Strong and formidable, he was a man willing to put himself between the innocent and whatever danger they may face. But there was also a softer, gentler side to him. One she'd seen more and more with each new day they spent together.

If only they could figure out the whole long-distance thing, then everything in her world would be damn near perfect.

Just like him.

Nicki swiped her finger across her screen and answered the call with a schoolgirl grin. "Hey, you."

"Hey, yourself."

God, would she ever get tired of hearing that deep, rumbly timbre of his? *Never.*

Turning to her side, Nicki settled into her pillow and grinned. "You just getting done for the day?"

"Yeah." A loud sigh filled the phone's speaker. "Between quarterly paperwork that had to be finished today, two separate meetings having to do with the insurance side of the business, and a video conference briefing us on a few precarious situations overseas, I barely had time to hit the head."

"Any news on Beñová?" Last she knew, the criminal mastermind had yet to be found.

"Still dark," Ethan practically growled.

His frustration was perfectly understandable. Beñová had already designed and built the dangerous software once before. With him running around free as a bird, it was only a matter of time before he built another.

"At least you have tomorrow off. That's something, right?"

"It definitely is." His smile was audible. "You're still flying in tomorrow morning, right?"

"My bags are already packed and sitting by the door." Nicki couldn't wait to see him again. "I have an early meeting at seven, but it'll be over with in plenty of time for me to make my flight."

"Good deal. That's at ten, right?"

"Yep." She nodded, even though he couldn't see her. "Air bound at ten, touchdown at CLT by eleven thirty-five."

"I'll be at the gate waiting."

Butterflies flittered about inside Nickie's stomach from just the thought of seeing him again. "You don't have to do that. I mean, I appreciate it and all, but doesn't the barbeque start at noon? I can get an Uber or something."

"Lunch is supposed to be at noon, but it's just the team getting together at Garrett and Avery's to eat, drink, and shoot the shit. Won't matter if we're a few minutes late, and there's not a chance in hell I'm letting you get into a car by yourself with a stranger and then hope you make it to Garrett's safe and sound."

"Yes, Sir," she teased, but didn't bother to argue.

When it came to her safety, the man could be relentless.

Nicki was both excited and nervous about spending time with the Tac-Ops guys outside her official DoD duties.

They'd all been great, so her nerves had nothing to do with them professionally. But this would be their first public outing as a couple.

The discussion of what they should call each other had yet to take place. Boyfriend and girlfriend seemed a bit juvenile, given their ages. But lovers suggested what they had between them was more about the physical connection than anything else.

For Nicki, she didn't need a label to tell her what they were or weren't. She knew in her heart that Ethan was the one for her.

But once she showed up at Garrett's tomorrow—as his *date*—this thing between them would be official. And if something happened and things didn't work out…

It will. You heard what he said. He wants you, Nic. Only you, remember? Get out of your own way and let yourself be happy.

"I still hate to risk making you late," she finally spoke up again. "What if something happens, and my flight gets delayed?"

"Then it's delayed." There was a slight touch of humor in his voice. "Relax, Nic. It's going to be fine."

He was right. She was worrying over nothing.

"They know I'm coming, right? I don't want to spring that on them at the last minute."

"The guys know, and they're looking forward to seeing you again. Avery, too. Garrett said her sister, Alex, is planning on coming. She's an artist, too."

"Really?"

"Yep. Owns her own gallery right here in Charlotte."

"That's awesome!"

"Yeah, she's pretty cool. Oh, and you'll get to meet Colt, too."

"Colt?"

"Garrett's brother," Ethan clarified. "He's a complete smartass, but funny as hell and totally harmless. But you've been warned."

A soft chuckle had her shoulders shaking beneath the covers. "Sounds like it should be a lot of fun."

"As long as you're there, it will be."

See? Sexy, Superman strong, and sweet.

The man really was the whole package. A tall, dark, deliciously handsome package she couldn't wait to unwrap again in a few short hours.

Another huge yawn had Nicki covering her mouth and waiting for it to pass. "Sorry. Guess I'm more tired than I thought."

"I'll let you go. Get some rest," Ethan ordered softly before adding a wicked, "Trust me, you're gonna need it."

With all thoughts of sleep temporarily placed on hold, she smiled wide. "Oh, yeah? You got something planned I don't know about?"

"Oh, sweetheart." His voice dropped to a panty-melting level. "I have all sorts of things planned for you."

"Mmm…" she crooned. "Do tell."

"Nope. You're just going to have to wait and see."

"Well that's plain mean." Nicki pretended to pout.

A low chuckle vibrated against her ear. "I'll make it up to you tomorrow night."

Her core began to swell with an incessant need that had her thighs rubbing together in an attempt to relieve the pressure. "Promise?"

"Damn straight."

For some reason, his answer made her chuckle. "I'll call you when I land."

"I'll already be there."

Seriously, could the guy be more perfect?

How he was still single was beyond all comprehension, but Nicki never had been one to look a gift horse in the mouth. Other women's loss was her gain. And she wasn't going to take a single second of it for granted.

Not ever.

"Sleep tight, sweetheart. I…" Ethan started to say something but cut himself short.

"Ethan?"

He cleared his throat, the raspy growl that made her toes

curl suddenly gone. "Sorry. I was just going to say I'll see you tomorrow."

Oh. She thought maybe he was going to say something else.

Refusing to let her imagination ruin her giddy mood, Nicki responded with a genuine, "Can't wait."

A beat of silence passed before she heard a soft, "Night, Nic."

"Goodnight, Ethan."

And with that, Nicki ended the call. After a disappointing self-gratification session—her own hand had nothing on the real thing—she settled herself back in and fell asleep.

Two hours later, she woke to a loud banging coming from either the living room or kitchen. Shooting straight up in bed, Nicki's heart raced from the unpleasant awakening.

For several seconds, she sat stock still, tilting her head toward her bedroom door, hoping to make out whatever had pulled her from an amazing dream. A glorious, wonderful dream starring none other than her favorite Tac-Ops operator.

It's nothing, Nic. You were dreaming. Go back to sleep.

A moment longer, after hearing nothing other than her own frantic heartbeat, Nicki chocked it up to her imagination and laid back down. Her lids fell shut, her lungs bringing in and then releasing a deep, calming breath.

Sooner you get back to sleep, the sooner you'll be with Ethan.

With a smile spread wide across her sleepy face, Nicki had just started to relax when she heard another noise. It was different than before, softer and less obvious. But she'd heard it, all the same.

Her eyes flew open, but she didn't sit straight up this time. Instead, she forced her breathing to remain steady, reminding herself that panicking would only make things worse.

It's probably just an ordinary field mouse.

Yes. That's probably all it was. A harmless, adorable little mouse that had found its way inside her house in search of food and warmth.

They used to get them now and then when she was little. Nicki and her dad would make a game of trying to find it. There was this one mouse she remembered that had scared the wits out of her.

For days, she and her dad had searched high and low without any luck. Eventually her dad moved to a different plan, building a makeshift trap that wouldn't harm the mouse. Only capture it.

That night, the two of them set up a camera in the kitchen—where they kept finding incriminating evidence of the little guy's presence—and kept watch from the other room. They munched on junk food and told each other funny stories... It was like their own little stakeout.

And it worked.

Nicki remembered running into the kitchen to see. There, trapped beneath the three-sided box with a mesh wire top, was a gray mouse with a white stomach, beady black eyes, and an adorable set of ears.

She could still see it staring up at her, the fear the tiny creature felt as real as any she'd experienced at that point in her life. Thinking petting it would make it feel better, Nicki lifted the box just enough to stick her hand inside so she could give the tiny rodent some comfort.

She still had the scar on her finger where that mouse bit her.

While she screamed and cried and begged her dad to kill it, he calmly cleaned the superficial wound, bandaged her up, and the two of them drove the mouse to a nearby field where her dad proceeded to set it free.

On the way back home, Nicki asked her dad why he'd gone to all that trouble for a mouse that was so mean. To this day, she could still hear her dad's caring tone when he answered with...

That mouse wasn't mean, baby girl. Animals are just like people. When they get cornered, they'll do whatever it takes to survive.

Another shuffling sound reached her ears from somewhere down the hall, sending Nicki's pulse racing with fear.

That's not a damn mouse, Nicolette. Someone's here!

Reaching for her glasses and phone, Nicki rushed to duck under the covers. With her glasses in place, she ignored the desperate urge to call Ethan and did the more practical, logical thing.

She dialed nine-one-one. It rang once...twice...

"Nine-one-one, can you tell me the nature of your emergency?"

Oh, thank god!

"My name is Nicki Castille." She whispered softer than she ever had in her life. Keeping her voice hushed, she quickly relayed her address before telling the operator, "There's someone inside my house."

"Nicki, my name is Nancy. I had a hard time hearing that last part. Did you say someone broke into your home?"

Tears threatened to fall as Nicki nodded her head. "Y-yes."

"Okay, Nicki. I have a unit on the way. Do you have a safe pathway out of the house?"

She thought of the window directly behind where she lay. "I might be able to climb out my bedroom window."

It was either that or try for the front door, which would put her directly in the path of the intruder.

"Do it. If you can, take your phone with you. I'll stay on the line."

"O-okay. I'm going to the window now."

Moving as quickly as she could while trying to remain silent was a lot harder than it looked in the movies. But Nicki could hear soft footfalls crossing over her hardwood floor, and though she didn't have a clear view of the hallway, she instinctually knew whoever had broken into her house was heading in her direction.

Please, please *let me get away before he finds me.*

With ice running through her veins, Nicki slid out of the side of her bed nearest the wall and raced to open the window. Setting her phone onto the wide, wooden sill, she flipped the locks free—first one and then the other. Then she pushed.

Nothing happened.

No!

She spun her head toward her half-opened door. Her heart leaped into her throat when she saw a dark shadow marring the part of the hallway wall she could see.

And it was moving.

No longer giving thought to how loud she was being, Nicki began smacking the heels of her palms against the window's jammed frame, praying with every painful shove it would come loose so she could be free.

"Hello, Nicolette."

She froze at the sound of her name. This wasn't some random thief looking to make a quick buck. This man *knew* her.

His shadowy reflection appeared in the window's upper pane. A rush of bile hit the base of her throat, but she refused to give into her fear. If she let it take over, this man would win.

What his prize would be, she didn't dare guess. Instead, she collected her racing thoughts and tried to come up with a plan.

I'm the mouse. I'm trapped and desperate.

And just like that mouse, Nicki knew she would do whatever it took to survive.

There isn't a screen on that window. You kept forgetting to get it replaced.

She still had a chance to escape.

She glanced down at the small accent table positioned next to the window. Grabbing the softball-size geode her dad had bought her one year at the county fair, she lifted it into the air, turned her face away from the window, and slammed it hard against the lower pane.

Deadly shards of broken glass fell around her as the cool night breeze shocked her flushed skin. Some of the glass had flown outside on impact while others fell on and around her bare feet.

Several remained secured inside the window frame, their jagged edges pointing toward her only means of escape.

This is going to hurt.

But given the alternative…

Using the side of her fist and forearm, Nicki did her best to make a hole big enough for her to crawl through with relative safety. From her peripheral, she could see the man walking slowly toward her.

Please, God. Please don't let him hurt me!

She swung one leg up over the window's frame. Ignoring the scrapes and cuts from the busted glass, Nicki dipped her head down to fit through the makeshift exit.

She was halfway to safety when a gloved hand curled painfully around her wrist and yanked her back inside.

"Ah!" Nicki cried out as she was thrown unceremoniously to the floor. The impact forced the air from her lungs, but she immediately pushed herself back up to her feet and ran.

"There's nowhere to go, Nicolette."

She hadn't noticed it at first, but the man definitely had an accent. Russian maybe? Or German?

It doesn't matter, goddamnit! Just get your ass in gear and run!

Nicki nearly stumbled when she heard Ethan's stern voice rolling through her frantic mind. Even though she knew he wasn't there, it had sounded as clear and concise as if he'd been standing right beside her.

And she'd received the imaginary message loud and clear.

The sound of bare feet slapping against wood sounded as she sprinted out of her bedroom and toward her home's front door. Nicki rounded the corner at the end of the hall, her palm smacking loudly against the wall to keep from toppling over when she lost her footing.

She managed to stay upright but knocked down two custom wooden frames in the process. They slid straight down to the floor, breaking apart on impact as she ran past.

Nicki reached her front door. Barely able to control her fine motor skills, she spent seconds she didn't have struggling with the locks.

Come on! Come on! Come on!

With a calming breath, she refocused her efforts, slowing her hysterical movements just enough to do what needed to be done.

She released the small lock centered on the bulbous knob. The deadbolt came second, followed by the added measure of the brass door chain.

With hope blooming in her chest, Nicki felt much more confident in the odds of her escaping. Yanking the door open, she started to run outside, where she planned to scream for help and flag down the first neighbor or passerby she spotted.

But as she started to cross the metal threshold, a second man stepped directly into her path.

Much larger than the one in her bedroom, the man filling her vision towered over her by at least a foot. Built much like Ethan's boss, Nicki didn't stand a chance if she tried to physically fight him.

With only one very *bad* option left, she spun on her bare heels and ran back into the house. The man who knew her name appeared at the hallway's entrance, essentially blocking her in.

And when people get cornered, they'll do whatever it takes to survive.

Nicki ran to the wicker basket resting decoratively on the stone hearth beneath the small brick fireplace. Grabbing the solid steel poker, she turned just in time to see the bigger of the two men start to reach for her.

With one hand, she swung the poker into the in air as if it were a baseball bat. Using as much force as she could muster, Nicki brought it down in a forceful slope toward the man's leg.

He cried out in pain as the rod's pointed edge sliced across his shin.

"You bitch!" The man's statuesque face twisted with anger, the injury to his leg doing little to stop him.

Run, Nicolette! You have to run!

She used her next breath to assess her options. If she went right, she'd have to face the pissed off wall of muscle. Left wasn't much better, since the shorter man was there, but if these were her only choices…

Please don't let me die!

The silent prayer played through her mind as her legs began to move. Charging forward, Nicki released an animalistic scream, the poker swinging back and forth wildly in front of her as she moved.

A lamp fell noisily to the ground, a flash of light and a loud *pop* filling the space as it shattered. Pictures, a vase, and a few porcelain figurines she'd only just started to collect were inadvertently knocked to the floor by the rod's flailing tip.

The shorter man jumped back to avoid being struck, and for half a breath, Nicki felt as though she were finally gaining the upper hand. But she was so busy trying to force Short Man to remain at arm's length, she failed to keep a constant eye on Square Jaw.

A set of massively strong arms wrapped around her from

behind. Pinning her upper arms beneath his biceps, Square Jaw squeezed her so hard, it made it nearly impossible for Nicki to breathe.

As she fought in vain to get free, the man lifted her off her feet as if she were weightless.

"Save your strength, pretty Nicolette." Short man stayed in the shadows. "We're not here to kill you."

"W-who…are…you?" Nicki kicked and twisted, but it was no use. The giant holding her was simply too strong.

"Ah, yes, we haven't been formally introduced. My name is Andrei Beňová." He took another step closer, his face appearing as he moved into a thin ray of moonlight shining through her living room windows.

Beňová? As in the man Ethan's team—along with every alphabet agency in the country—have been trying to find?

Dear god.

Realizing she was in serious trouble, Nicki managed to ground out a rough, "What do you…want from me?"

"Oh, I don't want anything from you." The madman shook his head slowly. "But your boyfriend and his team took something that belongs to me, and you're going to help me get it back."

He's talking about the flash drive.

Play dumb.

"I don't know…what you're…talking about." Nicki's fingertips began to tingle as the circulation in her arms began to fade. "And if you're not…going to…kill me…could you maybe have your…goon let me…go?"

Seriously, dude. You've made your point. You can win a fight with a woman less than half your size. Aren't you a stud?

Beňová dipped his chin, a silent signal to the man behind her. As the order was given, Square Jaw opened his arms and set her free.

Dropping to her feet, Nicki had to put both arms out to

the side to keep control of her wavering balance while also gulping in several deep, desperate breaths.

Once she felt sure-footed again, she straightened her spine and shot a glare in Beñová's direction. "Thanks." *Asshole.*

"As I was saying…" Beñová moved toward her. "Your boyfriend—"

"I don't have a boyfriend." Nicki figured it wasn't exactly a lie, since they hadn't had the whole 'what are we' discussion yet.

"You want to be very careful with me, pretty Nicolette." He took another step closer. "I can be a very patient man, but I do not tolerate lies."

"I'm not lying. I don't know what it is you think has been stolen, and I have no idea what team you're referring to." She put on her best acting chops and schooled her expression. "You have the wrong person."

A look of disappointment crossed over the evil man's face. Giving another silent order, Nicki had no time to decipher its meaning before Square Jaw spun her around by her shoulders and slammed his fist into the side of her head.

Pain exploded across her temple and cheekbone as the blow knocked her off her feet and into the air. Tipping over a wooden accent chair on her way down, a starburst of colors clouded her vision as she landed with a hard thud against the unforgiving floor.

Nicki groaned, her face already feeling swollen and tight. *Get up, Nic. You have to keep fighting!*

"As I said before, I don't tolerate liars." Beñová stood over her, his expression almost that of boredom. "Mr. McCallister and his team took possession of something that does not belong to them, and I want it back."

Dazed from the massive blow to her head, she moved at a pathetically slow pace in her feeble attempt to show these men she wasn't some damsel in distress that would cower down to bullies like them.

"If they're the ones who...stole from you..." She slowly attempted to push herself to her feet, only getting as far as her quivering hands and knees. "Then why did you...come after...me?"

Am I slurring my words? And why is everything in the room spinning?

Pinching the material covering his thighs, Beňová adjusted his pantlegs before lowering himself closer to her level "We're here, because what they took from me is worth more money than your feeble brain can even begin to comprehend. And you..." He started to move some hair from her face, but Nicki jerked her head from his reach at the last minute. "You're going to help me get it back."

CHAPTER SIXTEEN

Ethan watched as the final passenger from Flight 819 exited the secured area outside the gate where he was supposed to meet Nicki. She was supposed to be on this flight. He'd double-checked it this morning before he left for the airport, and then triple-checked it when he realized she hadn't made her flight.

He pulled up her number and tried calling her again. As it had the previous twelve times he'd tried reaching her, it went straight to voicemail. She also hadn't answered her work phone or responded to his multitude of texts.

A giant knot began to form deep in his gut. Something wasn't right. He could feel it.

Maybe she changed her mind.

The thought gave Ethan pause but only briefly. Yes, this thing between them was still really new—but also old—and everything in-between. But while their relationship may not have begun in the most conventional of ways, it didn't make it any less real.

And what they'd shared during their long-distance weekend visits was the realest thing he'd ever known.

She didn't change her mind. She wouldn't.

And on the off chance that is what had happened, Nicki would never intentionally leave him standing in the middle of a bustling airport looking like a lost puppy searching for its owner.

She does own you.

Now that was true. Nicki owned him body, heart, and soul. And unless he'd completely misread her during his most recent trip to D.C., she was his.

If that's true, why isn't she here?

It was a very good question, and one he intended on answering right the fuck now.

Stepping out of the path of traffic, Ethan stood near one of the floor-to-ceiling windows giving passers by a clear view of the arriving flights. He tapped another number in his list of contacts and put his phone to his ear.

Before now, he'd never called this person from his personal phone. The number was simply there in case of emergency.

The woman I love is missing. Can't think of a bigger emergency than that.

The familiar voice answered on the second ring. "Apollo?" Shadow sounded about as confused as he'd expected. "This is a surprise. Is everything okay?"

"I don't know," he answered honestly. "That's why I'm calling."

After sharing his reason for concern, he could hear the team's tech analyst clicking on her keyboard. "Give me a second to access the airline's mainframe. Flight 819, correct?"

"Yeah." Ethan ran a hand over his jaw, doing his damnedest not to overreact. Not exactly an easy task for men like him.

After seeing all the shit he had over the years, overreacting was almost second-nature.

"Okay, so it looks like Nicki was on the original flight manifest, but she never boarded the plane."

The tightening in his chest worsened. "You're sure?"

"I mean, yeah. I'm looking right at a digital copy of the complete manifest. That's about as definitive as you can get."

Ethan cursed beneath his breath. "I know this isn't work related, but if I give you Nicki's cell number, do you think you could—"

"Already on it." A few clicks and then, "Got it. It's still on, so that's good. Looks like it's at her house."

Her house? That didn't make any sense. Not unless she really did change her mind about spending the weekend with him.

"When was the last time you talked to her?"

"Last night around nine-thirty."

Memories of their conversation rose to the surface. In particular, his near-miss with the whole I love you declaration.

He'd come so damn close to saying it before they'd ended the call. The words had almost rolled right off his tongue without any thought or conscious effort on his part.

It was only by the grace of God that he'd caught himself in time to prevent it. Not because he didn't love her.

Ethan would lay his own life down for the woman and not think twice about it.

The reason he'd stopped himself from saying those three not-so-little words was because something that big needed to be done in person. He wanted to be standing in front of her, looking deep into those heart stopping eyes so she could see the truth in his.

Which is exactly what he'd planned to do. Tonight, in fact. As soon as the barbeque was over.

The barbeque.

Ethan glanced at his watch. He was officially past the *dude, where've you been* stage, but hadn't quite reached the peak of *why'd-you-even-bother*. But until he knew what was going on with Nicki...

"You said you talked to Nicki at nine-thirty last night?" Shadow's voice caught his attention once again.

"Yeah. She'd just gotten into bed. We talked about her flight and going to Falcon's for lunch...that was about it. We were on the phone like ten minutes, max. Why?"

"I'm showing an outgoing call from her number at eleven forty-two p.m. last night."

"Outgoing?" Ethan frowned. "Who'd she call?"

A slight pause ensued, raising the tiny hairs on the back of his neck. Shadow was one of the smartest, most confident women he'd met. She rarely hesitated, and when she did...

Ah, hell.

"Shadow, who did Nicki call?" he demanded so sharply a couple walking past turned and stared.

"It might not mean anything," her reply was cryptic as fuck. "I'm gonna need a couple more minutes to get all the details so just try not to freak out on me, okay?"

"Shadow..."

"Apollo..."

His back teeth ground together as he reigned in his heightened frustration. Normally he respected Shadow's refusal to back down. But this day was turning out to be anything but normal.

"Sorry," she apologized. Another rare occurrence that left him anxious as hell. "According to this, the outgoing call from your girl's phone was made to...nine-one-one."

Nic called nine-one-one two hours after she and I talked?

Just like that, the weighted feeling in his gut exploded into full-blown panic. "Shadow, can you check to see if—" Ethan's phone alerted him to an incoming call. "Shit." He glanced at the screen. "It's Owens. I'll call you back."

"Apollo, wait! There's something else you should—"

"Hey, Boss," Ethan greeted Owens after switching calls.

"Listen, this isn't really the best—"

"Where are you right now?"

Rafe's tone was even more serious than normal. "The airport why?"

"You need to come into the office."

"Now?"

"Yes."

Fuck. "Actually I was about to call and ask if I could borrow the jet again. Not for personal use, but…well, technically it is personal, but…"

He blew out a breath, stealing himself to say the words aloud. Once they were out there, this was real. Nicki would really be missing. Possibly worse.

"Nicki's missing." Ethan ripped the band aid off in one go. "She was supposed to be here by now, and she's not. I've been trying all morning, but I can't reach her, even though her phone's still showing at her house, and I—"

"I know."

Ethan cut his worried rambling short. "You know? What are you—"

"I just got off the phone with SecDef. Someone in his office called the police to request a well check for Miss Castille when she didn't show up for an important meeting."

She'd missed her meeting?

Moving in long, purposeful strides, Ethan walked swiftly toward the nearest exit. In rapid-fire style which was completely out of character for him, he began asking his boss questions faster than the other man could answer.

"And? What did they find? Did something happen to her?"

"I don't have all the details yet, but SecDef is sending over everything now, including the initial police report. He's also cleared his schedule so we can connect via video call as soon as you get here."

So many what-the-fucks filled Ethan's head at once he didn't have a clue where to start.

He'd woken up happy this morning. Excited, even. Because Nicki was coming to see him. Now she was missing, and the police and SecDef were involved, though he didn't know why because no one would tell him what the fuck was going on.

Feeling like he was going to lose his goddamn mind if someone didn't give him a straight answer, Ethan opened his mouth to demand his boss quit beating around the bush when Owens' English accent filled the phone's speaker once again.

"Do you love her, son?"

The man's intrusive question caused Ethan's steps to faulter as he hurried across the parking lot to his car. "Sir?"

"Miss Castille. I'm asking if you're in love with her."

"Uh…" He began walking again. "All due respect, Boss, but that's not really something I feel comfortable discussing—"

"If you love this woman…" Owens interrupted him again. "If you care about her at all, you'll hold your questions and get your ass here. You copy?"

Whatever had happened must be really fucking bad if Owens was worried about discussing it over their encrypted phones.

"I'll be there in twenty."

"Here's what we know."

Secretary Bradford's stone-cold face filled the smart board's big screen at the front of Tac-Ops' conference room. The concern behind his weary eyes was like a punch to Ethan's gut.

"At seven forty-five morning"—the man in charge of the room continued— "several of Miss Castille's co-workers became concerned when she didn't show up for an important meeting. As I'm sure Mr. McAllister knows, it's not in

Miss Castille's nature to be late, let alone miss without so much as a word. Which is why, after an hour with no contact, one of my staff called the police and requested a well-check."

"What did they find?" Ethan asked point-blank. Because he and the others wouldn't be here if there hadn't been something for the cops to find.

"It's more about what they *didn't* find." Bradford's image shrunk as several digital crime scene photos appeared, filling the other half of the screen. "This was the state of Miss Castille's living room when the unit from the Capitol Police arrived."

"What the hell?"

The blurted comment came from Bones, who was sitting in the chair to his right, but Ethan's entire focus was locked on those fucking pictures.

Nicki's quaint, neatly kept home was in shambles. Pictures had been knocked from the walls. Lamps were over-turned. Several of the books and figurines she kept on the small table against the living room's east wall appeared to have been swept right off the table's surface and onto the floor.

More pictures appeared; the newest collection all taken in Nicki's bedroom.

The window next to her bed had been broken from what appeared to be the inside out. Glass littered the immediate area, and several of the broken shards sticking up from inside the window's wooden frame had smears of dried blood on them.

A set of red eyeglasses lay haphazard on the floor below.
Oh, God.

"The good news is Miss Castille's body wasn't found in or around the crime scene."

"Meaning if they wanted to kill her, they probably would have just done the deed and left her there," Bones surmised.

"Exactly." Bradford nodded. "All we know for sure is that someone broke into the home late last night; there was as struggle, and now Miss Castille is missing."

The room grew silent as each of the men absorbed the reality of the situation. After a stretch of silence, Digger pointed to one of the pictures showing a close-up of the busted window.

"Looks like she tried using the window as her means of escape. Do we know if that's her blood?"

"It's been confirmed that it's her type," SecDef clarified. "We're still waiting to hear back on the DNA."

Ethan tried not to picture the way Nicki had been forced to fight for her life. Her fucking *life*.

As if that wasn't enough, she was out there somewhere, going through God only knows what, and he didn't have a fucking clue how to find her.

"Any leads on where she was taken?" He finally found his ability to speak again, his voice deadpan.

It was the only question he really needed the answer to. The only one that truly mattered.

"Unfortunately, we don't know. As of right now, there's been no attempt to make contact by an HT. Not to the family or law enforcement."

"What about CCTV?" Falcon asked. "Or even those doorbell cameras everyone seems to have these days. You pick up anything from any of those?"

"Our analysts are working around the clock hoping to catch either a glimpse of Miss Castille or whoever did this, or…if we're lucky…a plate. But as I'm sure you're aware, this is D.C. There's a lot of traffic that moves in and out of this city every hour of the day."

"You're point?" Ethan challenged.

So help me, he even thinks about passing this off to a bunch of techs and forgetting about it…

"My point, Mr. McAllister, is that this could take some

time. But rest assured, finding Miss Castille is my department's number one priority."

Ethan's muscles relaxed slightly, grateful to hear Nicki's boss was taking charge of the investigation.

Investigation.

He leaned forward, placing his elbows onto the table in front of him and linking his fingers together. Bowing his head, Ethan rested his forehead against his joined hands and tried like hell not to puke.

I'm so sorry, baby. So fucking sorry.

Christ Almighty, how could something like this even *happen?*

He was the one with the dangerous job, not her. Nicki was an innocent. A beautiful, creative spirit who saw the world in ways he only wished he could.

A world without Nicki was a world he had no desire to be in. If they couldn't find her...or God forbid, they found her too late...

No!

With his head cradled against his steepled hands, Ethan shook the unthinkable, earthshattering thought away.

God wouldn't be so cruel as to take her from him now. Not when they'd only just found each other again. And in many ways, for the very first time.

Please, please don't take her from me.

"So what's the plan?" Bones directed the question to Bradford while Owens stood off to the side.

"For now?" The powerful man stared back at him from the oversized screen. "We wait."

An unprecedented fury had Ethan shoving himself to his feet and away from the table. Without uttering a single word, he stormed out of the conference room, through the office, and out into the large, open area at the end of the hall.

Slapping a hand to the *down* button, he stood in the same spot he and Nicki had when she'd been here working on the model for their op. Her smiling face flashed before his eyes, the memory of her hugging him goodbye as clear as if it were yesterday.

More memories threatened to assault him. The tentative way he'd caressed her back when he'd finished fixing her zipper. The unbridled passion with which she made love to him that very first time...and all the other times that followed.

Fuck this.

Ethan turned and headed for the stairwell. Floor after floor, he pushed himself harder. Willed his booted feet to move faster.

No matter how hard he tried, he couldn't outrun his own personal hell. The pain and fear coursing through him with every beat of his shattered heart until it was a living, breathing thing.

Like a monster sinking its jagged teeth into his flesh, that same fear threatened to rip apart a future he'd never thought possible. A future he had no desire to have unless it meant sharing it with the woman he loved.

I should have told her. I should've said the words when I had the chance.

Tears stung the corners of his eyes as they did their damnedest to escape. Blinking quickly, Ethan managed to stave them off as he reached the main floor.

Shoving the heavy door out of his way, he ignored the wide eyes and second glances turning his way as he stormed through the building's main doors and out onto the sidewalk.

Ethan sucked in as much air as his lungs would hold. He repeated the move. Once...twice... He continued using the training he'd learned a lifetime ago to return his breathing—and his heartrate—to a normal, steady pace.

When he no longer felt as if he were suffocating, Ethan took off down the street rather than returning to his team.

There was nothing in that room that could help him and

sitting on his ass sure as hell wasn't helping Nicki. So he decided instead to walk.

Taking off with no real destination in mind, Ethan's white-knuckled fists remained tense at his sides. So help him, if he ever found the person who'd dared to touch what was his...

I'll fucking kill them.

"Ethan!" Bones hollered his name from somewhere behind him. "Wait up!"

He didn't wait. Didn't even try to slow his pace.

If he did, if he allowed himself to really stop and think about what happened, he'd have to acknowledge the fact that he may never see Nicki's smiling face again. May never hear her sweet voice or relish in the joy of her laughter.

For Ethan, that was a fate worse than death.

"Dude!" Bones jogged up beside him. "Jesus, man. Would you slow down, already?"

He didn't slow down.

"Where the hell are you going?"

"I don't know." He clenched his jaw together. "But I can't just sit around with my thumb up my ass while she's still out there somewhere."

"We're not just sitting on our asses, but you know how this shit works. It's all hurry up and wait."

"Exactly."

He switched gears, spinning round so suddenly Bones had to do a little side-step to keep from slamming into him. Standing in the other man's personal space, Ethan let his teammate—and anyone else within earshot—know what he thought of SecDef's plan.

"Some son of a bitch breaks into Nicki's house...he *hurts* her..." Raw emotions left his voice cracking, forcing him to clear his throat before continuing. "She's one of his, Bones. Nicki is one of Bradford's own people, and his so-called plan is to *wait?* Is he fucking serious with that shit?"

To his credit, Bones didn't try to defend Nicki's boss or offer empty platitudes. Instead the former SEAL put a comforting hand on one of Ethan's shoulders and gave it a squeeze. "What do you need?"

Her.

The truth in his unspoken answer had Bones' features blurring behind a fresh well of unshed tears. And this time, no matter how hard he tried, he couldn't keep them from falling.

"I can't lose her, Beck." Ethan's breath hitched as he swiped an angry palm across his damp skin. "Nicki is…she's my…" He swallowed hard, clearing his clogged throat enough to choke out a whispered, "She's everything."

"Ah, hell, brother." A flash of empathetic pain marred the other man's features as he made a promise he had no business making. "I know how important Nicki is to you. We *all* do. And me, Digger, Falcon… we're going to help you find her. I promise you're gonna get your girl back, Ethan. You just have to keep the faith, yeah?"

"We have no idea who took her." Ethan's jaw clenched. "We don't even know where to start *looking*."

"Hey." The man's face twisted into an angry scowl that demanded attention. "We went balls to the wall for Falcon when Avery was taken. Do you really think we won't do the same for you?"

Well, hell. "I've never doubted the team, Beck." Not ever. "I know you all have my six. But sitting around waiting for a lead to magically fall into our laps…that's not going to bring Nicki back."

And he desperately, *desperately* needed her back.

"Look, man. I won't pretend to understand what you're feeling right now, but you heard SecDef. They've got their best people on this one. Between them and us, our pooled resources are the best chance Nicki has."

Ethan knew his friend was right, but fuck. He wasn't built

for the sidelines. Not when it was his woman's life that hung in the balance.

"You good?" Bones stared back at him expectantly.

Good wasn't exactly the word he'd use for what he was feeling. Scared...confused...pissed as hell... Those were just the tip of the iceburg where Ethan was concerned.

But the man was right. Sitting on his hands wouldn't help bring Nicki home, but neither would losing his shit. So as far as that was concerned...

"I'm good."

"That's what I'm talking about." Bones flashed a boyish grin and slapped him on the back. "Now what do you say we get back upstairs. Who knows? Maybe they caught a break while we were out here gettin' all up in our feels and shit."

"Up in our feels?" Ethan arched a brow as the two men started back toward their building's main entrance. "What are you, twelve?"

"Don't hate me 'cuz you can't keep up with the trends. Speaking of which, did you see the one where you feed your cat a—"

Ethan's phone began to ring, the blaring tone drowning out whatever idiotic *trend* Bones was about to share. Pulling his phone from his denim pocket, he saw a number he didn't recognize.

"Who's that?" Bones asked without looking.

"No clue." He answered the call. "McAllister."

"Ethan?"

Ethan stopped mid-stride, grabbing hold of Bones' arm to keep him from walking past. *"Nicki?"*

"Y-yeah," she whispered softly. "It's me."

The relief he felt from hearing her voice again left him feeling dizzy and weak. "Jesus, baby. Are you okay?"

"I-I'm fine."

She didn't exactly sound it, but at least she was alive.

Thank you, God! "Sweetheart, where are you?" Ethan

demanded as he put the call on speaker.

Standing close by, Bones pulled up the tracking app Shadow designed specifically for their government phones. Didn't matter how intricate the protective encryptions were, eventually somebody always figured out a way to break through.

Hence the tracking app.

If the caller stayed on the phone long enough, the app would automatically begin pinpointing the caller's location. Once the coordinates were locked in, the program would then send the data to Shadow with a special alert notification to ensure she didn't miss it.

"Nic?" Ethan repeated her name when he realized she hadn't answered his question. "Baby, are you still there?"

"I'm here."

"Where are you?"

"I-I don't know." Her voice cracked and trembled as she started to cry. "I asked, but h-he won't tell me."

His spine stiffened, his gaze sliding to Bones. "Who's he?"

"Andrei Beñová."

Son of a...

Bones cursed beneath while Ethan closed his eyes and hung his head between his shoulders. With his fist squeezing the phone with near-shattering strength, he asked, "Is Beñová with you right now?"

A slight pause and then a soft, "Yes"

"Put him on the phone."

"He won't talk to you. Only me."

Chickenshit bastard. "What does he want?"

"The flash drive and plans your team took from Kozlov's compound." He could hear her throat working. "Me for the jump drive and plans."

"Done." It wasn't even a question.

They'd set up the trade, take Beñová out once and for all, and he'd have his Nicki back.

"You and I both know what will happen if he uses it."

"Tell Beňová to send me the address, and I'll be there."

"Ethan, no!" Nicki's denial sounded rushed. Almost frantic. "Please. You can't. If he uses that drive, he'll—"

The sound of flesh hitting flesh replaced her sweet, terrified voice. Nicki's cry of pain sliced through his soul.

Nicki!

Ethan looked to Bones, both men understanding what had just taken place.

You're a dead man, Beňová. Fucking. Dead.

"Sweetheart, listen to me. I'm not losing you over a fucking software program, you hear me? So you tell Beňová to set up the meet. I get you back in one piece; he'll get his precious flash drive. He has my word on that."

"O-okay." Nicki's voice shook with tears. "I-I'm sorry."

"Nothing to be sorry about, baby. I just need you to hang in there a little longer, okay? Just do what he says, and it'll all be okay. I'm coming for you, Nic. I swear I will find you."

Now who's making promises they might not be able to keep?

Ethan would keep this one. Come hell or high water, he *would* find her.

Sensing their call was coming to an end, he decided to make good on his earlier thought. If God forbid this was the last time she'd ever hear his voice, Ethan wanted his next words to count.

He didn't think about their audience or the fact that they weren't face-to-face. The only thing he cared about was making sure she knew exactly how he felt about her.

"I love you, Nicolette. I love you so fucking much." Ethan held his breath and waited, but when several seconds passed without a response, he said, "Nic? You still there?"

"Ethan, man.."

Bones motioned toward the screen. Heart sinking, Ethan realized Nicki hadn't responded to his declaration of love because Beňová had already ended the call.

CHAPTER SEVENTEEN

Two days later...

I LOVE YOU, Nicolette. I love you so fucking much.

Sitting on the stained mattress she could barely see, in the corner of what may as well be her jail cell, Nicki replayed Ethan's words through her mind for what had to be the millionth time over the past two days.

Only they weren't just any words.

They were raw and real. Deep and soulful. To Nicki, those words were...*everything.* And they'd come at a time when she'd needed them most.

But Ethan hadn't heard her own shouted declaration. She *had* told Ethan she loved him, but thanks to Beñová, her words had come too late for him to hear.

The jerk had been standing right beside her during the entire phone call. And during that time, his gun had been pressed snuggly against the back of her head.

I love you, Nicolette. I love you so fucking much.

She continued replaying those words, as they gave her strength. A reminder of why she couldn't give up hope.

ANNA BLAKELY

Tac-Ops would come for her. Ethan had promised as much.

Despite her efforts to the contrary, her strong, stubborn protector had chosen her over everything else. Because he loved her.

The door to her own personal prison swung inward, and Andrei Beňová's blurred image appeared. "Hope you're hungry." He stepped into the room where she was being held and handed her a peanut butter sandwich.

That was it. No jelly. Just bread and peanut butter.

Oh, she wasn't complaining, mind you. Given her circumstances, Nicki was fully aware that she could have it so much worse. It was just that, that particular type of sandwich always made her heart sad.

Her mom had loved peanut butter sandwiches. Nicki remembered her eating them when she was little and telling her the jelly was too sweet for her tastebuds.

Looking back now, she couldn't help but wonder if it had more to do with the poison her mom's doctors had put into her body to try to fight off the cancer that continued to spread, eventually stealing her mother from her and her dad forever.

I miss you, mom.

"Eat up." Beňová's order put a stop to her wandering thoughts. "You're going to need your strength for the long flight back to the states."

Back to the...

Nicki's humorless chuckle filled the musty space. "You expect me to believe you're going to keep your word and let me go?"

Beňová swung his confused gaze to hers. With a look that seemed quite genuine, he told her, "You *will* be let go, Nicolette. I already told you; the only reason you're here is to help me get that flash drive back. I'll admit, I considered killing you once I had what I needed. But I have to say..." He put a dramatic hand to his chest and sighed. "After hearing that heartwarming exchange between you and your boyfriend, I realized I simply couldn't separate two souls who were clearly meant to be together."

And this guy was supposed to be a genius?

Sure does give average I.Q. fellas a leg up on the competition, huh ladies?

Deciding to try her hand at playing the part of the grateful hostage, Nicki swallowed back the urge to scream and shout, instead going for a soft, "Thank you. For the sandwich and for keeping your word."

Because that's what you were supposed to do in situations like this, right? Wasn't that part of the whole hostage survival handbook?

Don't draw attention to yourself or say or do things that might agitate the hostage taker. Treat them with kindness and respect, even when those are the last things they deserve. Make the captives see you as a human being rather than a pawn in their sick and twisted games.

And who knows? Maybe he really *was* planning to let her go after he got what he wanted from Ethan. He'd sounded sincere when he'd made that promise a few minutes before.

On the flip side, Beňová had already proven himself to be a cold-hearted son of a bitch.

Just ask my swollen face and demolished home.

"See?" Beňová smiled down at her. "There's no reason at all why we can't conduct ourselves like the reasonable adults we are."

Reasonable? Nicki had to work not to roll her eyes.

The man clearly defined the word differently than she did. Apparently in his version, it meant she was to do what he said, when he said it, and exactly *how* he said it.

"Your boyfriend should be here soon, you know." Her captor changed the subject in the blink of an eye. Eyes lighting up with anticipation, Beňová's smile grew wide. "The trade is set for tomorrow. Noon sharp."

Nicki was taken off guard when the strange, eccentric man ended their little visit by abruptly disappearing back through the door as quickly as he'd appeared. The sound of the lock being engaged from the outside causing her to flinch.

She immediately regretted the movement but ignored the incessant pounding in her head and thought about Beňová's excited demeanor just now. His sole focus was on getting that drive back and conquering the world, but didn't he know?

Team or not, when Ethan finds you, he's going to drop you where you stand. And that's if you're lucky.

Her own twisted excitement began to build as she imagined Ethan and his team storming in and filling Beňová full of holes. It wasn't like her to fantasize about death and violence, but something Nicki had discovered about herself since being locked away in this room the past two days...

I want Andrei Beňová to die.

Not only that, but *she* wanted to be the one to pull the trigger.

Nicki had taken a firearms safety class the DoD had offered employees a couple years ago. She'd done okay, but that was the last time she'd shot a gun.

Sure wish I'd had one when those jerks broke into my house.

If she had, Nicki would most likely be lying in Ethan's bed, his warmth enveloping her as he held her body close to his. And her captors, well...

They'd be lying six feet underground.

Funny thing, her reasoning had nothing to do with what he and his wall of muscle had done to *her*, although breaking into her home and knocking her around sure didn't help his cause any.

Nicki didn't even wish the man dead for what his terrifyingly intelligent mind had created, or what he'd planned to do with it. Prison? Yes. Solitary confinement for the rest of his days? Absolutely. But Nicki didn't think he should be *killed* for those crimes.

What he did deserve to die for, what Nicki's *true* motive was for wanting Andrei Beňová wiped from the face of the earth forever...

Ethan.

He was hands down, without a doubt, the love of her life.

His was the face she wanted to see when she woke up in the morning. And it was his face she wanted to be the last thing she saw when she closed her eyes and went to sleep.

She wanted him to be her partner for life. A husband. Father. And someday, many years from now, she wanted his hand to be the one she held while sitting on the porch swing, drinking iced tea, and watching the sun set for the day.

That was what Ethan McAllister meant to her. He was one of the most important parts of her past...good and bad. He was also her future. And twice now, Andrei Beňová had played an intricate role in putting the man who owned her in harm's way.

The first time was during Tac-Op's raid on Kozlov's compound. The second hadn't happened yet. But it would. Tomorrow at noon, apparently.

Her headstrong hero was willing to risk his life to make the trade. Her life for the flash drive. And all she could do but sit in this small storage room and pray.

For Ethan. His teammates. The life she wanted to build with the man who meant more to her than life itself.

Please, Ethan. Please don't get yourself killed trying to save me.

Nicki didn't think she'd survive losing him again. Not now. Not like this. And if the worst happened...if God forbid something did happen to Ethan...

Beňová may as well kill me, too.

* * *

ETHAN STARED at the generic-looking flash drive Owens had just handed him, praying like hell the plan they'd spent the last two days formulating would work.

It *had* to.

Nicki's life depended on it.

The constant ache that had been present since he'd first learned of her abduction worsened. Raising the heel of his hand to the area where his shattered heart used to be, he pressed and rubbed there. A feeble attempt to ease a pain that ran much, much deeper than muscle or bone.

The pain he'd carried the past forty-eight hours was a part of him now. A parasite feeding off the anger, rage, and fear that was the driving force behind his need to find Andrei Beňová and end him.

Slowly. Painfully. With his bare fucking hands.

I will find him, and when I do, I will rid the world of him for good.

Because a man who would dare touch his woman, who'd cause *harm* to her… Those men weren't men at all. They were animals. Feral, disease-ridden animals who deserved to be put down.

And Ethan couldn't wait to put Beňová in the ground.

That was assuming, of course, that their mission was a success. Which brought him back to the small rectangular drive still pinched between his thumb and forefinger.

"And you're sure this is going to work?" The question was directed toward the multi-function conference phone in the center of the table.

"I sure hope so." Shadow's bubbly voice filled the Tac-Ops conference room via speaker phone. "That little sucker cost me about a year's worth of favors, and Tex…y'all remember him? He helped me out when all that went down with poor Avery…" She barely waited a breath and then, "Anyway, Tex is an even bigger genius than I am. But what might interest you more, especially where this mission is concerned, is that my amazingly awesome friend can outsmart the likes of one Andrei Beňová. He already did actually. Tex is the one who made it."

"Really?" Bones tilted his head. "I figured something like that would be all you."

"Normally, yes. But even I have my limits, though it pains me to admit that to a super stud group such as yourselves. Trust me. For software as sophisticated as the one your team took from Kozlov's compound, Tex is the man for the job."

"Speaking of sophisticated software..." Bones sat up a little straighter. "Can we go back over that part for us non-techies of the group?"

Bones looked to Digger, who looked at Owen, who passed the ball back to...

"Shadow, would you please do a quick rundown of our flash-drive's functions and what that means for the op?"

"Sure thing, Boss Man. Okay, boys and gents, pay attention to the teacher because we'll have to go quick if you want to get those boots of yours in the air in time to make the meet."

Fuck yes, they needed to make that meet. They miss that, it was anyone's guess as to how Beňová would react. If he became angry enough, there was a very real possibility he would take it out on Nicki.

Ethan would rather die than put her in more danger than she already was.

"So for all you non-techies out there, I'll try to keep it straight and to the point. Basically we took Beňová's original flash drive, which the CIA loaned to us so Tex could make the dupe but is now back under the CIA's protection. Anyway—"

"Shadow..." Digger used what the team called his dad

voice to bring their brilliant-but-sometimes-flighty over-watch queen back on point.

"Don't get your knickers in a twist, Dig." The sassy woman returned their team leader's attitude and raised him one, "I said straight to the point by my standards. Not yours."

"Oooh...ouch!" Bones shot Digger a look from across the room that said the man had just been burned. "Kinda hard to argue with that logic, ain't it Dig?" Then, because that was just the kind of man Bones was, the smartass leaned in toward the centralized phone and said, "Go on, sugar. The rest of us are listenin'."

With a wink and a waggle of his brows, Bones gave Digger a shit-eating grin as he settled himself back into his chair.

"Thanks, Bones. Aaaand...that is why you are my favorite."

"Let's stay focused, shall we?" Owens reminded them all. "Like Shadow said, we're on a bit of a time crunch."

"Right. Sorry, Boss Man. Anyway, the device you will be passing off as Beňová's pet project is identical to the real one in every single way except one."

"Which is?"

"There's an added component to the code that Tex designed specifically for this op. A failsafe, if you will. And the best part is, there is absolutely no way for Beňová to know it until it's too late."

"Too late as in…" Ethan listened with intense purpose.

"If the op goes off as planned, which it will because you guys are awesome, then the fact that the drive looks and feels identical to the original is all you need. But Tex being Tex, he suggested implementing an added layer of protection. Basically, in a worst-case-scenario-situation, Beňová escapes with the duped drive and tries using it the way he'd intended, it will appear to be doing everything exactly as he wrote it, except, when he hits the final command to transfer the funds he's trying to steal, the code Tex added will be activated. Beňová's software will be fried. Figuratively, of course."

"That's…pretty freakin' cool." Bones grinned.

"Right?" Shadow sounded as impressed as Bones. "Oh, I almost forgot the creme de la creme of the whole thing… Tex also installed an undetectable alert system that will automatically tell us the second the program is opened. Not only will we get real-time confirmation that Beňová is accessing the drive, it will also give us the drive's GPS coordinates at the time of access." Finishing up, she released a dramatic sigh and then, "You're welcome, gentlemen. The applause may now commence."

Two things Ethan gleaned from Shadow's mini-tutorial. One, the woman clearly didn't understand the meaning of straight to the point. Not by *anyone's* standards. And two…

"In case I forget to say it later, Shadow…you're amazing." *A fucking rock star.*

"Awww, thanks, Apollo. But again, this one's all Tex. I was just the go-between."

"Either way, it's your connection to him that made this possible. So thank you."

"You're welcome, Ethan." Her voice softened at the rare use of his real name. "For what it's worth, if Beňová was holding someone I loved, this is the exact plan I'd follow to get them back."

"You really trust this Tex guy that much?" Because he had to be sure. For Nicki.

For us.

"I trust Tex with my life." Shadow answered without hesitating.

Something about the way she said it made Ethan wonder about the history between their trusted analyst and the mysterious Tex. But that was a conversation for another day.

Rubbing the drive between his fingers, he nodded his

acceptance. "Good enough for me." To Owens he asked, "When do we leave?"

"Jet's fueled and ready to go. Pilot's been instructed to leave as soon as Digger gives the green light. Ghost and his team are already enroute to meet you at the safehouse."

"Delta's our assist?" Falcon seemed pleased.

Owens nodded his salt-and-pepper head. "They were finishing up an op nearby, so I gave Colonel Robinson a call. Asked if we could borrow them, *purely* as back-up. In fact, Robinson prefers to leave them out of the action unless their assistance becomes vital. Politics and all."

Ethan didn't give a rat's ass about politics. Not when it came to the most important mission of his life.

"There's still one thing I don't get." Digger looked to Owens. "If Beňová's such a genius, why didn't he make a backup copy of the software? Or keep his design plans in an electronic file instead of on paper?"

Ethan had wondered the same thing.

"I've got this one," Shadow answered for their boss. "Why Beňová didn't keep extra copies of his design is as confounding to me as it is all of you, but as we already know, the guy doesn't exactly reside on Common Sense Mountain. Plus, he sees himself as being so intellectually advanced, he probably convinced himself one was enough. The man's clearly a narcissistic asshole, and we all know the way those guys think."

"Ain't that the truth," Bones scoffed.

"According to our source"—Shadow continued—"Kozlov was the only person who could keep Beňová somewhat grounded. So it's possible the decision to keep the design to the one prototype very well could have been his."

"Why not make another one now?"

"Doesn't matter." Ethan took control of the pointless conversation. "The asshole has Nicki, and we have a way to get her back. Trying to make sense of Beňová's psyche is a waste of time."

Time Nicki didn't have.

"Apollo's right." Owens addressed the group. "Let's stay focused on the plan and leave the rest on the table for now."

Looking at his boss, Ethan gave the man a slight nod before checking with his team. "Everyone good?"

There was no room for errors. Not on this op. Not when Nicki was the one at risk.

"We're good, Apollo." Falcon met his gaze. "The team brought Avery back home to me." The other man's Adam's apple bobbed. "We'll get Nicki back to you."

Pinpricks stung the corners of Ethan's eyes, but he kept the tears at bay. Nicki was right. These men weren't just his team; they were his family. Since Nic was with him, that made her family, too.

And one thing Ethan had learned about the other men standing in this room...

For them, nothing was more important than family.

CHAPTER EIGHTEEN

Ethan sat casually on a bench in the middle of Vermane Garden, the oldest public garden in the city of Riga, Latvia. Dressed in a cream, long-sleeved Henley, well-worn jeans, and boots, he looked like the average Joe taking advantage of the enjoyable weather.

It was unseasonably warm for this time of year, which meant the park was a steady buzz of activity. Dog-walkers, bike-riders, flying kites, and strollers filled with cooing, crying, giggling babies joined the soft chirps of birds flying high above. The combination created a symphony of harmonizing sounds that were the perfect soundtrack for creating lasting memories.

The grasses were already turning a vibrant green, and a few select plants and trees had the start of several tiny buds. The sun was shining, and there wasn't a cloud in the sky, and with a cup of coffee in one hand and an ankle crossed over one knee, Ethan couldn't remember a more picture-perfect day.

For killing.

Giving the scene a slow, panoramic scan, he kept his eyes peeled for his target. A ballcap and shades not only aided in his goal of appearing unmemorable to passersby, but they also prevented the blinding afternoon sun from impeding his vision.

Anxiety running on-point, Ethan lifted his outstretched arm resting on the back of the bench and glanced at his watch. *Eleven fifty-eight.*

Two minutes. One hundred-twenty seconds. That was how long he had to wait. That's how long it would take for him to be able to see Nicki, to confirm with his own damn eyes that she really was okay.

A snapshot of the violent scene at her apartment filled his mind's eye, but he flipped that shit over and put it out of his head.

Emotions off. Guns on.

Ethan thought of the gun on his hip, concealed by his jacket's loose hem. With a full mag and one in the chamber, it was ready and waiting.

He looked at his watch again. Speaking into the tiny, undiscernible two-way mic nestled in his left ear, he spoke to his and Ghost's team.

"Anyone have eyes on Beñová or Nicki?" The question was concealed by another sip of his still-steaming brew.

"Negative for Digger."

"Negative for Bones."

"Hold up," Falcon alerted them of a possible ID, but then, "Never mind. That's a negative for Falcon."

Beñová's instructions were for Ethan to come alone, but unlike the fictional heroics shown on TV, Ethan would have to be insane to think he could pull this off without the help of his team.

Like him, their casual attire of jeans, joggers, T's, and hoodies allowed them to blend in with the local crowd. And though he couldn't see them from where he was sitting, he knew they were there, watching his six.

Same with Delta.

Ghost, Hollywood, Fletch, Beatle, Coach, and Truck were all here—somewhere. The Delta Force team's orders were to engage only as a last resort. Ethan hoped like hell it wouldn't come to that, but if things went sideways, there wasn't another team out there he'd rather have watching Tac-Ops' back.

"I've got 'em," Bones relayed to both teams and Shadow, who was watching from wherever the mysterious women lived. "Apollo's nine o'clock. Yep, that's definitely our boy. Heads up, he brought a friend."

Beñová's attempt at throwing off the balance of power. For all he knew, Ethan was here alone. Bringing backup gave Beñová a sense of security, making him believe he had the upper hand.

Ethan couldn't wait to see the look on the asshole's face when he realized how very wrong he was.

"Got him," Shadow chimed in. "Running facial rec on our third wheel now."

"Bones, you got Nicki?" Ethan could barely control the overwhelming need to see her.

The other man's confirmation couldn't come soon enough. "Affirmative. Your girl's walking beside Beñová's buddy. Shoulder-to-shoulder if you catch my drift."

Meaning the fucker probably had a gun on Nicki to keep her from trying to run.

Wrong move, asshole.

"Third wheel is armed." Ethan repeated the intel he'd found tucked between the lines. "That's a hard copy."

"Still have a clear view from bird's eye," Shadow joined back in, letting them know she was using satellite imagery to watch from overhead. "HT is coming up the sidewalk west of Apollo's location. Hostage and second target are following approximately three yards behind."

"We got ID on our third wheel?"

"Just came in. Guy's name is Vladimir Ozols, and from

what I've been able to find, he's Beňová's recently hired muscle. And I do mean that literally, so keep an eye on him."

"Copy that." Ethan's shift in position and adjustment of his baseball cap afforded him the opportunity of an unrecognizable glance to his left.

Seeing him would come as no surprise to Beňová since he was the one who'd chosen Ethan to do the trade in the first place. But there was a difference in being seen and *allowing* someone to see you.

"Get ready, Apollo," Shadow alerted him. "HT is cresting the hill now."

Ethan slid his focus to the portion of the sidewalk that dropped off into a decline. He watched and waited for the enemy. Seconds later, Andrei Beňová came into view.

Wearing a light blue button-up beneath a dark brown sweater vest, tan pants, and brown loafers, the less-than-impressive man looked more like a high school math teacher than the mastermind behind a menacing world-altering plan.

"Got him."

"Let him come to you, Apollo," Digger reminded him.

The man was probably afraid Ethan would lose his shit and attack Beňová on sight. A tempting thought, but he'd never risk a hostage like that. Especially when that hostage was the woman he loved.

Keeping an eye on the deceptively benign-looking man strolling casually down the sidewalk, Ethan's attention was pulled to a wave of blonde breaking the top of the small hill.

It's her!

His heart kicked against his ribs when Nicki came fully into his view. Dressed in baggy jeans and a sweatshirt that was two sizes too big, her hair was hanging loosely around her shoulders. Uncharacteristically disheveled, the long locks partially hiding her gorgeous face, and it took a Herculean effort Ethan didn't know he possessed not to go to her.

Emotions out, McAllister.

Giving himself a mental slap, Ethan pulled his focus back in place. Just like Bones described, Nicki was walking next to the man Shadow identified as Vladimir Ozols. After a quick assessment of the man's stance in relation to Nicki's, Ethan came to the same conclusion as his teammate.

The son of a bitch was definitely holding a weapon against Nicki's side.

While Ethan couldn't confirm it from his current vantage point, he'd bet his next paycheck that weapon was a gun.

Don't worry, sweetheart. I've got you.

Ethan knew she had to be terrified, but she was alive. Right now, that was all that mattered.

Hating to do it, Ethan pulled his focus away from Nicki and her guard, and back to their main target. Closer now, he could see that Andrei Beñová was much shorter and leaner in person than he'd expected.

A passing breeze lifted a section of Nicki's hair as the trio continued moving closer to where he waited. Keeping both targets and Nicki in view, Ethan saw when Nicki brushed the wayward strands from her face.

Though no one else would probably notice, the tiny changes in her expression and stance told Ethan she'd spotted him.

A slight lift of her chest from a hitched breath. The subtle way her lips had parted when she'd found him sitting on that bench. The way her body immediately tensed, followed by the slight fall of her shoulders as she became more relaxed...

It was the solace he'd needed to see, and it told Ethan everything he needed to know. She knew she wasn't alone, and she trusted him to keep her safe.

And that was exactly what he intended to do.

Beñová's stride shortened, his pace slowing as his beady gaze began a search of the man's immediate area. Putting on his game face, Ethan locked down every thought and

ANNA BLAKELY

emotion that didn't belong on an op and put his team's plan in motion.

"Showtime." A signal to Shadow and his team to be ready.

Taking a small sip of his coffee, Ethan lifted the cup in the air to grab Beňová's attention. Seeing this, Beňová left the concrete path and began walking through the grass to where Ethan still sat.

"Mr. McAllister." He stopped a few feet away, well out of Ethan's reach.

Well played.

Ethan removed his sunglasses to look the man square in the eyes as he tipped his chin. "Andrei."

From his peripheral, Ethan could see Ozols and Nicki following Beňová's same path across the grass. Disappointment coursed through him when Ozols halted their movements several feet behind Beňová.

Staring at Ethan from behind a set of thinly wired eyeglasses, Beňová got right down to business. "I believe you have something that belongs to me."

Sure do, you arrogant prick.

"And I believe you have something that's mine."

Still seated, Ethan gave his head a slight tilt to the side so he could have a direct line of sight between him and Nicki. With a tip of his chin, he lifted his voice enough for her to hear him ask, "You okay?"

Nicki nodded her head, the jerky movement appearing to be causing her pain. When another breeze blew past, the shift in her golden locks revealing a nasty bruise on the left side of her face.

Even from here, Ethan could tell her cheek and eye were swollen.

His muscles tensed, his spine straightening as he brought his deadly gaze back to their target. Nearly shaking with the urge to kill, he had to remind himself where he was and what was at stake.

Guns on, emotions off.

It was a phrase he'd learned in boot camp, back in the day. Even now, he could hear his old drill sergeant shouting the mantra during every one of the man's weapons trainings.

Guns kill people on the field. Emotions on the field kill people.

Ethan had never felt the truth in those words as much as he did right now. Despite his desire to pull his gun from his waistband and shoot Beňová right in the forehead—and he really, *really* wanted to shoot the bastard in the forehead—he kept his heart tucked away and his head in the game.

Speaking of games…

Leaning to the side, he made a show of taking in Nicki's appearance before sitting back up straight. With a schooled expression, he told the other man, "The items I brought to trade are in perfect condition." A muscle in his jaw twitched. "Doesn't look like you can say the same about yours."

On the outside, Ethan appeared aloof. Almost indifferent. But on the inside…

I'll fucking kill him for the bruises alone.

"Yes, well…" Beňová wore a look of feigned regret. "An unfortunate byproduct that happened during the package's pickup. Occupational hazard. I'm sure you understand."

Oh, he understood all right. Someone had punched Nicki. More than once, by the looks of those bruises. And by the rough hold the son of a bitch had on Nicki's arm, Ethan's money was on Ozols.

Guess who just graduated to the do-not-let-live list?

"Well, I don't know about you, but I have a very busy day planned. Let's get on with it, shall we? I'm assuming you have the notebook and flash drive with you?"

Ready to get Nicki as far away from this place—and this man—as possible, Ethan pulled a rolled-up composition notebook from his jacket pocket. A notebook that had been found with the intel gathered from Kozlov's office.

He held it out for the other man to take.

Without a word, Beňová excitedly began thumbing through the pages of 'his' notes mapping out the software's design from start to finish. What the man didn't know—what Ethan prayed he wouldn't discover—was the notebook in Beňová's hands was a fake.

The entire collection had been duplicated right down to the smallest equation. According to the information Director Barnes passed on to Owens, the CIA artist who'd spent twenty-two painstaking hours copying Beňová's handwriting exactly was a retired forger hired by the government to help catch active forgers and thieves.

The best part? The CIA had added a few special touches to Beňová's plans along the way. A number change here. A symbol change there...

It would take the self-proclaimed genius days, if not weeks, to figure out all the new changes and put the plans back to their original design. And that was assuming he was ever given the chance.

Not on my watch.

"Excellent." Beňová held the notebook to his chest. "Thank you, Mr. McAllister. I thought this was lost to me forever."

The crazed genius was talking to him as if they were pals or some shit. Not that it mattered to Ethan.

Beňová could invite him over for a fucking tea party if he wanted. And if it meant getting Nicki back, Ethan would accept the invitation with a smile.

One dupe down, one to go.

"Your turn. Let her go." His gaze bounced from the man standing in front of him, to Nicki, and back.

"Not until I have my drive."

"No drive until Nicki is back with me." Ethan didn't so much as flinch. "Take it or leave it."

"You see, I *might* be compelled to take it if it weren't for the pistol my friend is pointing at your girlfriend's liver."

Beňová turned to the side and flashed Nicki a smile. After everything he'd put her through, the asshole had the balls to fucking *smile*.

But it was his next move—or words, really—that sent a rush of ice racing through Ethan's veins.

"Do you remember what I told you earlier? About what would happen to you once I had my things back?"

Nicki nodded, her voice rough with fear. "You said you'd let me go."

"You're right." Beňová smiled again. "I did. Unfortunately for you, your boyfriend didn't play by the rules, so I'm afraid I'll have to go back on my word."

What the—

"Teams be advised we have possible situation with the HT," Shadow announced in Ethan's ear.

At the same time, Ethan shot up from the bench and took a step toward Beňová.

"Bullshit." He scowled. "I did everything exactly as you asked."

"Did you, now?"

"I'm here, aren't I? You have your precious notebook, and…" Ethan sat the coffee down onto the ground before slowly reaching into his pocket and pulling out the drive. "See? It's right here. You take this and your notes, and I take her home. It's a win-win for us both."

Rather than respond to him, Beňová continued to speak to Nicki as if Ethan wasn't there.

"Mr. McAllister was supposed to come alone, but instead he brought an entire team. Two, in fact, if Vlad counted correctly."

Ethan's gut tightened, his ear filling with Shadow's voice once again.

"HT is claiming to have spotted two teams. I repeat, Tac-Ops and Delta, you have both been made. Delta, begin following retreat protocol. Tac-Ops, hold steady."

"That's a hard copy on holding steady." Digger responded for their team.

Ghost answered for theirs next, his frustration about having to pull back. "Copy that. Delta following retpro. Sorry boys."

Retpro—or retreat protocol—consisted of the team pulling back in a calm, non-threatening manner to avoid putting the hostage at greater risk. Which meant Digger, Falcon, and Bones were the only three left with eyes still on them.

Fuck, fuck, fuck!

Ethan's mind raced to decipher his best next move. Beñová, the son of a bitch, must've had men in place at the park prior to his arrival. And the real kick in the nuts…

Not a single fucking one of them knew it before now.

Chill the fuck out, McAllister. You've been in a helluva lot worse situations than this.

The mental reminder to keep cool was true. He and the others had faced some of the world's most dangerous men during ops with a much lower chance of survival than this one.

The difference being, Nicki was nowhere near any of those.

"I may be a bit peculiar, Mr. McAllister," Beñová spoke up again. "But I'm not stupid. Of course, you would bring backup You'd have been a fool not to. But I, too, have a team of men who work for me now. And like in your wonderfully entertaining American movies, they, too, enjoy a good, what do you call it? Oh, yes. A stake out."

Well, fuck me.

Ethan and the others had been thoroughly and royally played. This man may come off as a total whack job—which he was—but Ethan was beginning to realize much of Beñová's quirky persona was an act. One designed to fool others into underestimating the son of a bitch.

Which Ethan had done in spectacular fashion.

"Here's what's going to happen, Ethan. May I call you Ethan? Good."

Never actually answered you, you smug piece of shit.

"Like I was saying…" Beñová continued, "This is what's going to happen. I am going to take my notes and the jump drive you're still holding, and then my friend and I are going to leave. And we're taking pretty Nicolette with us."

"Like hell you are."

Unphased by Ethan's lethal tone, the other man removed his glasses and began cleaning them with the hem of his wool vest. "You seem to think you're the one in charge here, Ethan." He slid his glasses back on and smiled. "But that would actually be me."

"I still have the drive, remember?"

"And I still have your girl." Beñová didn't so much as flinch. "One signal from me, and Vlad will pull the trigger on that gun he's holding, and you'll be forced to watch while poor Nicolette bleeds out right here in the grass."

The image the man's words created was like a sucker-punch to Ethan's soul.

"You're not taking her anywhere." He stared Beñová down.

"You honestly didn't think I'd simply take you at your word that the drive you have is mine, did you? I need time to check it. To ensure that the program is still intact, and in good working order." Looking around, the little man's tone grew rhetorical as he asked, "I don't see a computer here, do you?"

"You're not. Taking. Her."

"I am taking her, Ethan. And you're going to let me. Otherwise, I'll have no choice but to give Vlad the order to shoot."

"You do that, you'll both be dead before you hit the ground."

"Perhaps." Beñová shrugged. "But so will pretty Nicolette. And something tells me you aren't willing to take that chance."

Fucking son of a bitch!

"He's right, Apollo." Digger's voice filled Ethan's ear. "You're going to have to let him take her."

"That can't happen."

His words were for Digger, but Beñová assumed differently.

"So we're agreed. Pretty Nicolette will come with me now. Once I confirm the software hasn't been tampered with, I will send you the address where she will be waiting for you."

"Give him the drive." Digger's deep voice was stern.

Shadow backed up his team leader's directive. "Listen to him, Apollo. Beñová's going to want to test the drive as soon as he can. The second he puts it into his computer, I'll have his location and we can take the offensive."

"They're both right, brother," Falcon agreed. "I know it sucks, but you're going to have to let this one play out a little longer."

Ethan couldn't believe what he was hearing. His teammates—his friends—expected him to just stand there and let this man take the love of his life away from him? Again?

If this were any other hostage, you'd go with the odds and trust the team to do what they do best. But goddamnit, this wasn't just another hostage.

This was Nicki. She was *his*.

Fuck. Shit. Fuck!

Swallowing back the urge to put a bullet in the asshole's brain and be done with it, Ethan asked Beñová, "How do I know you aren't going to kill her the second you leave the park?"

"You don't." The asshole shrugged one of his narrow shoulders. "Guess you're just going to have to trust me."

Not a fucking chance.

"Ethan?"

His eyes went to Nicki who was looking back at him with a fear he tried like hell to erase. "Do you trust me?"

Unshed tears had her baby blues glistening in the afternoon sun. "Yes."

"Then trust me on this." Then, as much as it burned his ass to do it, he told her, "Go. Do as they say, and everything will be okay."

"What?" A look of panic marred her pretty face as she began shaking her head in wild despair. "No. I-I can't—"

"You can," he assured her. "I don't know if you heard me on the phone the other day, but I—"

"I heard you." Twin tears fell, streaking two silver lines down her terrified face. "And I love you, too, Ethan. So much."

Ah, baby. "I love you, too, sweetheart." He blinked away his own fresh tears before they could fall. "You have to go with them now, Nic. Just for a little while longer."

"Ethan..."

"I *will* come for you, Nicolette. Whatever it takes. I swear it."

The tiny nod of her head nearly broke him. Using it as fuel for the revenge he was mentally planning to extract on the man before him, Ethan stepped directly into his personal space.

"This isn't over." Not by a long shot.

"No, I don't suppose it is."

"Go. Check your precious software. When you find everything is in order, and you will, you'd better keep up your end of the bargain. Oh, and one more thing." Ethan leaned in so close, his breath fogged the lenses of the dickhead's glasses. "If you or *Vlad* lay a hand on her again, you won't have to worry about whether or not the software works. You'll be too dead to care."

For the first time since their meeting began, Beñová showed a flicker of real, honest emotion... Fear.

That's right, asshole. You should be afraid.

With a quick blink of his eyes, Beñová regained his composure and jutted his pointy chin. "Duly noted. Now I have a warning of my own. That team I mentioned earlier? They have a very specific order to follow. Would you like to know what it is?"

Ethan's only response was to continue staring down at the little fuck.

"If anything happens to me or Vlad before we leave the park..." Beñová continued, "If, for example, a sniper's bullet was to somehow make its way into either of our heads... The team *I* have here will open fire on everyone in this park. Women...children...their orders are to kill them all. Starting with her." He looked over at where Nicki was still standing.

They had no way of confirming if there really was a team of men waiting to follow Beñová's orders, but he didn't have to. Knowing there was even a possibility was enough.

"We have to assume he's telling the truth." Digger relayed that same thought to the team. "Keep position but stand down. Only fire if Beñová or his man initiates. Do you copy?"

"Falcon, copy."

"Bones, copy."

Apollo...copy.

"Keep your phone on, Mr. McAllister." The sadistic prick waved a hand in the air to give his man the order to leave.

With no other choice, Ethan watched as Beñová and Vladimir Ozols turned and walked away, taking his future with them.

CHAPTER NINETEEN

Nicki sat on the dirty mattress, back against the cool concrete wall, legs pulled tightly to her chest. With her head back and her eyes closed, she pictured Ethan's handsome face.

The relief she'd felt when she saw him sitting on that bench had been so all-consuming, she'd wanted nothing more than to go to him. To run across that grass, jump into his arms, and never leave.

She thought she'd be there by now. In his arms, safely on her way back home. She thought they'd get to the meeting, make the trade, and that would be the end of this horrific, terrifying nightmare.

Instead, Ethan had asked the impossible of her...to willingly leave him behind and go with Beňová and his henchman.

I didn't want to leave him.

It was the hardest thing she'd ever had to do. But Nicki had spoken the truth before. She *did* trust Ethan. Implicitly. And if the look he'd given her was any indication, the brave, sweet man had a plan.

He'd find her. Of that, Nicki was unequivocally certain. Ethan loved her, and he wouldn't stop until he found her.

She just prayed he didn't get himself killed in the process.

* * *

ETHAN PACED across the carpeted floor, his restless legs refusing to still. It had already been over an hour since they'd left the park to come back to their hotel in Riga. The rooms here didn't offer much, but it had given them a place to rest, and now...to wait.

More fucking waiting.

He pictured Nicki's face. That beautiful, sweet, dimpled face. She was an angel trapped in the midst of hell.

And he'd sent her right back there with the Devil himself.

"Goddamnit!" Ethan spun around, raised his fist, and punched a hole in the nearest wall. His breathing picked up, and his stomach threatened to revolt, but he ignored it.

He ignored *everything* except the fact that the woman he loved was right there, just out of his reach. And now...

"We're going to get her back, brother." Bones looked over at him from across the room. Sitting with Digger at the room's small, two-person table, the man split his focus between the damaged wall and Ethan. "We just have to give it more time."

"Nicki doesn't have more time," Ethan shot back.

He didn't care what sort of promises Beňová had made. Once he believed the flash drive they'd given him was legit, Nicki was dead.

Ethan felt that truth to the depths of his soul.

"We don't have a choice." Digger stared back at him. "Our orders are to stay here and wait for Shadow's call."

"I don't give a flying fuck about orders!" Ethan shouted. "This is taking too long. We have to figure out another way to find where Beňová is hiding. We need to have boots on the ground and do whatever it takes to pinpoint Beñová's location."

The tips of his fingers tingled, and his limbs felt heavy. His body's reaction to the extra adrenaline filling his cells. Running a hand over his weary face, he began tossing out every Hail Mary he could think of that might give them a chance at figuring out where Nicki was being held.

"We can flash his picture to people on the streets. Maybe Shadow can put us in touch with the CIA's source. We could—"

Digger's phone began to ring.

"It's Shadow." The man rushed to answer the call. "Putting you on speaker." He tapped the screen. "Okay, go."

"We got him!"

The excitement in the woman's voice gave Ethan the hope he'd so desperately needed. "Where?"

"Sending the coordinates now. It's an abandoned granary outside the city. I'm sending Ghost and his men the same intel."

Bones frowned. "I thought Delta was out on this one."

"They were," Shadow confirmed. "Guess Colonel Robinson didn't approve of the way Beñová liked to play. Once he found out the guy reneged on the original deal, he rescinded the order for Delta to remain in the shadows and gave them the green light to aid in whatever way is needed."

The tension in Ethan's neck eased slightly. Knowing the other team would be on sight and ready for action upped Nicki's chance of making it out of there alive. Assuming she wasn't already—

No!

Ethan physically shook the thought away. He couldn't think like that. Not even for a second. Nicki was alive, and he was going to get her back.

"Once I have a go-time from you, I'll pass it along to

Delta," Shadow's voice filled the speaker again. "They're locked and ready, so as soon as you say when—"

"Now." Ethan looked at his teammates. "We have our weapons, and we're ready. We go *now.*"

"Digger?" Shadow posed the question to their team lead. "I need to know if that's the official answer. Do you concur with Apollo's plan to move on Beňová now?"

With a solemn nod in Ethan's direction, Digger said, "Call Ghost. Let him know we're gearing up and heading out in five."

TWENTY MINUTES LATER, Ethan was standing along a side-road a hundred yards from Beňová's location. With a low grassy field separating them from the run-down building, Ethan and the others had a fairly clear view of the structure.

Dressed in their civilian clothes, each member of Tac-Ops One had on jeans and T's, their combat vests, thigh holsters, and sheaths filled with a slew of weapons and ammo.

Gathered between their respective vehicles, he and his teammates went over the plan with the men of Delta, who were dressed in nearly identical clothing and gear.

"How do you want to play this one?" Ghost looked to Digger.

Digger glanced at his tablet's screen that showed a real-time bird's eye view of the abandoned building. "Shadow, you got any activity?"

"Negative, Team One. The building's constructed of concrete blocks, so I can't get a look inside. As far as the perimeter, I'm showing no heat signatures anywhere around the structure. In fact, there hasn't been any activity outside since I first got the alert that the drive had been activated."

"I don't get it." Bones looked at the others. "If he has a team of men who were ready and willing to shoot up a park full of kids, why aren't they there, protecting the asshole's... well...ass?"

Ethan looked across the blowing grass to the granary. Tiny pinpricks of pain fired through every nerve ending in his body, his need for action a rising monster eating him alive from the inside out. Nicki was in there, right now, waiting for him to come get her.

I'm right here, baby. Just need you to hang on a little longer.

"There is no team." Ethan turned to face Bones. "I think Beñová was bluffing."

"I don't disagree, but there's no way to know that for sure," Hollywood—the good-looking one Ghost's team—pointed out.

"Which is why I didn't try to call him out on it at the park. But think about it." Ethan pointed toward the building behind him. "Why would a guy who has a team full of deadly sharpshooters be holed up in some shithole building with no water or lights? And he's in there, holding an American woman hostage while testing out this software that could essentially destroy civilization as we know it, yet there isn't a single man anywhere near the building's perimeter?"

"His men could be inside," Ghost countered.

"And we'll plan as if they are." They'd be stupid not to. "But there's only one vehicle from what I can see, and my gut is telling me the guy's full of shit. I think the only people in that building are Beñová and Nicki. Maybe Ozlos. And Beñová ... he already thinks he's won." Which meant the prick most likely had his guard down.

All good things for us.

Truck, the tall operator standing next to Hollywood joined the debate. "Have to say, I'm with Apollo on this one. If I'm Beñová and I knew y'all were coming after me?" He huffed out a breath. "I'd have every inch of that building covered. If I actually had a team of men to fill the job, that is."

Sharing an appreciative glance with the brickhouse of a

man, Ethan turned to Digger, sending his team leader an expectant look.

"Dig, I have to go with Apollo and Hollywood." Shadow joined in the cause. "I've looked at Beňová's finances, and unless he's got a stash of cash hidden somewhere, the guy doesn't have the funds to keep a team like the one he claims to have on his payroll."

All eyes shifted to Digger, who finally put their plan into action.

"We go low and slow," the former SEAL instructed. "Shadow will keep eyes on the perimeter to alert us of any incoming threats there. We approach high and tight, and once we reach the structure, Ghost and his team will split up into two groups."

When no one questioned the order, Digger continued by instructing Ghost on his team's play.

"Half of your team will go east; the other half take the west, and meet out back. You guys clear this section here." He pointed to a second building located behind the main target. "Unlike the granary, it's only one story, but it's approximately fifty by two hundred. My guess is it was a stable back in the day, which means there could be any number of blind spots in there, so watch your sixes. Once that's clear, enter the main target from this door here."

Ghost followed the line of Digger's index finger and nodded. "Copy that."

Returning his focus to Tac-Ops, Digger said, "We'll breach entry from the front and proceed to clear and search." The man paused, his gaze flickering to Ethan for a brief moment before taking in the team as a whole. "I know we all want to take down Beňová, but our priority is locating and freeing the hostage. We do that, it means mission success, regardless of what happens with the HT. Copy?"

Several muttered agreements rolled through the combined group of trained killers.

Digger knew what was at stake for him, and Ethan understood what needed to be done.

Circling back to their earlier point, the man in charge finished giving Tac-Ops their orders. "As far as we know, there are twenty men behind those walls ready to kill on sight. We go in as if that were fact until we prove otherwise, got it?" He looked to Ethan. "We all want to get your girl back, but we have to be smart about it. That means we treat this like any other mission."

He knew Digger was right. Nicki needed him to be at his best. He couldn't think about who the hostage was or what it would do to him if he lost her.

Ethan sent his team leader a look. A silent message between friends that said it all.

Guns on, emotions off.

Putting his game face on, Ethan dipped his chin and acknowledged Digger's order. "Copy that."

"Any questions?"

He watched and waited, thankful as fuck when no one else spoke up. Holding his rifle across his chest, Digger finally gave the nod Ethan had been waiting for.

"All right, boys. Let's do this."

Leaving their vehicles behind, both teams moved as one as they crossed the abandoned field. Every man was on alert, their weapons held out in front of them, their fingers resting near the rifles' triggers.

Blades of tall, wheat-colored grass brushed against Ethan's legs, the tips of some reaching his knees as he moved. Making his way closer and closer to the building—to Nicki—he kept his head on a swivel, expertly assessing the area around them for anything that could be considered a threat.

The others did the same.

After what felt like an eternity, the teams finally reached the dirt-clad area surrounding the building. Low clouds of dust grew behind each man's boots as they covered the distance separating them from the stone structure.

"Perimeter is still showing clear," Shadow announced through their shared comms. "You're good to make entry."

"Copy that, Shadow," Digger acknowledged with a hushed breath. Using hand signals both teams were familiar with, he let Ghost and his men know it was time to make the split.

With Hollywood, Coach, Beatle, and Blade taking the left, Ghost, Fletch, and Truck went right. Ethan and the others watched and waited as both groups of SF operators disappeared around their respective corners of the building.

Ethan's heart felt as though it was trying to pound its way out his chest, and he had to make a conscious effort to control his breathing. This was it. The most pivotal moment of his existence.

The next few minutes would determine the rest of his life. Every decision. Every memory. Every single moment of his future hinged on what happened once they walked through that door.

I love you, Nicolette.

Locking the thought away—for now—Ethan tightened his hold on his weapon and waited for his team leader to give the order. Luckily, he didn't have to wait long.

With their shoulders pressed against the building's front wall, Ethan risked a glimpse through one of the broken windows. Dirt and grime clouded the scene, but he could make out a small table, desk lamp, computer, and what appeared to be a gas generator on the floor nearby.

Beňová's workstation.

Ethan took a closer look but saw no sign of movement. Either Beňová had spotted them and was hiding, or he was already in another part of the building.

With Nicki?

He looked away from the window and waited for his

team leader to give the signal. On cue, Digger raised a hand and pointed toward the wooden door up ahead. Moving single file, the team silently covered the distance.

Digger stopped, and Ethan and the others followed suit. Since the door was wooden and not in the best of shape—and the fact that, even old, grain dust was highly combustible—the demolitions expert had chosen a less explosive entrance.

Lifting his right foot, Digger slammed the boot of his heel against the weathered slats beneath the knob.

The door blew inward, a cloud of dust and splinters disrupting the air around them.

Motioning toward the now-open door, Digger gave the order to enter.

He stepped in first, followed by Ethan, Bones, and Falcon. The interior was large and open, and the only thing impeding their line of sight were several thick wooden beams supporting the structure's second floor.

With only three additional rooms with access from the main area, the team was fast and efficient in their clearing of the first floor.

"Shadow, this is Team One," Digger spoke through the comms. "First floor is clear with no sign of our HT. There are two sets of stairs we can see. Apollo and Bones will take the basement"—Digger looked to them both for acknowledgement—"and Falcon and I will cover upstairs."

Sounds like a plan to me.

"Copy that, Team One. Delta, do you have a SITREP?"

"Affirmative, overwatch," Ghost's voice filled Ethan's ear. "Just finished clearing. Found Ozlos dead in one of the stalls. Making our way back to the main house from the far south end now."

"Copy that, Delta. Showing Target Two down and your team en route to main target via annex. Perimeter still showing clear."

Guess good old Vlad outlived his usefulness.

With the back part of the property covered by Ghost's team and Shadow watching from overhead, Tac-Ops initiated the second part of the plan.

Digger and Falcon headed for the wooden staircase adjacent to the west wall several yards from where they stood. At the same time, Ethan and Bones made their way across the expansive space to the open stairwell to their right.

Basement.

Using two fingers, Ethan silently told his teammate to keep his eyes peeled and took the lead. The sound of his own rushing blood filled his ears as his boots hit the dusty, decrepit concrete steps.

He moved with purpose, his rifle up and ready to kill. Reaching the bottom, he and Bones each took a side of the open doorway. After flipping on the tactical lights mounted atop their guns, Ethan gave Bones a quick nod, letting him know they were a go.

Bones went low and Ethan went high as they swung their weapons around the door jam in opposite directions. To the right was a small niche and nothing else, so he brought his rifle to the left to cover his teammate.

Son of a...

Running the length of the building was a long, dark hallway. From where he stood, Ethan could make out at least three shadowed doorways, which meant there was a hell of a lot more space to clear than they'd originally thought.

And Nicki could be anywhere.

One bite at a time.

Shadow's age-old adage of how to eat an elephant came rushing to the forefront of his mind. Despite the timing, Ethan damn near smiled. The woman was always watching over them.

Even when she wasn't.

Focusing on clearing one space at a time, Ethan stepped

past Bones and tapped his shoulder, letting the man know he was good to stand and follow. One by one, they cleared the first three rooms they came to with ease.

And little by little, Ethan's hope of finding Nicki began to wane.

Don't give up now. She's here. You just have to find her.

With the mental reminder spurring him on, Ethan and Bones cleared yet another empty room. Ethan lowered his weapon and reported in.

"This is Apollo. Basement's clear."

"Copy that, Apollo. Digger?"

"Top floor's clear. No sign of HT or hostage. Making our way back to the main floor now."

"Goddamnit!" Ethan's fists clenched as he fought the urge to punch another wall.

"They have to be here, Ethan." Bones assured him. "We just have to keep lookin'."

"We've checked the entire place, Beck. If they were here, we would've—"

A loud, high-pitched scream echoed from somewhere behind them. Ethan's heart flew into his throat even as his legs began to move.

"This is Apollo. We just heard a woman's scream. En route to locate now."

"We heard it, too," Digger sounded breathy, as if he were running. "Sounded like it came from the main floor."

"Approaching the back entrance now," Ghost relayed.

"Hard copy from all." Shadow let them know she'd heard and understood each man's report.

"What the fuck?" Bones talked as the two of them sprinted back down the hall toward the stairs. "How the hell did we miss them?"

"They must have seen us and double-backed." It was the only thing that made sense.

The renewed sense of fear for the woman he loved threatening to overtake, but Ethan pushed it back and forged on. Leg muscles burned, the tendons in his neck growing taut as he held his gun steady and started back up the stairs they'd only recently traveled down.

He reached the top as another shrill scream pierced the otherwise silent air. The terrorized sound was abruptly cut off, and Ethan refused to let himself think about why.

"There!" Bones pointed toward the door leading to the back of the building.

When Ethan turned to follow the man's line of sight, he caught a flash of blonde just as the door drew shut.

"Nicki!" He shouted for her as he took off in that direction.

With Bones on his heels, Ethan could see Digger and Falcon in his peripheral, both men running across the open space to join them.

He reached the door, shoving it open with the right side of his body. Swinging his rifle back up, he kept it at the ready as he stepped outside...and straight into a nightmare.

Standing off with Ghost and his teammates, Beñová had stopped halfway between the two buildings. Each member of Delta had their weapons drawn; their barrels aimed at their target.

A target who was using a limp and unconscious Nicki as a human shield.

Ah, Christ!

"Stay back!" Beñová warned Ghost and his men.

Ethan took several slow, careful steps forward, keeping Beñová's head centered in his sights. If it wasn't for Nicki, the man would already be dead. But the way he was holding her—and his intermittent shifting of her unmoving form— made it impossible for him or anyone else to get a clean shot.

And he wouldn't risk Nicki. Not her.

Never her.

"Let her go, Beñová!"

The panicked man spun halfway around, his eyes growing as wide as saucers when he realized he was surrounded. Holding Nicki with a tight arm around her waist, Beňová pressed the barrel of his pistol against Nicki's cheek.

"I'll kill her!" he warned. "Come another step closer, and she's dead!"

"Take it easy, Andrei." Ethan kept his gun trained on his target. "There are still choices to be made, here. You haven't done anything that can't be undone."

Beňová let loose with a hysterical laugh. "I kidnapped an American woman, brought her to Latvia, and held her against her will for ransom. I know you're not just going to let me walk away a free man."

"No." Ethan answered honestly. "You'll walk out of here in our custody."

Alive or dead. Your choice, asshole.

Their target considered this but shook his head. "You said I have choices. Plural. What's my other option?"

He was starting to panic. Ethan could see it in his beady little eyes, the man was becoming desperate. And desperate men made mistakes.

"You can either walk out or be carried," Ethan laid it out for the man. "Those are your two choices."

"I can't go to prison." Beňová stared back at him as if he'd lost his damn mind. With his head moving back and forth to keep both groups of operators in his sights, he asked, "Do you have any idea what they do to men like me in prison?"

Oh, I have a pretty good idea.

"It's over, Andrei." Ethan took a hesitant step closer. And then another. He continued closing the gap between him and Beňová. "Look around you. There's no way out this time, so just drop your weapon and let her go before someone gets hurt."

Their target took a step back, away from Ethan and inad-

ANNA BLAKELY

vertently closer to where Ghost and Hollywood were standing.

"Drop the gun, Beňová!" Ethan shouted. "I won't say it again."

The man was like a caged animal, his crazed eyes sliding back and forth in a hopeless search of a way out. But there was no way out. Not this time.

And he knew it.

With his next breath, the look in Beňová's eyes morphed from panic to acceptance. It was a look Ethan had seen more times than he cared to remember.

It was the look of a man who knew he was about to die.

Ethan almost missed the slight twitch of Beňová's trigger finger as the man tightened the grip on his gun. He may have accepted his impending death, but he wasn't about to go alone.

He's going to kill her first.

"Don't do it, Andrei!" Ethan's shouted warning escaped through a set of clenched teeth. "Don't you fucking do it!"

Several other growled warnings traveled through the air, but Ethan couldn't hear them. He couldn't hear anything but the sound of his own frantically beating heart.

A look of peace fell over the man holding onto all that Ethan held dear. The gun pressed against Nicki's cheek lifted, the move stealing every molecule of air left in Ethan's lungs.

"No!"

But just when Ethan thought he was about to watch the only woman he'd ever loved die, Beňová did the unexpected.

In one swift move, he lifted Nicki's ragdoll form and threw her to the side. At the same time, Beňová raised his weapon high, its barrel aiming straight at Ethan.

Ethan pulled his trigger as a barrage of bullets from his and Ghost's team began filling Beňová's body with holes.

Landing with a dull thud, the psychopathic genius was dead before he hit the ground.

"Nicki!" Ethan ran to where she lay, relieved as fuck when he saw she was starting to move. He dropped to his knees beside her. "Baby? Are you okay?"

A soft moan reached his ears as Nicki began pushing herself into a seated position.

"Easy, Nic," he crooned. "Go slow."

"I-I'm...okay." She blinked; her lids squinting with an effort to focus. "Is it really you?"

Her voice was strained and weak but fuck if it wasn't the most beautiful thing he'd ever heard. Fighting tears, he gave her a watery smile. "Yeah, sweetheart. It's really me."

A smile began to form on her bow-shaped lips, but then it fell, fear returning in her beautiful eyes. "Beň...ová?" She squinted in pain as she did a visual search for her captor.

"Dead." Ethan used a gentle hand to guide her gaze back to his. "Beňová's dead, Nic. It's over. You're safe."

He could say it a million more times, and he probably still wouldn't believe it to be true.

"Jesus, that was close." Bones and the others began filtering in around them. "She okay?"

Lifting her left hand to that side of her head, she winced. "Jerk slammed my head into a wall."

Ethan and Bones shared a look, and Ethan knew the man was thinking the same as him...

Bastard's lucky he's already dead.

"Can we go home now?" The soft question had every man there smiling.

But it was Ethan who answered.

"Yeah, baby. We're going home."

EPILOGUE

One week later...

NICKI SAT on Ethan's lap as they enjoyed the beautiful spring day.

The barbeque at Falcon's house had been rescheduled as an impromptu party in Nicki's honor. Bones had even made a custom banner to drape across the patio wall. It's big, bold print letters reading *Welcome to the Family!*

She smiled, reading the words again. Bones had teased her when she'd first seen it. Said she was stuck with them now. But the joke was on him because they were the ones who were stuck.

Especially this one right here.

"I still can't believe I slept through a shootout." She languidly raked the tips of her fingers thought the short hair at his temple.

"Wouldn't exactly call having your head slammed into a wall and getting knocked out 'sleeping'."

Meeting his gaze, Nicki found a mixture of pain, anger, and fear staring back at her. It was the same look that came into his eyes any time the incident with Beñová was brought up.

Not that she didn't feel those things and more.

A week had gone by since Ethan and his team—along with the same group of men who had aided in the evacuation at the Athens embassy—rescued her from that awful place. Nicki still woke up at least once in the night, her memories colliding together to create a nightmarish world starring Andrei Beñová.

Sometimes he killed her. Sometimes he ordered his bodyguard to beat her. And sometimes…during the very worst of her nightmares…Beñová would shoot and kill Ethan.

Those were the ones that had her scared to fall asleep. The ones that sent her shooting straight up in bed, her throat raw from the screams. And through it all, no matter how bad it got, Ethan had been there.

Every nightmare. Every scream. Every tear.

Secretary Bradford had given her a month off with pay with the option to take more time if needed. He'd also put a buzz in her ear about the possibility of working from home, should she decide she needed a change of scenery.

Meaning, should she decide to move to Charlotte to be with Ethan.

Leaning down, she pressed her lips to his. "I'm okay, Ethan." A quick brush of his nose with the tip of hers. "Thanks to you and your team."

"Don't forget Ghost's team."

"Ghost's. Right." Nicki smiled.

Although she had yet to get out of the stubborn man exactly what team Ghost and his men were on. She'd guessed everything, from SEALs, to Delta Force, to private-pay mercenaries…and everything in between.

Ethan's response each and every time…a tight-lipped smile.

Better get used to being with a man who keeps secrets.

"I almost lost you." His Adam's apple bobbed in the afternoon sun, his watering eyes shimmering as they saw into her soul. "Do you have any idea what it would do to me if that happened?"

Ah, baby.

"You won't lose me." She caressed his rugged cheek with her thumb. "Not ever."

"Don't say that if you don't mean it, Nic." He blinked quickly, a tear catching at the very corner of one of his eyes.

"I mean it." Nicki kissed him again, letting her lips linger a bit longer this time. "I love you, Ethan."

"Forever."

His answer was instant; not a smidge of hesitation laced around it anywhere. She studied him for any signs of regret or uncertainty, her heart blooming when she found none.

"What are you saying?" She prayed he was headed in the direction she thought he might be.

Ethan nodded toward Bones' sign. "That's what I'm saying." He brought his dark gaze to hers. "This is your home now, Nic. Maybe not physically, but in here..." A warm palm came to rest over her heart. "In here, this is your home. We're your home."

"The team?"

"You're stuck with them." He grinned.

Nicki wondered if he could feel the rapid beating of her heart, and just how much that crooked lift of his lips affected her.

"And you?" She teased. "Am I stuck with you, too?"

"That depends on you."

Before Nicki could ask what he meant, Ethan guided her from his lap and stood.

"What are you—"

"I was going to wait to do this until later, when we were alone. But I meant what I said. These guys are family, and I want them to see just how much I love you."

He pulled a small black box from his jacket pocket and dropped to his knee.

"Ethan!" Nicki gasped. "What are you—"

"Holy shit!"

Nicki and Ethan both turned to see Alex—Falcon's sister-in-law—staring wide-eyed with a hand covering her mouth. "Sorry." The pretty brunette put a hand up. "Please…continue."

"Way to go, Al." Colt, Falcon's brother-in-law teased the other woman. "Ruin their moment, why don't you?"

Alex sent the man a sharp scowl and a middle finger, to which Colt threw his hands up as if to ask an innocent *what?*

With a watery chuckle, Nicki turned back to find Ethan staring up at her with a smile of his own.

God, I love that smile.

But then that smile fell, his expression becoming serious.

"Nicolette Castille, I have loved you for so long, I can hardly remember a time when I didn't. I know we can't make up the time we lost, but I'd damn sure'd like to try." He blinked, sending a tear streaking slowly down his face. "Marry me, Nicki. Let me spend the rest of my life showing you how much I love you."

Nicki dropped to her knees in front of him and cupped his face. With her own tears streaming, she stared into her love—her *everything*—and said, "Yes."

Ethan slammed his lips to hers as cheers and whistles erupted around them.

"Are we really getting married?" She pulled back to ask because…

It's my dream come true.

Ethan's face lit up with the biggest smile she'd ever seen. "Hell yeah, we are."

He opened the box and pulled out another one. This one covered in velvet.

Lifting the satin-lined lid, he revealed the most beautiful sapphire and diamond ring she'd ever seen.

"Oh, Ethan," Nicki breathed.

With his thumb and forefinger, he carefully plucked the delicate ring from its protective valley and slid it onto her left ring finger.

It was a perfect fit.

"Blue's your favorite color," Ethan explained his choice in gems. "And I remember you saying once that you didn't want a traditional wedding ring. You said wanted one with color, because love should be filled with color."

Nicki's lips parted, her jaw growing slack with shock. "Ethan, I said that when I was like seventeen."

One of her friend's older sisters had gotten engaged, and everyone had gone on and on about how gorgeous the giant diamond solitaire had been. But Nicki had thought it was missing something.

She'd thought it needed color.

Later that night, she'd shared her thoughts with Ethan's mom while she'd been at his house for a movie night. Ethan had come into the room and popped off with some smartass comment about how rings were a waste of money, blah, blah, blah.

And yet...

"I remember it as if it were yesterday." He took her hand in his. "That was the day I knew, if I ever got lucky enough to marry you, I was buying you a sapphire ring."

A collective *Awww* came courtesy of Avery and Alex...and maybe Bones. But Nicki couldn't be sure about that last one.

"If I had every ring in the world to choose from, this is the one I would have picked." She blinked to clear her vision. "And of all the men in the world, you're the only one I want."

"Forever?"

For Nicki, there was no question.

Leaning up, she wrapped her arms around his neck and

kissed him slowly. Thoroughly. In front of God and everyone.

And when they finally came up for air, she stared back at the love of her life and whispered, "Forever."

* * *

BECKETT "BONES" Stone sat in his usual chair at the Tac-Ops conference table and waited for the meeting to begin.

Their boss had called the team in for a last-minute briefing on what would most likely be their next op. It was about time, as far as Beckett was concerned.

He was getting a little tired of hearing about how great married life was.

Not that he wasn't happy for Ethan and Nicki, who'd chosen to get married at the courthouse less than a week after his impromptu barbeque proposal. Beck had been rooting for the two of them since seeing how his boy was around the sweet artist.

So yeah, he was happy for Apollo and Nicki. Just as he was happy for Falcon and Avery. But he was starting to grasp the whole *too much of a good thing* concept. Especially when all the talk about marital bliss reminded him of what he was missing.

Ethan's words from the man's wedding day came rushing back….

Your time will come, Bones. Probably when you least expect it.

Beckett knew his day would come. It wasn't like he was in a massive rush to settle down or anything. It was just something he'd been thinking about a little more lately. That's all.

Keep telling yourself that, Stone.

Now that was *his* voice, and just as he was going to do with Falcon's, Beckett chose to ignore it.

"Let's get started." Rafe Owens, Beckett's boss entered the room with a small stack of folders in his hands. Setting them down onto the table, he picked up a small remote and turned on the big white screen mounted on the wall behind him.

"We have a hostage situation that needs our attention."

"Where we going?" Beckett asked.

Owens clicked the remote and brought up a digital map of...

"Afghanistan?" Falcon spoke up next.

The man in charge of the room nodded.

Digger studied the map before asking, "Who's the HT?"

"A group of insurgents revolting against the local Taliban's decision to yield to educating girls."

"Ah, hell." Beckett got a bad feeling in his gut. "Who are the hostages?"

His boss changed the image on the screen, and that gut-churning feeling turned to rage.

A small group of young Afghani girls—he guessed them to be eight or nine—were gathered together and smiling for the camera. Their faces filled with joy and peace.

And now some sons of bitches with hate in their hearts have filled those same faces with terror.

"This group of third graders and their teacher were taken at gunpoint from their classroom two days ago."

"Demands?" Falcon spoke up next.

"None yet." Owens shook his head. "So far, they've only posted pictures with captions praising their cause."

"They're using them to gain traction," Apollo surmised.

Beckett agreed. "What about the teacher?"

"Her name is Evelynn Mitchell." Owens clicked the remote a third time, but the image took longer than it should have to load. While they waited, their boss went on with the intel. "Miss Mitchell is a thirty-one-year-old American school teacher who signed up for a semester-long program abroad. One that focuses on the areas in Afghanistan where the Taliban is allowing girls to be taught."

For years, it was illegal for any girls in Afghanistan to

learn how to read or write. Things got better for a while, but after the Taliban regained control, they put the archaic law back in place.

Only a few locations existed where the local insurgents decided to back down and look the other way.

Beckett's attention was pulled back to the screen as the teacher's picture finally came into view. When it did, it was as if every ounce of oxygen had been sucked out of the room.

He couldn't talk. Couldn't breathe. Beckett couldn't think. All he could do was sit there and stare.

Long brown hair that fell in waves around the most beautiful face he'd ever seen. Big hazel eyes with specks of browns and greens he could see from here. An adorable button nose and cheeks with a slight kiss of pale freckles. And a set of lips full enough to get the job done.

She wasn't supermodel, skin-and-bones, sharp-features beautiful. More girl-next-door, sweet-as-cherry-pie beautiful.

And cherry pie was Beckett's favorite.

Taken aback by his confusing reaction to a *picture*, he sat up straight and shook whatever the hell that was off.

"So what's the plan? We going in and taking these fuckers out, or…"

"Actually, the choice on this one is yours."

"Ours?" Falcon frowned. "Why do we get to choose?"

"Because this one's gonna be dangerous." Owens didn't pull any punches. "That area is extremely volatile, and the group we're dealing with plays by a whole different set of rules than everyone else. And…there's one more thing."

"Well, that sounds ominous," Beckett half-teased.

"Because it is, Bones." The silver fox of a man in charge turned his stoic gaze in his direction. "Due to political unrest in that area, the government has been rotating special ops teams from all branches to remain stationed in nearby areas where Americans are welcome."

"And..." Ethan prompted.

"If you agree to go, you'll be with one of those teams as a joint op."

Work with a team they'd never met? That wasn't ideal by any stretch, but...

"We're going." All eyes turned to look at him, but Beckett didn't back down. "Those girls are what, eight? Nine? And now a group of assholes ripped them out of a place that should have been safe, stole them away from their families, and for what? Because they wanted to learn to read and write?"

"Nobody's arguing against the fact that this is a totally fucked-up situation, Bones," Digger spoke to him from across the table. "We're just listening to all the facts before making a solid decision."

"There's only one decision to make." He glanced around the room. "Those kids are innocent and helpless. And the teacher..." Beckett looked back up at the screen, the pull he felt for a woman he'd never met unexplainable. "Her only crime is having a heart so big it put her in the exact wrong place at the exact wrong time." When no one said anything, he threw his hands out to the side. "Seriously. How is this even a discussion?"

"He's right." Digger nodded. "This is what we do. It's why this team exists."

"What about the rest of you?" Owens posed the question to the group. "This one has to be a team decision."

"I'm in." Apollo was the first to answer.

Guilt assaulted Beckett when he thought of his friend's new wife. "You sure? You and Nic have only been married three weeks. I doubt she's ready to send you off to Bumfuck-istan when the honeymoon's barely over."

"Are you kidding?" Apollo scoffed. "Nic would have my ass if she knew we had a chance to help those girls and didn't take it."

"I'm in." Digger confirmed his decision.

"Avery would feel the same as Nicki." Falcon looked to Apollo and nodded. "I say we go."

"Then we're agreed." Owens began passing around the folders he'd prepared pre-emptively. "I'll let the President know. For now, you're free to go but stay close and study up." He pointed to the folders each man had been given. "That's enough to get us started. Once I have all the details, we'll need to start formulating a plan. I'll also make contact with the team you'll be working with and get their information as well. At least have some idea of who has your backs out there."

"Copy that, Boss." Ethan scooped up his folder and stood.

Following his lead, Beckett and the others stood, as well. He hung back, letting his teammates and boss ahead of him on their way to the door. As he started to leave, Beckett looked back at the giant screen...and the woman still smiling back at him.

He knew nothing about her other than the fact that she clearly loved kids. She had to, right? Who else would volunteer to go to that part of the world, to do *that* job, knowing the risks?

A teacher, that's who.

Beckett's mom had been a teacher, so he understood better than most the time and energy that particular job required. More importantly, Beck knew the love and passion a teacher's heart held. The light they brought to every student who came into their path, whether they realized it or not.

The thought of someone extinguishing the light shining behind those heart stopping, colorful eyes on that screen...

Not happening, sweetheart.

Beckett wouldn't let it. Not to her. Not to those kids.

Despite not wanting to, he turned away from the teacher's frozen image and walked out of that room. And later, hours after having left the office to come home, there was one thought that kept rolling through his mind.

Something he wished like hell he had a way to let Evelynn Mitchell know. A message he wished he could somehow get to her...

Stay strong, darlin'. We're coming for you.

* * *

Want to more Tac-Ops? GARRETT'S DESTINY (Tac-Ops #1) is available now!

Join Anna's reader group to be the first to know when ***BECKETT'S DESIRE (Tac-Ops #3)*** is available for pre-order! www.facebook.com/groups/blakelysbunch/

ABOUT THE AUTHOR

Author Anna Blakely brings you stories of love, action, and edge-of-your-seat suspense. As an avid reader of romantic suspense herself, Anna's dream is to create stories her readers will enjoy and characters they'll fall in love with as much as she has. She believes in true love and happily-ever-after, and that's what she will always bring to you.

Anna lives in rural Missouri with her husband, children, and several rescued animals. When she's not writing, Anna enjoys reading, watching action and horror movies (the scarier the better), and spending time with her amazing husband, four wonderful children, and her adorable grand-daughter.

FB Author Page: facebook.com/annablakely.author.7
Blakely's Bunch (reader group): https://www.facebook.com/groups/354218335396441/
Instagram: https://instagram.com/annablakely
BookBub: https//www.bookbub.com/authors/anna-blakely
Amazon: amazon.com/author/annablakely
Twitter: @ablakelyauthor
Goodreads: https://www.goodreads.com/author/show/18650841.Anna_Blakely

facebook.com/annablakely.author.7

twitter.com/ablakelyauthor

instagram.com/annablakely

amazon.com/author/annablakely

WANT TO CONNECT WITH ANNA?

Newsletter signup (with FREE Bravo Team prequel novella!)
BookHip.com/ZLMKFT
Join Anna's Reader Group: www.facebook.com/groups/
blakelysbunch/
BookBub: https://www.bookbub.com/authors/anna-blakely
Amazon: amazon.com/author/annablakely
Author Page: https://www.facebook.com/
annablakelyromance
Instagram: https://instagram.com/annablakely
Goodreads: https://www.goodreads.com/author/show/
18650841.Anna_Blakely

ALSO BY ANNA BLAKELY

Check it out! Anna Blakely has three new series:

TAC-OPS Series

Garrett's Destiny

Ethan's Obsession

Beckett's Desire (TBA)

Creed's Future (TBA)

Marked Series

Marked For Death

Marked for Revenge

Marked for Deception

Marked for Obsession

Marked for Danger

Marked for Disaster

Charlie Team

(R.I.S.C. Spinoff Series)

Kellan

Asher

Rhys

Other Books by Anna

R.I.S.C. Series

Taking a Risk, Part One (Jake & Olivia's HFN)

Taking a Risk, Part Two (Jake & Olivia's HEA)

Beautiful Risk (Trevor & Lexi)

Intentional Risk (Derek & Charlie)

Unpredictable Risk (Grant & Brynnon)

Ultimate Risk (Coop & Mac)

Targeted Risk (Mike & Jules)

Savage Risk (Eric & Riley)

Undeniable Risk (Ryker & Sophie)

His Greatest Risk

Bravo Team Series

Rescuing Gracelynn (Nate & Gracie)

Rescuing Katherine (Matt & Katherine)

Rescuing Gabriella (Zade & Gabby)

Rescuing Ellena (Gabe & Elle)

Rescuing Jenna (Adrian & Jenna)

There are many more books in this fan fiction world than listed here, for an up-to-date list go to www.AcesPress.com

You can also visit our Amazon page at:
http://www.amazon.com/author/operationalpha

Special Forces: Operation Alpha World
Christie Adams: Charity's Heart
Linzi Baxter: Dangerous Rescue
Misha Blake: Flash
Anna Blakely: Rescuing Gracelynn
Julia Bright: Saving Lorelei
Cara Carnes: Protecting Mari
Kendra Mei Chailyn: Beast
Melissa Kay Clarke: Rescuing Annabeth
Samantha A. Cole: Handling Haven
Lorelei Confer: Protecting Sara
KaLyn Cooper: Spring Unveiled
Janie Crouch: Storm
Jordan Dane: Redemption for Avery
Tarina Deaton: Found in the Lost
Riley Edwards: Protecting Olivia
Dorothy Ewels: Knight's Queen
Lila Ferrari: Protecting Joy
Nicole Flockton: Protecting Maria
Hope Ford: Rescuing Karina
Amy Gamet: Guarded by the SEAL
Desiree Holt: Protecting Maddie
Danielle Haas: Crossroads of Betrayal
Jesse Jacobson: Protecting Honor
Rayne Lewis: Justice for Mary
Ireland Lorelei: The Detective
Kristin Lynn: Worth the Risk
Callie Love & Ann Omasta: Hawaii Hottie

Delta Team Three Series

Police and Fire: Operation Alpha World
Freya Barker: Burning for Autumn
B.P. Beth: Scott
Jane Blythe: Salvaging Marigold
Julia Bright, Justice for Amber
Hadley Finn: Exton
Emily Gray: Shelter for Allegra
Danielle M. Haas: Crossroads of Betrayal
Deanndra Hall: Shelter for Sharla
Jenna Harte: Dead But Not Forgotten
Amber Kuhlman: Protecting Paisley
Reina Torres: Justice for Sloane
Aubree Valentine, Justice for Danielle
Maddie Wade: Finding English

Tarpley VFD Series
Silver James, Fighting for Elena
Deanndra Hall, Fighting for Carly
Haven Rose, Fighting for Calliope
MJ Nightingale, Fighting for Jemma
TL Reeve, Fighting for Brittney
Nicole Flockton, Fighting for Nadia

As you know, this book included at least one character from Susan Stoker's books. To check out more, see below.

SEAL Team Hawaii Series
Finding Elodie
Finding Lexie
Finding Kenna
Finding Monica
Finding Carly
Finding Ashlyn
Finding Jodelle (July 2023)

Eagle Point Search & Rescue
Searching for Lilly
Searching for Elsie
Searching for Bristol
Searching for Caryn
Searching for Finley (Sept 2023)
Searching for Heather (Jan 2024)
Searching for Khloe (TBA)

The Refuge Series
Deserving Alaska
Deserving Henley
Deserving Reese
Deserving Cora (Nov 2023)
Deserving Lara (Feb 2024)
Deserving Maisy (TBA)
Deserving Ryleigh (TBA)

Delta Team Two Series
Shielding Gillian
Shielding Kinley

BOOKS BY SUSAN STOKER

Shielding Aspen
Shielding Jayme (novella)
Shielding Riley
Shielding Devyn
Shielding Ember
Shielding Sierra

SEAL of Protection: Legacy Series

Securing Caite (FREE!)
Securing Brenae (novella)
Securing Sidney
Securing Piper
Securing Zoey
Securing Avery
Securing Kalee
Securing Jane

Delta Force Heroes Series

Rescuing Rayne (FREE!)
Rescuing Aimee (novella)
Rescuing Emily
Rescuing Harley
Marrying Emily (novella)
Rescuing Kassie
Rescuing Bryn
Rescuing Casey
Rescuing Sadie (novella)
Rescuing Wendy
Rescuing Mary
Rescuing Macie (novella)
Rescuing Annie

Badge of Honor: Texas Heroes Series

Justice for Mackenzie (FREE!)

Justice for Mickie
Justice for Corrie
Justice for Laine (novella)
Shelter for Elizabeth
Justice for Boone
Shelter for Adeline
Shelter for Sophie
Justice for Erin
Justice for Milena
Shelter for Blythe
Justice for Hope
Shelter for Quinn
Shelter for Koren
Shelter for Penelope

SEAL of Protection Series

Protecting Caroline (FREE!)
Protecting Alabama
Protecting Fiona
Marrying Caroline (novella)
Protecting Summer
Protecting Cheyenne
Protecting Jessyka
Protecting Julie (novella)
Protecting Melody
Protecting the Future
Protecting Kiera (novella)
Protecting Alabama's Kids (novella)
Protecting Dakota

New York Times, *USA Today* and *Wall Street Journal* Bestselling Author Susan Stoker has a heart as big as the state of Tennessee where she lives, but this all American girl has also spent the last fourteen years living in Missouri, California,

Colorado, Indiana, and Texas. She's married to a retired Army man who now gets to follow *her* around the country.

www.stokeraces.com
www.AcesPress.com
susan@stokeraces.com

Made in United States
North Haven, CT
01 June 2024

53200573R00161